THE VOICE OF THE NIGHT
"A fearsome tour of an adolescent's psyche. Terrifying, knee-knocking suspense." —*Chicago Sun-Times*

THE BAD PLACE
"A new experience in breathless terror." —UPI

THE SERVANTS OF TWILIGHT
"A great storyteller." —*New York Daily News*

MIDNIGHT
"A triumph." —*New York Times*

LIGHTNING
"Brilliant . . . a spine-tingling tale . . . both challenging and entertaining." —Associated Press

THE MASK
"Koontz hones his fearful yarns to a gleaming edge." —*People*

WATCHERS
"A breakthrough for Koontz . . . his best ever." —*Kirkus Reviews*

TWILIGHT EYES
"A spine-chilling adventure . . . will keep you turning pages to the very end." —*Rave Reviews*

DEAN KOONTZ

The Eyes of Darkness

Originally published under the pseudonym Leigh Nichols

BERKLEY BOOKS, NEW YORK

Originally published under the
pseudonym Leigh Nichols.

THE EYES OF DARKNESS

A Berkley Book / published by arrangement with
Nkui, Inc.

PRINTING HISTORY
Pocket Books edition / February 1981
Berkley edition / July 1996

The Putnam Berkley World Wide Web site address is
http://www.berkley.com

ISBN: 0-425-15397-5

BERKLEY®
Berkley Books are published by The Berkley Publishing Group,
200 Madison Avenue, New York, New York 10016.
BERKLEY and the "B" design
are trademarks belonging to Berkley Publishing Corporation.

PRINTED IN THE UNITED STATES OF AMERICA

10 9 8 7 6 5 4 3 2 1

This better version is for Gerda,
with love.

After five years of work,
now that I'm nearly finished improving
these early novels first published under pen names,
I intend to start improving myself.

Considering all that needs to be done,
this new project will henceforth be known
as the *hundred*-year plan.

The Eyes of Darkness

Tuesday,

December 30

1

AT SIX MINUTES PAST MIDNIGHT, TUESDAY MORN-
ing, on the way home from a late rehearsal of her new stage
show, Tina Evans saw her son, Danny, in a stranger's car.
But Danny had been dead more than a year.

Two blocks from her house, intending to buy a quart of
milk and a loaf of whole-wheat bread, Tina stopped at a
twenty-four-hour market and parked in the dry yellow
drizzle of a sodium-vapor light, beside a gleaming, cream-
colored Chevrolet station wagon. The boy was in the front
passenger seat of the wagon, waiting for someone in the
store. Tina could see only the side of his face, but she
gasped in painful recognition.

Danny.

The boy was about twelve, Danny's age. He had thick
dark hair like Danny's, a nose that resembled Danny's, and
a rather delicate jawline like Danny's too.

She whispered her son's name, as if she would frighten
off this beloved apparition if she spoke any louder.

Unaware that she was staring at him, the boy put one
hand to his mouth and bit gently on his bent thumb knuckle,

3

which Danny had begun to do a year or so before he died. Without success, Tina had tried to break him of that bad habit.

Now, as she watched this boy, his resemblance to Danny seemed to be more than mere coincidence. Suddenly Tina's mouth went dry and sour, and her heart thudded. She still had not adjusted to the loss of her only child, because she'd never wanted—or tried—to adjust to it. Seizing on this boy's resemblance to her Danny, she was too easily able to fantasize that there had been no loss in the first place.

Maybe . . . maybe this boy actually *was* Danny. Why not? The more that she considered it, the less crazy it seemed. After all, she'd never seen Danny's corpse. The police and the morticians had advised her that Danny was so badly torn up, so horribly mangled, that she was better off not looking at him. Sickened, grief-stricken, she had taken their advice, and Danny's funeral had been a closed-coffin service. But perhaps they'd been mistaken when they identified the body. Maybe Danny hadn't been killed in the accident, after all. Maybe he'd only suffered a mild head injury, just severe enough to give him . . . amnesia. Yes. Amnesia. Perhaps he had wandered away from the wrecked bus and had been found miles from the scene of the accident, without identification, unable to tell anyone who he was or where he came from. That was possible, wasn't it? She had seen similar stories in the movies. Sure. Amnesia. And if that were the case, then he might have ended up in a foster home, in a new life. And now here he was sitting in the cream-colored Chevrolet wagon, brought to her by fate and by—

The boy became conscious of her gaze and turned toward her. She held her breath as his face came slowly around. As they stared at each other through two windows and through the strange sulphurous light, she had the feeling that they were making contact across an immense gulf of space and time and destiny. But then, inevitably, her fantasy burst, for he wasn't Danny.

Pulling her gaze away from his, she studied her hands, which were gripping the steering wheel so fiercely that they ached.

"Damn."

She was angry with herself. She thought of herself as a tough, competent, levelheaded woman who was able to deal with anything life threw at her, and she was disturbed by her continuing inability to accept Danny's death.

After the initial shock, after the funeral, she *had* begun to cope with the trauma. Gradually, day by day, week by week, she had put Danny behind her, with sorrow, with guilt, with tears and much bitterness, but also with firmness and determination. She had taken several steps up in her career during the past year, and she had relied on hard work as a sort of morphine, using it to dull her pain until the wound fully healed.

But then, a few weeks ago, she had begun to slip back into the dreadful condition in which she'd wallowed immediately after she'd received news of the accident. Her denial was as resolute as it was irrational. Again, she was possessed by the haunting feeling that her child was alive. Time should have put even more distance between her and the anguish, but instead the passing days were bringing her around full circle in her grief. This boy in the station wagon was not the first that she had imagined was Danny; in recent weeks, she had seen her lost son in other cars, in schoolyards past which she had been driving, on public streets, in a movie theater.

Also, she'd recently been plagued by a repeating dream in which Danny was alive. Each time, for a few hours after she woke, she could not face reality. She half convinced herself that the dream was a premonition of Danny's eventual return to her, that somehow he had survived and would be coming back into her arms one day soon.

This was a warm and wonderful fantasy, but she could not sustain it for long. Though she always resisted the grim truth, it gradually exerted itself every time, and she was repeatedly brought down hard, forced to accept that the dream was not a premonition. Nevertheless, she knew that when she had the dream again, she would find new hope in it as she had so many times before.

And that was not good.

Sick, she berated herself.

She glanced at the station wagon and saw that the boy was still staring at her. She glared at her tightly clenched hands again and found the strength to break her grip on the steering wheel.

Grief could drive a person crazy. She'd heard that said, and she believed it. But she wasn't going to allow such a thing to happen to her. She would be sufficiently tough on herself to stay in touch with reality—as unpleasant as reality might be. She couldn't allow herself to hope.

She had loved Danny with all her heart, but he was gone. Torn and crushed in a bus accident with fourteen other little boys, just one victim of a larger tragedy. Battered beyond recognition. *Dead.*

Cold.

Decaying.

In a coffin.

Under the ground.

Forever.

Her lower lip trembled. She wanted to cry, needed to cry, but she didn't.

The boy in the Chevy had lost interest in her. He was staring at the front of the grocery store again, waiting.

Tina got out of her Honda. The night was pleasantly cool and desert-dry. She took a deep breath and went into the market, where the air was so cold that it pierced her bones, and where the harsh fluorescent lighting was too bright and too bleak to encourage fantasies.

She bought a quart of nonfat milk and a loaf of whole-wheat bread that was cut thin for dieters, so each serving contained only half the calories of an ordinary slice of bread. She wasn't a dancer anymore; now she worked behind the curtain, in the production end of the show, but she still felt physically and psychologically best when she weighed no more than she had weighed when she'd been a performer.

Five minutes later she was home. Hers was a modest ranch house in a quiet neighborhood. The olive trees and lacy melaleucas stirred lazily in a faint Mojave breeze.

In the kitchen, she toasted two pieces of bread. She spread a thin skin of peanut butter on them, poured a glass of nonfat milk, and sat at the table.

Peanut-butter toast had been one of Danny's favorite foods, even when he was a toddler and was especially picky about what he would eat. When he was very young, he had called it "neenut putter."

Closing her eyes now, chewing the toast, Tina could still see him—three years old, peanut butter smeared all over his lips and chin—as he grinned and said, *More neenut putter toast, please.*

She opened her eyes with a start because her mental image of him was too vivid, less like a memory than like a *vision.* Right now she didn't want to remember so clearly.

But it was too late. Her heart knotted in her chest, and her lower lip began to quiver again, and she put her head down on the table. She wept.

● ● ●

That night Tina dreamed that Danny was alive again. Somehow. Somewhere. Alive. And he needed her.

In the dream, Danny was standing at the edge of a bottomless gorge, and Tina was on the far side, opposite him, looking across the immense gulf. Danny was calling her name. He was lonely and afraid. She was miserable because she couldn't think of a way to reach him. Meanwhile, the sky grew darker by the second; massive storm clouds, like the clenched fists of celestial giants, squeezed the last light out of the day. Danny's cries and her response became increasingly shrill and desperate, for they knew that they must reach each other before nightfall or be lost forever; in the oncoming night, something waited for Danny, something fearsome that would seize him if he was alone after dark. Suddenly the sky was shattered by lightning, then by a hard clap of thunder, and the night imploded into a deeper darkness, into infinite and perfect blackness.

Tina Evans sat straight up in bed, certain that she had heard a noise in the house. It hadn't been merely the thunder from the dream. The sound she'd heard had come as she was waking, a real noise, not an imagined one.

She listened intently, prepared to throw off the covers and slip out of bed. Silence reigned.

Gradually doubt crept over her. She *had* been jumpy lately. This wasn't the first night she'd been wrongly convinced that an intruder was prowling the house. On four or five occasions during the past two weeks, she had taken the pistol from the nightstand and searched the place, room by room, but she hadn't found anyone. Recently she'd been under a lot of pressure, both personally and professionally. Maybe what she'd heard tonight *had* been the thunder from the dream.

She remained on guard for a few minutes, but the night was so peaceful that at last she had to admit she was alone. As her heartbeat slowed, she eased back onto her pillow.

At times like this she wished that she and Michael were still together. She closed her eyes and imagined herself lying beside him, reaching for him in the dark, touching, touching, moving against him, into the shelter of his arms. He would comfort and reassure her, and in time she would sleep again.

Of course, if she and Michael were in bed right this minute, it wouldn't be like that at all. They wouldn't make love. They would argue. He'd resist her affection, turn her away by picking a fight. He would begin the battle over a triviality and goad her until the bickering escalated into marital warfare. That was how it had been during the last months of their life together. He had been seething with hostility, always seeking an excuse to vent his anger on her.

Because Tina had loved Michael to the end, she'd been hurt and saddened by the dissolution of their relationship. Admittedly, she had also been relieved when it was finally over.

She had lost her child and her husband in the same year, the man first, and then the boy, the son to the grave and the husband to the winds of change. During the twelve years of their marriage, Tina had become a different and more complex person than she'd been on their wedding day, but Michael hadn't changed at all—and didn't like the woman that she had become. They began as lovers, sharing every detail of their daily lives—triumphs and failures, joys and frustrations—but by the time the divorce was final, they were strangers. Although Michael was still living in town, less than a mile from her, he was, in some respects, as far away and as unreachable as Danny.

She sighed with resignation and opened her eyes.

She wasn't sleepy now, but she knew she had to get more rest. She would need to be fresh and alert in the morning.

Tomorrow was one of the most important days of her life: December 30. In other years that date had meant nothing special. But for better or worse, *this* December 30 was the hinge upon which her entire future would swing.

For fifteen years, ever since she turned eighteen, two years before she married Michael, Tina Evans had lived and worked in Las Vegas. She began her career as a dancer—not a showgirl but an actual dancer—in the Lido de Paris, a gigantic stage show at the Stardust Hotel. The Lido was one of those incredibly lavish productions that could be seen nowhere in the world but Vegas, for it was only in Las Vegas that a multimillion-dollar show could be staged year after year with little concern for profit; such vast sums were spent on the elaborate sets and costumes, and on the enormous cast and crew, that the hotel was usually happy if the production merely broke even from ticket and drink sales. After all, as fantastic as it was, the show was only a come-on, a draw, with the sole purpose of putting a few thousand people into the hotel every night. Going to and from the showroom, the crowd had to pass all the craps tables and blackjack tables and roulette wheels and glittering ranks of slot machines, and *that* was where the profit was made. Tina enjoyed dancing in the Lido, and she stayed there for two and a half years, until she learned that she was pregnant. She took time off to carry and give birth to Danny, then to spend uninterrupted days with him during his first few months of life. When Danny was six months old, Tina went into training to get back in shape, and after three arduous months of exercise, she won a place in the chorus line of a new Vegas spectacle. She managed to be both a fine dancer and a good mother, although that was not always easy; she loved Danny, and she enjoyed her work and she thrived on double duty.

Five years ago, however, on her twenty-eighth birthday, she began to realize that she had, if she was lucky, ten years left as a show dancer, and she decided to establish herself in the business in another capacity, to avoid being washed up at thirty-eight. She landed a position as choreographer for a two-bit lounge revue, a dismally cheap imitation of the multimillion-dollar Lido, and eventually she took over the costumer's job as well. From that she moved up through a series of similar positions in larger lounges, then in small showrooms that seated four or five hundred in second-rate hotels with limited show budgets. In time she directed a revue, then directed and produced another. She was steadily becoming a respected name in the closely knit Vegas entertainment world, and she believed that she was on the verge of great success.

Almost a year ago, shortly after Danny had died, Tina had been offered a directing and co-producing job on a huge ten-million-dollar extravaganza to be staged in the two-thousand-seat main showroom of the Golden Pyramid, one of the largest and plushest hotels on the Strip. At first it had seemed terribly wrong that such a wonderful opportunity should come her way before she'd even had time to mourn her boy, as if the Fates were so shallow and insensitive as to think that they could balance the scales and offset Danny's death merely by presenting her with a chance at her dream job. Although she was bitter and depressed, although—or maybe because—she felt utterly empty and useless, she took the job.

The new show was titled *Magyck!* because the variety acts between the big dance numbers were all magicians and because the production numbers themselves featured elaborate special effects and were built around supernatural themes. The tricky spelling of the title was not Tina's idea, but most of the rest of the program was her creation, and she remained pleased with what she had wrought. Exhausted too. This year had passed in a blur of twelve- and fourteen-hour days, with no vacations and rarely a weekend off.

Nevertheless, even as preoccupied with *Magyck!* as she was, she had adjusted to Danny's death only with great difficulty. A month ago, for the first time, she'd thought that at last she had begun to overcome her grief. She was able to think about the boy without crying, to visit his grave without being overcome by grief. All things considered, she felt reasonably good, even cheerful to a degree. She would never forget him, that sweet child who had been such a large part of her, but she would no longer have to live her life around the gaping hole that he had left in it. The wound was achingly tender but healed.

That's what she had thought a month ago. For a week or two she had continued to make progress toward acceptance.

Then the new dreams began, and they were far worse than the dream that she'd had immediately after Danny had been killed.

Perhaps her anxiety about the public's reaction to *Magyck!* was causing her to recall the greater anxiety she had felt about Danny. In less than seventeen hours—at 8:00 P.M., December 30—the Golden Pyramid Hotel would present a special, invitational, VIP premiere of *Magyck!*, and the following night, New Year's Eve, the show would open to the general public. If audience reaction was as strong and as positive as Tina hoped, her financial future was assured, for her contract gave her two and one-half percent of the gross receipts, minus liquor sales, after the first five million. If *Magyck!* was a hit and packed the showroom for four or five years, as sometimes happened with successful Vegas shows, she'd be a multimillionaire by the end of the run. Of course, if the production was a flop, if it failed to please the audience, she might be back working the small lounges again, on her way down. Show business, in any form, was a merciless enterprise.

She had good reason to be suffering from anxiety attacks. Her obsessive fear of intruders in the house, her disquieting dreams about Danny, her renewed grief—all of those things might grow from her concern about *Magyck!* If that were the case, then those symptoms would disappear as soon as the fate of the show was evident. She needed only to ride out the next few days, and in the relative calm that would follow, she might be able to get on with healing herself.

In the meantime she absolutely *had* to get some sleep. At ten o'clock in the morning, she was scheduled to meet with two tour-booking agents who were considering reserving eight thousand tickets to *Magyck!* during the first three months of its run. Then at one o'clock the entire cast and the crew would assemble for the final dress rehearsal.

She fluffed her pillows, rearranged the covers, and tugged at the short nightgown in which she slept. She tried to relax by closing her eyes and envisioning a gentle night tide lapping at a silvery beach.

Thump!

She sat straight up in bed.

Something had fallen over in another part of the house. It must have been a large object because, though muffled by the intervening walls, the sound was loud enough to rouse her.

Whatever it had been . . . it hadn't simply fallen. It had been knocked over. Heavy objects didn't just fall of their own accord in deserted rooms.

She cocked her head, listening closely. Another and softer sound followed the first. It didn't last long enough for Tina to identify the source, but there was a stealthiness about it. This time she hadn't been imagining a threat. Someone actually was in the house.

As she sat up in bed, she switched on the lamp. She pulled open the nightstand drawer. The pistol was loaded. She flicked off the two safety catches.

For a while she listened.

In the brittle silence of the desert night, she imagined that she could sense an intruder listening too, listening for *her*.

She got out of bed and stepped into her slippers. Holding the gun in her right hand, she went quietly to the bedroom door.

She considered calling the police, but she was afraid of making a fool of herself. What if they came, lights flashing and sirens screaming—and found no one? If she had summoned the police every time that she imagined hearing a prowler in the house during the past two weeks, they would have decided long ago that she was scramble-brained. She was proud, unable to bear the thought of appearing to be hysterical to a couple of macho cops who would grin at her and, later over doughnuts and coffee, make jokes about her. She would search the house herself, alone.

Pointing the pistol at the ceiling, she jacked a bullet into the chamber.

Taking a deep breath, she unlocked the bedroom door and eased into the hall.

TINA SEARCHED THE ENTIRE HOUSE, EXCEPT FOR Danny's old room, but she didn't find an intruder. She almost would have preferred to discover someone lurking in the kitchen or crouching in a closet rather than be forced to look, at last, in that final space where sadness seemed to dwell like a tenant. Now she had no choice.

A little more than a year before he had died, Danny had begun sleeping at the opposite end of the small house from the master bedroom, in what had once been the den. Not long after his tenth birthday, the boy had asked for more space and privacy than was provided by his original, tiny quarters. Michael and Tina had helped him move his belongings to the den, then had shifted the couch, armchair, coffee table, and television from the den into the quarters the boy had previously occupied.

At the time, Tina was certain that Danny was aware of the nightly arguments she and Michael were having in their own bedroom, which was next to his, and that he wanted to move into the den so he wouldn't be able to hear them bickering. She and Michael hadn't yet begun to raise their voices to each other; their disagreements had been conducted in normal tones, sometimes even in whispers, yet Danny probably had heard enough to know they were having problems.

She had been sorry that he'd had to know, but she hadn't said a word to him; she'd offered no explanations, no reassurances. For one thing, she hadn't known what she *could* say. She certainly couldn't share with him her appraisal of the situation: *Danny, sweetheart, don't worry about anything you might have heard through the wall. Your father is only suffering an identity crisis. He's been acting like an ass lately, but he'll get over it.* And that was another reason she didn't attempt to explain her and Michael's problems to Danny—she thought that their estrangement was only temporary. She loved her husband, and she was sure that the sheer power of her love would restore the luster to their marriage. Six months later she and Michael separated, and less than five months after the separation, they were divorced.

Now, anxious to complete her search for the burglar— who was beginning to look as imaginary as all the other burglars she had stalked on other nights—she opened the door to Danny's bedroom. She switched on the lights and stepped inside.

No one.

Holding the pistol in front of her, she approached the closet, hesitated, then slid the door back. No one was hiding there, either. In spite of what she had heard, she was alone in the house.

As she stared at the contents of the musky closet—the boy's shoes, his jeans, dress slacks, shirts, sweaters, his blue Dodgers' baseball cap, the small blue suit he had worn on

special occasions—a lump rose in her throat. She quickly
slid the door shut and put her back against it.

Although the funeral had been more than a year ago, she
had not yet been able to dispose of Danny's belongings.
Somehow, the act of giving away his clothes would be even
sadder and more final than watching his casket being
lowered into the ground.

His clothes weren't the only things that she had kept: His
entire room was exactly as he had left it. The bed was
properly made, and several science-fiction-movie action
figures were posed on the deep headboard. More than a
hundred paperbacks were ranked alphabetically on a five-
shelf bookcase. His desk occupied one corner; tubes of glue,
miniature bottles of enamel in every color, and a variety of
model-crafting tools stood in soldierly ranks on one half of
the desk, and the other half was bare, waiting for him to
begin work. Nine model airplanes filled a display case, and
three others hung on wires from the ceiling. The walls were
decorated with evenly spaced posters—three baseball stars,
five hideous monsters from horror movies—that Danny had
carefully arranged.

Unlike many boys his age, he'd been concerned about
orderliness and cleanliness. Respecting his preference for
neatness, Tina had instructed Mrs. Neddler, the cleaning
lady who came in twice a week, to vacuum and dust his
unused bedroom as if nothing had happened to him. The
place was as spotless as ever.

Gazing at the dead boy's toys and pathetic treasures, Tina
realized, not for the first time, that it wasn't healthy for her
to maintain this place as if it were a museum. Or a shrine.
As long as she left his things undisturbed, she could
continue to entertain the hope that Danny was not dead, that

he was just away somewhere for a while, and that he would shortly pick up his life where he had left off. Her inability to clean out his room suddenly frightened her; for the first time it seemed like more than just a weakness of spirit but an indication of serious mental illness. She *had* to let the dead rest in peace. If she was ever to stop dreaming about the boy, if she were to get control of her grief, she must begin her recovery here, in this room, by conquering her irrational need to preserve his possessions in situ.

She resolved to clean this place out on Thursday, New Year's Day. Both the VIP premiere and the opening night of *Magyck!* would be behind her by then. She'd be able to relax and take a few days off. She would start by spending Thursday afternoon here, boxing the clothes and toys and posters.

As soon as she made that decision, most of her nervous energy dissipated. She sagged, limp and weary and ready to return to bed.

As she started toward the door, she caught sight of the easel, stopped, and turned. Danny had liked to draw, and the easel, complete with a box of pencils and pens and paints, had been a birthday gift when he was nine. It was an easel on one side and a chalkboard on the other. Danny had left it at the far end of the room, beyond the bed, against the wall, and that was where it had stood the last time that Tina had been here. But now it lay at an angle, the base against the wall, the easel itself slanted, chalkboard-down, across a game table. An Electronic Battleship game had stood on that table, as Danny had left it, ready for play, but the easel had toppled into it and knocked it to the floor.

Apparently, that was the noise she had heard. But she

couldn't imagine what had knocked the easel over. It couldn't have fallen by itself.

She put her gun down, went around the foot of the bed, and stood the easel on its legs, as it belonged. She stooped, retrieved the pieces of the Electronic Battleship game, and returned them to the table.

When she picked up the scattered sticks of chalk and the felt eraser, turning again to the chalkboard, she realized that two words were crudely printed on the black surface:

NOT DEAD

She scowled at the message.

She was positive that nothing had been written on the board when Danny had gone away on that scouting trip. And it had been blank the last time she'd been in this room.

Belatedly, as she pressed her fingertips to the words on the chalkboard, the possible meaning of them struck her. As a sponge soaked up water, she took a chill from the surface of the slate. Not *dead*. It was a denial of Danny's death. An angry refusal to accept the awful truth. A challenge to reality.

In one of her terrible seizures of grief, in a moment of crazy dark despair, had she come into this room and unknowingly printed those words on Danny's chalkboard?

She didn't remember doing it. If she had left this message, she must be having blackouts, temporary amnesia of which she was totally unaware. Or she was walking in her sleep. Either possibility was unacceptable.

Dear God, unthinkable.

Therefore, the words must have been here all along. Danny must have left them before he died. His printing was neat, like everything else about him, not sloppy like this scrawled message. Nevertheless, he must have done it. *Must* have.

And the obvious reference that those two words made to the bus accident in which he had perished?

Coincidence. Danny, of course, had been writing about something else, and the dark interpretation that could be drawn from those two words now, after his death, was just a macabre coincidence.

She refused to consider any other possibility because the alternatives were too frightening.

She hugged herself. Her hands were icy; they chilled her sides even through her nightgown.

Shivering, she thoroughly erased the words on the chalkboard, retrieved her handgun, and left the room, pulling the door shut behind her.

She was wide awake, but she had to get some sleep. There was so much to do in the morning. Big day.

In the kitchen, she withdrew a bottle of Wild Turkey from the cupboard by the sink. It was Michael's favorite bourbon. She poured two ounces into a water glass. Although she wasn't much of a drinker, indulging in nothing more than a glass of wine now and then, with no capacity whatsoever for hard liquor, she finished the bourbon in two swallows. Grimacing at the bitterness of the spirits, wondering why Michael had extolled this brand's smoothness, she hesitated, then poured another ounce. She finished it quickly, as though she were a child taking medicine, and then put the bottle away.

In bed again she snuggled in the covers and closed her eyes and tried not to think about the chalkboard. But an image of it appeared behind her eyes. When she couldn't banish that image, she attempted to alter it, mentally wiping the words away. But in her mind's eye, the seven letters reappeared on the chalkboard: NOT DEAD. Although she repeatedly erased them, they stubbornly returned. She grew dizzy from the bourbon and finally slipped into welcome oblivion.

T UESDAY AFTERNOON TINA WATCHED THE FINAL
dress rehearsal of *Magyck!* from a seat in the middle of the
Golden Pyramid showroom.

The theater was shaped like an enormous fan, spreading
under a high domed ceiling. The room stepped down toward
the stage in alternating wide and narrow galleries. On the
wider levels, long dinner tables, covered with white linen,
were set at right angles to the stage. Each narrow gallery
consisted of a three-foot-wide aisle with a low railing on
one side and a curving row of raised, plushly padded booths
on the other side. The focus of all the seats was the immense
stage, a marvel of the size required for a Las Vegas
spectacular, more than half again as large as the largest stage
on Broadway. It was so huge that a DC-9 airliner could be
rolled onto it without using half the space available—a feat
that had been accomplished as part of a production number
on a similar stage at a hotel in Reno several years ago. A
lavish use of blue velvet, dark leather, crystal chandeliers,
and thick blue carpet, plus an excellent sense of dramatic

lighting, gave the mammoth chamber some of the feeling of a cozy cabaret in spite of its size.

Tina sat in one of the third-tier booths, nervously sipping ice water as she watched her show.

The dress rehearsal ran without a problem. With seven massive production numbers, five major variety acts, forty-two girl dancers, forty-two boy dancers, fifteen showgirls, two boy singers, two girl singers (one temperamental), forty-seven crewmen and technicians, a twenty-piece orchestra, one elephant, one lion, two black panthers, six golden retrievers, and twelve white doves, the logistics were mind-numbingly complicated, but a year of arduous labor was evident in the slick and faultless unfolding of the program.

At the end, the cast and crew gathered onstage and applauded themselves, hugged and kissed one another. There was electricity in the air, a feeling of triumph, a nervous expectation of success.

Joel Bandiri, Tina's co-producer, had watched the show from a booth in the first tier, the VIP row, where high rollers and other friends of the hotel would be seated every night of the run. As soon as the rehearsal ended, Joel sprang out of his seat, raced to the aisle, climbed the steps to the third tier, and hurried to Tina.

"We did it!" Joel shouted as he approached her. "We made the damn thing work!"

Tina slid out of her booth to meet him.

"We got a hit, kid!" Joel said, and he hugged her fiercely, planting a wet kiss on her cheek.

She hugged him enthusiastically. "You think so? Really?"

"Think? I know! A giant. That's what we've got. A real giant! A gargantua!"

"Thank you, Joel. Thank you, thank you, thank you."

"Me? What are you thanking me for?"

"For giving me a chance to prove myself."

"Hey, I did you no favors, kid. You worked your butt off. You earned every penny you're gonna make out of this baby, just like I knew you would. We're a great team. Anybody else tried to handle all this, they'd just end up with one goddamn big *mishkadenze* on their hands. But you and me, we made it into a hit."

Joel was an odd little man: five-feet-four, slightly chubby but not fat, with curly brown hair that appeared to have frizzed and kinked in response to a jolt of electricity. His face, which was as broad and comic as that of a clown, could stretch into an endless series of rubbery expressions. He wore blue jeans, a cheap blue workshirt—and about two hundred thousand dollars' worth of rings. Six rings bedecked each of his hands, some with diamonds, some with emeralds, one with a large ruby, one with an even larger opal. As always, he seemed to be high on something, bursting with energy. When he finally stopped hugging Tina, he could not stand still. He shifted from foot to foot as he talked about *Magyck!*, turned this way and that, gestured expansively with his quick, gem-speckled hands, virtually doing a jig.

At forty-six he was the most successful producer in Las Vegas, with twenty years of hit shows behind him. The words "Joel Bandiri Presents" on a marquee were a guarantee of first-rate entertainment. He had plowed some of his substantial earnings into Las Vegas real estate, parts of two hotels, an automobile dealership, and a slot-machine casino downtown. He was so rich that he could retire and live the rest of his life in the high style and splendor for which he had a taste. But Joel would never stop willingly. He loved his work. He would most likely die on the stage, in the middle of puzzling out a tricky production problem.

He had seen Tina's work in some lounges around town, and he had surprised her when he'd offered her the chance to co-produce *Magyck!* At first she hadn't been sure if she should take the job. She was aware of his reputation as a perfectionist who demanded superhuman efforts from his people. She was also worried about being responsible for a ten-million-dollar budget. Working with that kind of money wasn't merely a step up for her; it was a giant leap.

Joel had convinced her that she'd have no difficulty matching his pace or meeting his standards, and that she was equal to the challenge. He helped her to discover new reserves of energy, new areas of competence in herself. He had become not just a valued business associate, but a good friend as well, a big brother.

Now they seemed to have shaped a hit show together.

As Tina stood in this beautiful theater, glancing down at the colorfully costumed people milling about on the stage, then looking at Joel's rubbery face, listening as her co-producer unblushingly raved about their handiwork, she was happier than she had been in a long time. If the audience at this evening's VIP premiere reacted enthusiastically, she might have to buy lead weights to keep herself from floating off the floor when she walked.

Twenty minutes later, at 3:45, she stepped onto the smooth cobblestones in front of the hotel's main entrance and handed her claim check to the valet parking attendant. While he went to fetch her Honda, she stood in the warm late-afternoon sunshine, unable to stop grinning.

She turned and looked back at the Golden Pyramid

Hotel-Casino. Her future was inextricably linked to that gaudy but undeniably impressive pile of concrete and steel. The heavy bronze and glass revolving doors glittered as they spun with a steady flow of people. Ramparts of pale pink stone stretched hundreds of feet on both sides of the entrance; those walls were windowless and garishly decorated with giant stone coins, a gushing torrent of coins flooding from a stone cornucopia. Directly overhead, the ceiling of the immense porte cochere was lined with hundreds of lights; none of the bulbs were burning now, but after nightfall they would rain dazzling, golden luminosity upon the glossy cobblestones below. The Pyramid had been built at a cost in excess of four hundred million dollars, and the owners had made certain that every last dime showed. Tina supposed that some people would say this hotel was gross, crass, tasteless, ugly—but she loved the place because it was here that she had been given her big chance.

Thus far, the thirtieth of December had been a busy, noisy, exciting day at the Pyramid. After the relative quiet of Christmas week, an uninterrupted stream of guests was pouring through the front doors. Advance bookings indicated a record New Year's holiday crowd for Las Vegas. The Pyramid, with almost three thousand rooms, was booked to capacity, as was every hotel in the city. At a few minutes past eleven o'clock, a secretary from San Diego put five dollars in a slot machine and hit a jackpot worth $495,000; word of that even reached backstage in the showroom. Shortly before noon, two high rollers from Dallas sat down at a blackjack table and, in three hours, lost a quarter of a million bucks; they were laughing and joking when they left the table to try another game. Carol Hirson, a cocktail waitress who was a friend of Tina's, had told her about the unlucky Texans a few minutes ago. Carol had been shiny-eyed and breathless because the high rollers had tipped her with green chips, as if they'd been winning instead of losing; for bringing them half a dozen drinks, she had collected twelve hundred dollars.

Sinatra was in town, at Caesar's Palace, perhaps for the last time, and even at eighty years of age, he generated more excitement in Vegas than any other famous name. Along the entire Strip and in the less posh but nonetheless jammed casinos downtown, things were jumping, sparking.

And in just four hours *Magyck!* would premiere.

The valet brought Tina's car, and she tipped him.

He said, "Break a leg tonight, Tina."

"God, I hope so."

She was home by 4:15. She had two and a half hours to fill before she had to leave for the hotel again.

She didn't need that much time to shower, apply her makeup, and dress, so she decided to pack some of Danny's belongings. Now was the right time to begin the unpleasant chore. She was in such an excellent mood that she didn't think even the sight of his room would be able to bring her down, as it usually did. No use putting it off until Thursday, as she had planned. She had at least enough time to make a start, box up the boy's clothes, if nothing else.

When she went into Danny's bedroom, she saw at once that the easel-chalkboard had been knocked over again. She put it right.

Two words were printed on the slate:

NOT DEAD

A chill swept down her back.

Last night, after drinking the bourbon, had she come back here in some kind of fugue and . . . ?

No.

She hadn't blacked out. She had not printed those words. She wasn't going crazy. She wasn't the sort of person who would snap over a thing like this. Not even a thing like *this*. She was tough. She had always prided herself on her toughness and her resiliency.

Snatching up the felt eraser, she vigorously wiped the slate clean.

Someone was playing a sick, nasty trick on her. Someone had come into the house while she was out and had printed those two words on the chalkboard again. Whoever it was, he wanted to rub her face in the tragedy that she was trying so hard to forget.

The only other person who had a right to be in the house was the cleaning woman, Vivienne Neddler. Vivienne had been scheduled to work this afternoon, but she'd canceled. Instead, she was coming in for a few hours this evening, while Tina was at the premiere.

But even if Vivienne had kept her scheduled appointment, she never would have written those words on the chalkboard. She was a sweet old woman, feisty and independent-minded but not the type to play cruel pranks.

For a moment Tina racked her mind, searching for someone to blame, and then a name occurred to her. It was the only possible suspect. Michael. Her ex-husband. There was no sign that anyone had broken into the house, no obvious evidence of forced entry, and Michael was the only other person with a key. She hadn't changed the locks after the divorce.

Shattered by the loss of his son, Michael had been irrationally vicious with Tina for months after the funeral, accusing her of being responsible for Danny's death. She had given Danny permission to go on the field trip, and as far as Michael was concerned, that had been equivalent to driving the bus off the cliff. But Danny had wanted to go to the mountains more than anything else in the world. Besides, Mr. Jaborski, the scoutmaster, had taken other groups of scouts on winter survival hikes every year for sixteen years, and no one had been even slightly injured. They didn't hike all the way into the true wilderness, just a reasonable distance off the beaten path, and they planned for every contingency. The experience was supposed to be good for a boy. Safe. Carefully managed. Everyone assured her there was no chance of trouble. She'd had no way of knowing that Jaborski's seventeenth trip would end in disaster, yet Michael blamed her. She'd thought he had regained his perspective during the last few months, but evidently not.

She stared at the chalkboard, thought of the two words that had been printed there, and anger swelled in her. Michael was behaving like a spiteful child. Didn't he realize that her grief was as difficult to bear as his? What was he trying to prove?

Furious, she went into the kitchen, picked up the telephone, and dialed Michael's number. After five rings she realized that he was at work, and she hung up.

In her mind the two words burned, white on black: NOT DEAD.

This evening she would call Michael, when she got home from the premiere and the party afterward. She was certain to be quite late, but she wasn't going to worry about waking him.

She stood indecisively in the center of the small kitchen, trying to find the willpower to go to Danny's room and box his clothes, as she had planned. But she had lost her nerve. She couldn't go in there again. Not today. Maybe not for a few days.

Damn Michael.

In the refrigerator was a half-empty bottle of white wine. She poured a glassful and carried it into the master bath.

She was drinking too much. Bourbon last night. Wine now. Until recently, she had rarely used alcohol to calm her nerves—but now it was her cure of first resort. Once she had gotten through the premiere of *Magyck!*, she'd better start cutting back on the booze. Now she desperately needed it.

She took a long shower. She let the hot water beat down on her neck for several minutes, until the stiffness in her muscles melted and flowed away.

After the shower, the chilled wine further relaxed her body, although it did little to calm her mind and allay her anxiety. She kept thinking of the chalkboard.

NOT DEAD.

$\mathbf{A}$T 6:50 TINA WAS AGAIN BACKSTAGE IN THE showroom. The place was relatively quiet, except for the muffled oceanic roar of the VIP crowd that waited in the main showroom, beyond the velvet curtains.

Eighteen hundred guests had been invited—Las Vegas movers and shakers, plus high rollers from out of town. More than fifteen hundred had returned their RSVP cards.

Already, a platoon of white-coated waiters, waitresses in crisp blue uniforms, and scurrying busboys had begun serving the dinners. The choice was filet mignon with Bernaise sauce or lobster in butter sauce, because Las Vegas was the one place in the United States where people at least temporarily set aside concerns about cholesterol. In the health-obsessed final decade of the century, eating fatty foods was widely regarded as a far more delicious—and more damning—sin than envy, sloth, thievery, and adultery.

By seven-thirty the backstage area was bustling. Technicians double-checked the motorized sets, the electrical connections, and the hydraulic pumps that raised and lowered portions of the stage. Stagehands counted and arranged props. Wardrobe women mended tears and sewed up unraveled hems that had been discovered at the last minute. Hairdressers and lighting technicians rushed about on urgent tasks. Male dancers, wearing black tuxedos for the opening number, stood tensely, an eye-pleasing collection of lean, handsome types.

Dozens of beautiful dancers and showgirls were backstage too. Some wore satin and lace. Others wore velvet and rhinestones—or feathers or sequins or furs, and a few were topless. Many were still in the communal dressing rooms, while other girls, already costumed, waited in the halls or at the edge of the big stage, talking about children and husbands and boyfriends and recipes, as if they were secretaries on a coffee break and not some of the most beautiful women in the world.

Tina wanted to stay in the wings throughout the performance, but she could do nothing more behind the curtains. *Magyck!* was now in the hands of the performers and technicians.

Twenty-five minutes before showtime Tina left the stage and went into the noisy showroom. She headed toward the center booth in the VIP row, where Charles Mainway, general manager and principal stockholder of the Golden Pyramid Hotel, waited for her.

She stopped first at the booth next to Mainway's. Joel Bandiri was with Eva, his wife of eight years, and two of their friends. Eva was twenty-nine, seventeen years younger than Joel, and at five foot eight, she was also four inches taller than he was. She was an ex-showgirl, blond, willowy, delicately beautiful. She gently squeezed Tina's hand. "Don't worry. You're too good to fail."

"We got a hit, kid," Joel assured Tina once more.

In the next semicircular booth, Charles Mainway greeted Tina with a warm smile. Mainway carried and held himself as if he were an aristocrat, and his mane of silver hair and his clear blue eyes contributed to the image he wished to project. However, his features were large, square, and utterly without evidence of patrician blood, and even after the mellowing influences of elocution teachers, his naturally low, gravelly voice belied his origins in a rough Brooklyn neighborhood.

As Tina slid into the booth beside Mainway, a tuxedoed captain appeared and filled her glass with Dom Pérignon.

Helen Mainway, Charlie's wife, sat at his left side. Helen was by nature everything that poor Charlie struggled to be: impeccably well-mannered, sophisticated, graceful, at ease and confident in any situation. She was tall, slender, striking, fifty-five years old but able to pass for a well-preserved forty.

"Tina, my dear, I want you to meet a friend of ours," Helen said, indicating the fourth person in the booth. "This is Elliot Stryker. Elliot, this lovely young lady is Christina Evans, the guiding hand behind *Magyck!*"

"One of *two* guiding hands," Tina said. "Joel Bandiri is more responsible for the show than I am—especially if it's a flop."

Stryker laughed. "I'm pleased to meet you, Mrs. Evans."

"Just plain Tina," she said.

"And I'm just plain Elliot."

He was a rugged, good-looking man, neither big nor small, about forty. His dark eyes were deeply set, quick, marked by intelligence and amusement.

"Elliot's my attorney," Charlie Mainway said.

"Oh," Tina said, "I thought Harry Simpson—"

"Harry's a hotel attorney. Elliot handles my private affairs."

"And handles them very well," Helen said. "Tina, if you need an attorney, this is the best in Las Vegas."

To Tina, Stryker said, "But if it's flattery you need—and I'm sure you already get a lot of it, lovely as you are—no one in Vegas can flatter with more charm and style than Helen."

"You see what he just did?" Helen asked Tina, clapping her hands with delight. "In one sentence he managed to flatter you, flatter me, and impress all of us with his modesty. You see what a wonderful attorney he is?"

"Imagine him arguing a point in court," Charlie said.

"A very smooth character indeed," Helen said.

Stryker winked at Tina. "Smooth as I might be, I'm no match for these two."

They made pleasant small talk for the next fifteen minutes, and none of it had to do with *Magyck!* Tina was aware that they were trying to take her mind off the show, and she appreciated their effort.

Of course no amount of amusing talk, no quantity of icy Dom Pérignon could render her unaware of the excitement that was building in the showroom as curtain time drew near. Minute by minute the cloud of cigarette smoke overhead thickened. Waitresses, waiters, and captains rushed back and forth to fill the drink orders before the show began. The roar of conversation grew louder as the sounds ticked away, and the quality of the roar became more frenetic, gayer, and more often punctuated with laughter.

Somehow, even though her attention was partly on the mood of the crowd, partly on Helen and Charlie Mainway, Tina was nevertheless aware of Elliot Stryker's reaction to her. He made no great show of being more than ordinarily interested in her, but the attraction she held for him was evident in his eyes. Beneath his cordial, witty, slightly cool exterior, his secret response was that of a healthy male animal, and her awareness of it was more instinctual than intellectual, like a mare's response to the stallion's first faint stirrings of desire.

At least a year and a half, maybe two years, had passed since a man had looked at her in quite that fashion. Or perhaps this was the first time in all those months that she had been *aware* of being the object of such interest. Fighting with Michael, coping with the shock of separation and divorce, grieving for Danny, and putting together the show with Joel Bandiri had filled her days and nights, so she'd had no chance to think of romance.

Responding to the unspoken need in Elliot's eyes with a need of her own, she was suddenly warm.

She thought: *My God, I've been letting myself dry up! How could I have forgotten this!*

Now that she had spent more than a year grieving for her broken marriage and for her lost son, now that *Magyck!* was almost behind her, she would have time to be a woman again. She would *make* time.

Time for Elliot Stryker? She wasn't sure. No reason to be in a hurry to make up for lost pleasures. She shouldn't jump at the first man who wanted her. Surely that wasn't the smart thing to do. On the other hand, he was handsome, and in his face was an appealing gentleness. She had to admit that he sparked the same feelings in her that she apparently enflamed in him.

The evening was turning out to be even more interesting than she had expected.

V IVIENNE NEDDLER PARKED HER VINTAGE 1955
Nash Rambler at the curb in front of the Evans house, being
careful not to scrape the whitewalls. The car was immacu-
late, in better shape than most new cars these days. In a
world of planned obsolescence, Vivienne took pleasure in
getting long, full use out of everything that she bought,
whether it was a toaster or an automobile. She enjoyed
making things last.

She had lasted quite a while herself. She was seventy, still
in excellent health, a short sturdy woman with the sweet
face of a Botticelli Madonna and the no-nonsense walk of
an army sergeant.

She got out of the car and, carrying a purse the size
of a small suitcase, marched up the walk toward the
house, angling away from the front door and past the
garage.

The sulfur-yellow light from the street lamps failed to
reach all the way across the lawn. Beside the front walkway
and then along the side of the house, low-voltage landscape
lighting revealed the path.

Oleander bushes rustled in the breeze. Overhead, palm fronds scraped softly against one another.

As Vivienne reached the back of the house, the crescent moon slid out from behind one of the few thin clouds, like a scimitar being drawn from a scabbard, and the pale shadows of palms and melaleucas shivered on the lunar-silvered concrete patio.

Vivienne let herself in through the kitchen door. She'd been cleaning for Tina Evans for two years, and she had been entrusted with a key nearly that long.

The house was silent except for the softly humming refrigerator.

Vivienne began work in the kitchen. She wiped the counters and the appliances, sponged off the slats of the Levolor blinds, and mopped the Mexican-tile floor. She did a first-rate job. She believed in the moral value of hard work, and she always gave her employers their money's worth.

She usually worked during the day, not at night. This afternoon, however, she'd been playing a pair of lucky slot machines at the Mirage Hotel, and she hadn't wanted to walk away from them while they were paying off so generously. Some people for whom she cleaned house insisted that she keep regularly scheduled appointments, and they did a slow burn if she showed up more than a few minutes late. But Tina Evans was sympathetic; she knew how important the slot machines were to Vivienne, and she wasn't upset if Vivienne occasionally had to reschedule her visit.

Vivienne was a nickel duchess. That was the term by which casino employees still referred to local, elderly women whose social lives revolved around an obsessive interest in one-armed bandits, even though the nickel machines were pretty much ancient history. Nickel duchesses always played the cheap slot machines—nickels and dimes in the old days, now quarters   never the dollar- or five-dollar slots. They pulled the handles for hours at a time, often making a twenty-dollar bill last a long afternoon. Their gaming philosophy was simple: *It doesn't matter if you win or lose, as long as you stay in the game.* With that attitude plus a few money-management skills, they were able to hang on longer than most slot players who plunged at the dollar machines after getting nowhere with quarters, and because of their patience and perseverance, the duchesses won more jackpots than did the tide of tourists that ebbed and flowed around them. Even these days, when most machines could be played with electronically validated value cards, the nickel duchesses wore black gloves to keep their hands from becoming filthy after hours of handling coins and pulling levers; they always sat on stools while they played, and they remembered to alternate hands when operating the machines in order not to strain the muscles of one arm, and they carried bottles of liniment just in case.

The duchesses, who for the most part were widows and spinsters, often ate lunch and dinner together. They cheered one another on those rare occasions when one of them hit a really large jackpot; and when one of them died, the others went to the funeral en masse. Together they formed an odd but solid community, with a satisfying sense of belonging. In a country that worshiped youth, most elderly

Americans devoutly desired to discover a place where they belonged, but unlike the duchesses, many of them never found it.

Vivienne had a daughter, a son-in-law, and three grand-children in Sacramento. For five years, ever since her sixty-fifth birthday, they had been pressuring her to live with them. She loved them as much as life itself, and she knew they truly wanted her with them; they were not inviting her out of a misguided sense of guilt and obligation. Nevertheless, she didn't want to live in Sacramento. After several visits there, she had decided that it must be one of the dullest cities in the world. Vivienne liked the action, noise, lights, and excitement of Las Vegas. Besides, living in Sacramento, she wouldn't be a nickel duchess any longer; she wouldn't be anyone special; she would be just another elderly lady, living with her daughter's family, playing grandma, marking time, waiting to die.

A life like that would be intolerable.

Vivienne valued her independence more than anything else. She prayed that she would remain healthy enough to continue working and living on her own until, at last, her time came and all the little windows on the machine of life produced lemons.

As she was mopping the last corner of the kitchen floor, as she was thinking about how dreary life would be without her friends and her slot machines, she heard a sound in another part of the house. Toward the front. The living room.

She froze, listening.

The refrigerator motor stopped running. A clock ticked softly.

After a long silence, a brief clattering echoed through the house from another room, startling Vivienne. Then silence again.

She went to the drawer next to the sink and selected a long, sharp blade from an assortment of knives.

She didn't even consider calling the police. If she phoned for them and then ran out of the house, they might not find an intruder when they came. They would think she was just a foolish old woman. Vivienne Neddler refused to give anyone reason to think her a fool.

Besides, for the past twenty-one years, ever since her Harry died, she had always taken care of herself. She had done a pretty damn good job of it too.

She stepped out of the kitchen and found the light switch to the right of the doorway. The dining room was deserted.

In the living room, she clicked on a Stifel lamp. No one was there.

She was about to head for the den when she noticed something odd about four framed eight-by-ten photographs that were grouped on the wall above the sofa. This display had always contained six pictures, not just four. But the fact that two were missing wasn't what drew Vivienne's attention. All four of the remaining photos were swinging back and forth on the picture hooks that held them. No one was near them, yet suddenly two photos began to rattle violently against the wall, and then both flew off their mountings and clattered to the floor behind the beige, brushed-corduroy sofa.

This was the sound she had heard when she'd been in the kitchen—this clatter.

"What the hell?"

The remaining two photographs abruptly flung themselves off the wall. One dropped behind the sofa, and the other tumbled onto it.

Vivienne blinked in amazement, unable to understand what she had seen. An earthquake? But she hadn't felt the house move; the windows hadn't rattled. Any tremor too mild to be felt would also be too mild to tear the photographs from the wall.

She went to the sofa and picked up the photo that had dropped onto the cushions. She knew it well. She had dusted it many times. It was a portrait of Danny Evans, as were the other five that usually hung around it. In this one, he was ten or eleven years old, a sweet brown-haired boy with dark eyes and a lovely smile.

Vivienne wondered if there had been a nuclear test; maybe *that* was what had shaken things up. The Nevada Nuclear Test Site, where underground detonations were conducted several times a year, was less than a hundred miles north of Las Vegas. Whenever the military exploded a high-yield weapon, the tall hotels swayed in Vegas, and every house in town shuddered a little.

But, no, she was stuck in the past: The Cold War was over, and nuclear tests hadn't been conducted out in the desert for a long time. Besides, the house hadn't shuddered just a minute ago; only the photos had been affected.

Puzzled, frowning thoughtfully, Vivienne put down the knife, pulled one end of the sofa away from the wall, and collected the framed eight-by-tens that were on the floor behind it. There were five photographs in addition to the one that had dropped onto the sofa; two were responsible for the noises that had drawn her into the living room, and the other three were those that she had seen popping off the picture hooks. She put them back where they belonged, then slid the sofa into place.

A burst of high-pitched electronic noise blared through the house: *Aiii-eee . . . aiii-eee . . . aiii-eee . . .*

Vivienne gasped, turned. She was still alone.

Her first thought was: *Burglar alarm.*

But the Evans house didn't have an alarm system.

Vivienne winced as the shrill electronic squeal grew louder, a piercing oscillation. The nearby windows and the thick glass top of the coffee table were vibrating. She felt a sympathetic resonance in her teeth and bones.

She wasn't able to identify the source of the sound. It seemed to be coming from every corner of the house.

"What in the blue devil is going on here?"

She didn't bother picking up the knife, because she was sure the problem wasn't an intruder. It was something else, something weird.

She crossed the room to the hallway that served the bedrooms, bathrooms, and den. She snapped on the light. The noise was louder in the corridor than it had been in the living room. The nerve-fraying sound bounced off the walls of the narrow passage, echoing and re-echoing.

Vivienne looked both ways, then moved to the right, toward the closed door at the end of the hall. Toward Danny's old room.

The air was cooler in the hallway than it was in the rest of the house. At first Vivienne thought that she was imagining the change in temperature. but the closer she drew to the end of the corridor, the colder it got. By the time she reached the closed door, her skin was goose-pimpled, and her teeth were chattering.

Step by step, her curiosity gave way to fear. Something was very wrong here. An ominous pressure seemed to compress the air around her.

Aiii-eee . . . aiii-eee . . .

The wisest thing she could do would be to turn back, walk away from the door and out of the house. But she wasn't completely in control of herself; she felt a bit like a sleepwalker. In spite of her anxiety, a power she could sense—but which she could not define—drew her inexorably to Danny's room.

Aiii-eee . . . aiii-eee . . . aiii-eee . . .

Vivienne reached for the doorknob but stopped before touching it, unable to believe what she was seeing. She blinked rapidly, closed her eyes, opened them again, but still the doorknob appeared to be sheathed in a thin, irregular jacket of ice.

She finally touched it. *Ice.* Her skin almost stuck to the knob. She pulled her hand away and examined her damp fingers. Moisture had condensed on the metal and then had frozen.

But how was that possible? How in the name of God could there be ice here, in a well-heated house and on a night when the outside temperature was at least twenty degrees above the freezing point?

The electronic squeal began to warble faster, but it was no quieter, no less bone-penetrating than it had been.

Stop, Vivienne told herself. *Get away from here. Get out as fast as you can.*

But she ignored her own advice. She pulled her blouse out of her slacks and used the tail to protect her hand from the icy metal doorknob. The knob turned, but the door wouldn't open. The intense cold had caused the wood to contract and warp. She put her shoulder against it, pushed gently, then harder, and finally the door swung inward.

MAGYCK! WAS THE MOST ENTERTAINING VEGAS show that Elliot Stryker had ever seen.

The program opened with an electrifying rendition of "That Old Black Magic." Singers and dancers, brilliantly costumed, performed in a stunning set constructed of mirrored steps and mirrored panels. When the stage lights were periodically dimmed, a score of revolving crystal ballroom chandeliers cast swirling splinters of color that seemed to coalesce into supernatural forms that capered under the proscenium arch. The choreography was complex, and the two lead singers had strong, clear voices.

The opening number was followed by a first-rate magic act in front of the drawn curtains. Less than ten minutes later, when the curtains opened again, the mirrors had been taken away, and the stage had been transformed into an ice rink; the second production number was done on skates against a winter backdrop so real that it made Elliot shiver.

Although *Magyck!* excited the imagination and commanded the eye, Elliot wasn't able to give his undivided attention to it. He kept looking at Christina Evans, who was as dazzling as the show she had created.

She watched the performers intently, unaware of his gaze. A flickering, nervous scowl played across her face, alternating with a tentative smile that appeared when the audience laughed, applauded, or gasped in surprise.

She was singularly beautiful. Her shoulder-length hair—deep brown, almost black, glossy—swept across her brow, feathered back at the sides, and framed her face as though it were a painting by a great master. The bone structure of that face was delicate, clearly defined, quintessentially feminine. Dusky, olive complexion. Full, sensuous mouth. And her eyes . . . She would have been lovely enough if her eyes had been dark, in harmony with the shade of her hair and skin, but they were crystalline blue. The contrast between her Italian good looks and her Nordic eyes was devastating.

Elliot supposed that other people might find flaws in her face. Perhaps some would say that her brow was too wide. Her nose was so straight that some might think it was severe. Others might say that her mouth was too wide, her chin too pointed. To Elliot, however, her face was perfect.

But her physical beauty was not what most excited him. He was interested primarily in learning more about the mind that could create a work like *Magyck!* He had seen less than one-fourth of the program, yet he knew it was a hit—and far superior to others of its kind. A Vegas stage extravaganza could easily go off the rails. If the gigantic sets and lavish costumes and intricate choreography were overdone, or if any element was improperly executed, the production would quickly stumble across the thin line between captivating show-biz flash and sheer vulgarity. A glittery fantasy could metamorphose into a crude, tasteless, and stupid bore if the wrong hand guided it. Elliot wanted to know more about Christina Evans—and on a more fundamental level, he just *wanted* her.

No woman had affected him so strongly since Nancy, his wife, who had died three years ago.

Sitting in the dark theater, he smiled, not at the comic magician who was performing in front of the closed stage curtains, but at his own sudden, youthful exuberance.

T HE WARPED DOOR GROANED AND CREAKED AS Vivienne Neddler forced it open.

Aiii-eee, aiii-eee . . .

A wave of frigid air washed out of the dark room, into the hallway.

Vivienne reached inside, fumbled for the light switch, found it, and entered warily. The room was deserted.

Aiii-eee, aii-eee . . .

Baseball stars and horror-movie monsters gazed at Vivienne from posters stapled to the walls. Three intricate model airplanes were suspended from the ceiling. These things were as they always had been, since she had first come to work here, before Danny had died.

Aiii-eee, aiii-eee, aiii-eee . . .

The maddening electronic squeal issued from a pair of small stereo speakers that hung on the wall behind the bed. The CD player and an accompanying AM-FM tuner and amplifier were stacked on one of the nightstands.

Although Vivienne could see where the noise originated, she couldn't locate any source for the bitterly cold air.

Neither window was open, and even if one had been raised, the night wasn't frigid enough to account for the chill.

Just as she reached the AM-FM tuner, the banshee wail stopped. The sudden silence had an oppressive weight.

Gradually, as her ears stopped ringing, Vivienne perceived the soft empty hiss of the stereo speakers. Then she heard the thumping of her own heart.

The metal casing of the radio gleamed with a brittle crust of ice. She touched it wonderingly. A sliver of ice broke loose under her finger and fell onto the nightstand. It didn't begin to melt; the room was *cold.*

The window was frosted. The dresser mirror was frosted too, and her reflection was dim and distorted and strange.

Outside, the night was cool but not wintry. Maybe fifty degrees. Maybe even fifty-five.

The radio's digital display began to change, the orange numbers escalating across the frequency band, sweeping through one station after another. Scraps of music, split-second flashes of disc jockeys' chatter, single words from different somber-voiced newscasters, and fragments of commercial jingles blended in a cacophonous jumble of meaningless sound. The indicator reached the end of the band width, and the digital display began to sequence backward.

Trembling, Vivienne switched off the radio.

As soon as she took her finger off the push switch, the radio turned itself on again.

She stared at it, frightened and bewildered.

The digital display began to sequence up the band once more, and scraps of music blasted from the speakers.

She pressed the ON-OFF bar again.

After a brief silence, the radio turned on spontaneously.

"This is crazy," she said shakily.

When she shut off the radio the third time, she kept her finger pressed against the ON-OFF bar. For several seconds she was certain that she could feel the switch straining under her fingertip as it tried to pop on.

Overhead, the three model airplanes began to move. Each was hung from the ceiling on a length of fishing line, and the upper end of each line was knotted to its own eye-hook that had been screwed firmly into the drywall. The planes jiggled, jerked, twisted, and trembled.

Just a draft.

But she didn't feel a draft.

The model planes began to bounce violently up and down on the ends of their lines.

"God help me," Vivienne said.

One of the planes swung in tight circles, faster and faster, then in wider circles, steadily decreasing the angle between the line on which it was suspended and the bedroom ceiling. After a moment the other two models ceased their erratic dancing and began to spin around and around, like the first plane, as if they were actually flying, and there was no mistaking this deliberate movement for the random effects of a draft.

Ghosts? A poltergeist?

But she didn't believe in ghosts. There were no such things. She believed in death and taxes, in the inevitability of slot-machine jackpots, in all-you-can-eat casino buffets for $5.95 per person, in the Lord God Almighty, in the truth of alien abductions and Big Foot, but she didn't believe in ghosts.

The sliding closet doors began to move on their runners, and Vivienne Neddler had the feeling that some awful *thing* was going to come out of the dark space, its eyes as red as blood and its razor-sharp teeth gnashing. She felt a *presence*, something that wanted her, and she cried out as the door came all the way open.

But there wasn't a monster in the closet. It contained only clothes. Only clothes.

Nevertheless, untouched, the doors glided shut . . . and then open again. . . .

The model planes went around, around.

The air grew even colder.

The bed started to shake. The legs at the foot rose three or four inches before crashing back into the casters that had been put under them to protect the carpet. They rose up again. Hovered above the floor. The springs began to sing as if metal fingers were strumming them.

Vivienne backed into the wall, eyes wide, hands fisted at her sides.

As abruptly as the bed had started bouncing up and down, it now stopped. The closet doors closed with a jarring crash—but they didn't open again. The model airplanes slowed, swinging in smaller and smaller circles, until they finally hung motionless.

The room was silent.

Nothing moved.

The air was getting warmer.

Gradually Vivienne's heartbeat subsided from the hard, frantic rhythm that it had been keeping for the past couple of minutes. She hugged herself and shivered.

A logical explanation. There had to be a logical explanation.

But she wasn't able to imagine what it could be.

As the room grew warm again, the doorknobs and the radio casing and the other metal objects quickly shed their fragile skins of ice, leaving shallow puddles on furniture and damp spots in the carpet. The frosted window cleared, and as the frost faded from the dresser mirror, Vivienne's distorted reflection resolved into a more familiar image of herself.

Now this was only a young boy's bedroom, a room like countless thousands of others.

Except, of course, that the boy who had once slept here had been dead for a year. And maybe he was coming back, haunting the place.

Vivienne had to remind herself that she didn't believe in ghosts.

Nevertheless, it might be a good idea for Tina Evans to get rid of the boy's belongings at last.

Vivienne had no logical explanation for what had happened, but she knew one thing for sure: She wasn't going to tell anyone what she had seen here tonight. Regardless of how convincingly and earnestly she described these bizarre events, no one would believe her. They would nod and smile woodenly and agree that it was a strange and frightening experience, but all the while they would be thinking that poor old Vivienne was finally getting senile. Sooner or later word of her rantings about poltergeists might get back to her daughter in Sacramento, and then the pressure to move to California would become unbearable. Vivienne wasn't going to jeopardize her precious independence.

She left the bedroom, returned to the kitchen, and drank two shots of Tina Evans's best bourbon. Then, with characteristic stoicism, she returned to the boy's bedroom to wipe up the water from the melted ice, and she continued housecleaning.

She refused to let a poltergeist scare her off.

It might be wise, however, to go to church on Sunday. She hadn't been to church in a long time. Maybe some churching would be good for her. Not every week, of course. Just one or two Masses a month. And confession now and then. She hadn't seen the inside of a confessional in ages. Better safe than sorry.

8

EVERYONE IN SHOW BUSINESS KNEW THAT NON-paying preview crowds were among the toughest to please. Free admission didn't guarantee their appreciation or even their amicability. The person who paid a fair price for something was likely to place far more value on it than the one who got the same item for nothing. That old saw applied in spades to stage shows and to on-the-cuff audiences.

But not tonight. *This* crowd wasn't able to sit on its hands and keep its cool.

The final curtain came down at eight minutes till ten o'clock, and the ovation continued until after Tina's wristwatch had marked the hour. The cast of *Magyck!* took several bows, then the crew, then the orchestra, all of them flushed with the excitement of being part of an unqualified hit. At the insistence of the happy, boisterous, VIP audience, both Joel Bandiri and Tina were spotlighted in their booths and were rewarded with their own thunderous round of applause.

Tina was on an adrenaline high, grinning, breathless, barely able to absorb the overwhelming response to her work. Helen Mainway chattered excitedly about the spectacular special effects, and Elliot Stryker had an endless supply of compliments as well as some astute observations about the technical aspects of the production, and Charlie Mainway poured a third bottle of Dom Pérignon, and the house lights came up, and the audience reluctantly began to leave, and Tina hardly had a chance to sip her champagne because of all the people who stopped by the table to congratulate her.

By ten-thirty most of the audience had left, and those who hadn't gone yet were in line, moving up the steps toward the rear doors of the showroom. Although no second show was scheduled this evening, as would be the case every night henceforth, busboys and waitresses were busily clearing tables, resetting them with fresh linen and silverware for the following night's eight o'clock performance.

When the aisle in front of her booth was finally empty of well-wishers, Tina got up and met Joel as he started to come to her. She threw her arms around him and, much to her surprise, began to cry with happiness. She hugged him hard, and Joel proclaimed the show to be a "gargantua if I ever saw one."

By the time they got backstage, the opening-night party was in full swing. The sets and props had been moved from the main floor of the stage, and eight folding tables had been set up. The tables were draped with white cloths and burdened with food: five hot hors d'oeuvres, lobster salad, crab salad, pasta salad, filet mignon, chicken breasts in tarragon sauce, roasted potatoes, cakes, pies, tarts, fresh fruits, berries, and cheeses. Hotel management personnel, showgirls, dancers, magicians, crewmen, and musicians crowded around the tables, sampling the offerings while Phillippe Chevalier, the hotel's executive chef, personally watched over the affair. Knowing this feast had been laid on for the party, few of those present had eaten dinner, and most of the dancers had eaten nothing since a light lunch. They exclaimed over the food and clustered around the portable bar. With the memory of the applause still fresh in everyone's mind, the party was soon jumping.

Tina mingled, moving back and forth, upstage and downstage, through the crowd, thanking everyone for his contribution to the show's success, complimenting each member of the cast and crew on his dedication and professionalism. Several times she encountered Elliot Stryker, and he seemed genuinely interested in learning how the splashy stage effects had been achieved. Each time that Tina moved on to talk to someone else, she regretted leaving Elliot, and each time that she found him again, she stayed with him longer than she had before. After their fourth encounter, she lost track of how long they were together. Finally she forgot all about circulating.

Standing near the left proscenium pillar, out of the main flow of the party, they nibbled at pieces of cake, talking about *Magyck!* and then about the law, Charlie and Helen Mainway, Las Vegas real estate—and, by some circuitous route, superhero movies.

He said, "How can Batman wear an armored rubber suit all the time and not have a chronic rash?"

"Yeah, but there are advantages to a rubber suit."

"Such as?"

"You can go straight from office work to scuba diving without changing clothes."

"Eat takeout food at two hundred miles an hour in the Batmobile, and no matter how messy it gets—just hose off later."

"Exactly. After a hard day of crime-fighting, you can get stinking drunk and throw up on yourself, and it doesn't matter. No dry-cleaning bills."

"In basic black he's dressed for any occasion—"

"—from an audience with the Pope to a Marquis de Sade memorial sock hop."

Elliot smiled. He finished his cake. "I guess you'll have to be here most nights for a long time to come."

"No. There's really no need for me to be."

"I thought a director—"

"Most of the director's job is finished. I just have to check on the show once every couple of weeks to make sure the tone of it isn't drifting away from my original intention."

"But you're also the co-producer."

"Well, now that the show's opened successfully, most of my share of the producer's chores are public relations and promotional stuff. And a little logistics to keep the production rolling along smoothly. But nearly all of that can be handled out of my office. I won't have to hang around the stage. In fact, Joel says it isn't healthy for a producer to be backstage every night . . . or even most nights. He says I'd just make the performers nervous and cause the technicians to look over their shoulders for the boss when they should have their eyes on their work."

"But will you be able to resist?"

"It won't be easy staying away. But there's a lot of sense in what Joel says, so I'm going to try to play it cool."

"Still, I guess you'll be here every night for the first week or so."

"No," she said. "If Joel's right—and I'm sure he is—then it's best to get in the habit of staying away right from the start."

"Tomorrow night?"

"Oh, I'll probably pop in and out a few times."

"I guess you'll be going to a New Year's Eve party."

"I hate New Year's Eve parties. Everyone's drunk and boring."

"Well, then . . . in between all that popping in and out of *Magyck!*, do you think you'd have time for dinner?"

"Are you asking me for a date?"

"I'll try not to slurp my soup."

"You *are* asking me for a date," she said, pleased.

"Yes. And it's been a long time since I've been this awkward about it."

"Why is that?"

"You, I guess."

"I make you feel awkward?"

"You make me feel young. And when I was young, I was very awkward."

"That's sweet."

"I'm trying to charm you."

"And succeeding," she said.

He had such a warm smile. "Suddenly I don't feel so awkward anymore."

She said, "You want to start over?"

"Will you have dinner with me tomorrow night?"

"Sure. How about seven-thirty?"

"Fine. You prefer dressy or casual?"

"Blue jeans."

He fingered his starched collar and the satin lapel of his tuxedo jacket. "I'm so glad you said that."

"I'll give you my address." She searched her purse for a pen.

"We can stop in here and watch the first few numbers in *Magyck!* and then go to the restaurant."

"Why don't we just go straight to the restaurant?"

"You don't want to pop in here?"

"I've decided to go cold turkey."

"Joel will be proud of you."

"If I can actually do it, *I'll* be proud of me."

"You'll do it. You've got true grit."

"In the middle of dinner, I might be seized by a desperate need to dash over here and act like a producer."

"I'll park the car in front of the restaurant door, and I'll leave the engine running just in case."

Tina gave her address to him, and then somehow they were talking about jazz and Benny Goodman, and then about the miserable service provided by the Las Vegas phone company, just chatting away as if they were old friends. He had a variety of interests; among other things he was a skier and a pilot, and he was full of funny stories about learning to ski and fly. He made her feel comfortable, yet at the same time he intrigued her. He projected an interesting image: a blend of male power and gentleness, aggressive sexuality and kindness.

A hit show . . . lots of royalty checks to look forward to . . . an infinity of new opportunities made available to her because of this first smashing success . . . and now the prospect of a new and exciting lover . . .

As she listed her blessings, Tina was astonished at how much difference one year could make in a life. From bitterness, pain, tragedy, and unrelenting sorrow, she had turned around to face a horizon lit by rising promise. At last the future looked worth living. Indeed, she couldn't see how anything could go wrong.

THE SKIRTS OF THE NIGHT WERE GATHERED
around the Evans house, rustling in a dry desert wind.

A neighbor's white cat crept across the lawn, stalking a
wind-tossed scrap of paper. The cat pounced, missed its
prey, stumbled, scared itself, and flashed lightning-quick
into another yard.

Inside, the house was mostly silent. Now and then the
refrigerator switched on, purring to itself. A loose window-
pane in the living room rattled slightly whenever a strong
gust of wind struck it. The heating system rumbled to life,
and for a couple of minutes at a time, the blower whispered
wordlessly as hot air pushed through the vents.

Shortly before midnight, Danny's room began to grow
cold. On the doorknob, on the radio casing, and on other
metal objects, moisture began to condense out of the air.
The temperature plunged rapidly, and the beads of water
froze. Frost formed on the window.

The radio clicked on.

For a few seconds the silence was split by an electronic
squeal as sharp as an ax blade. Then the shrill noise abruptly

stopped, and the digital display flashed with rapidly changing numbers. Snippets of music and shards of voices crackled in an eerie audio-montage that echoed and re-echoed off the walls of the frigid room.

No one was in the house to hear it.

The closet door opened, closed, opened. . . .

Inside the closet, shirts and jeans began to swing wildly on the pole from which they hung, and some clothes fell to the floor.

The bed shook.

The display case that held nine model airplanes rocked, banging repeatedly against the wall. One of the models was flung from its shelf, then two more, then three more, then another, until all nine lay in a pile on the floor.

On the wall to the left of the bed, a poster of the creature from the *Alien* movies tore down the middle.

The radio ceased scanning, stopping on an open frequency that hissed and popped with distant static. Then a voice blared from the speakers. It was a child's voice. A boy. There were no words. Just a long, agonized scream.

The voice faded after a minute, but the bed began to bang up and down.

The closet door slammed open and shut with substantially more force than it had earlier.

Other things began to move too. For almost five minutes the room seemed to have come alive.

And then it died.

Silence returned.

The air grew warm again.

The frost left the window, and outside the white cat still chased the scrap of paper.

WEDNESDAY,

DECEMBER 31

10

Tina didn't get home from the opening-night party until shortly before two o'clock Wednesday morning. Exhausted, slightly tipsy, she went directly to bed and fell into a sound sleep.

Later, after no more than two dreamless hours, she suffered another nightmare about Danny. He was trapped at the bottom of a deep hole. She heard his frightened voice calling to her, and she peered over the edge of the pit, and he was so far below her that his face was only a tiny, pale smudge. He was desperate to get out, and she was frantic to rescue him; but he was chained, unable to climb, and the sides of the pit were sheer and smooth, so she had no way to reach him. Then a man dressed entirely in black from head to foot, his face hidden by shadows, appeared at the far side of the pit and began to shovel dirt into it. Danny's cry escalated into a scream of terror; he was being buried alive. Tina shouted at the man in black, but he ignored her and kept shoveling dirt on top of Danny. She edged around the pit, determined to make the hateful bastard stop what he was doing, but he took a step away from her for every step that she took toward him, and he always stayed directly across the hole from her. She couldn't reach him, and she couldn't reach Danny, and the dirt was up to the boy's knees, and now up to his hips, and now over his shoulders. Danny wailed and shrieked, and now the earth was even with his chin, but the man in black wouldn't stop filling in the hole. She wanted to kill the bastard, club him to death with his own shovel. When she thought of clubbing him, he looked at her, and she saw his face: a fleshless skull with rotting skin stretched over the bones, burning red eyes, a yellow-toothed grin. A disgusting cluster of maggots clung to the man's left cheek and to the corner of his eye, feeding off him. Tina's terror over Danny's impending entombment was suddenly mixed with fear for her own life. Though Danny's screams were increasingly muffled, they were even more urgent than before, because the dirt began to cover his face and pour into his mouth. She had to get down to him and push the earth away from his face before he suffocated, so in blind panic she threw herself over the edge of the pit, into the terrible abyss, falling and falling—

Gasping, shuddering, she wrenched herself out of sleep.

She was convinced that the man in black was in her bedroom, standing silently in the darkness, grinning. Heart pounding, she fumbled with the bedside lamp. She blinked in the sudden light and saw that she was alone.

"Jesus," she said weakly.

She wiped one hand across her face, sloughing off a film of perspiration. She dried her hand on the sheets.

She did some deep-breathing exercises, trying to calm herself.

She couldn't stop shaking.

In the bathroom, she washed her face. The mirror

revealed a person whom she hardly recognized: a haggard, bloodless, sunken-eyed fright.

Her mouth was dry and sour. She drank a glass of cold water.

Back in bed, she didn't want to turn off the light. Her fear made her angry with herself, and at last she twisted the switch.

The returning darkness was threatening.

She wasn't sure she would be able to get any more sleep, but she had to try. It wasn't even five o'clock. She'd been asleep less than three hours.

In the morning, she would clean out Danny's room. Then the dreams would stop. She was pretty much convinced of that.

She remembered the two words that she had twice erased from Danny's chalkboard—NOT DEAD—and she realized that she'd forgotten to call Michael. She had to confront him with her suspicions. She had to know if he'd been in the house, in Danny's room, without her knowledge or permission.

It *had* to be Michael.

She could turn on the light and call him now. He would be sleeping, but she wouldn't feel guilty if she woke him, not after all the sleepless nights that he had given her. Right now, however, she didn't feel up to the battle. Her wits were dulled by wine and exhaustion. And if Michael *had* slipped into the house like a little boy playing a cruel prank, if he *had* written that message on the chalkboard, then his hatred of her was far greater than she had thought. He might even be a desperately sick man. If he became verbally violent and abusive, if he were irrational, she would need to have a clear head to deal with him. She would call him in the morning when she had regained some of her strength.

She yawned and turned over and drifted off to sleep. She didn't dream anymore, and when she woke at ten o'clock, she was refreshed and newly excited by the previous night's success.

She phoned Michael, but he wasn't home. Unless he'd changed shifts in the past six months, he didn't go to work until noon. She decided to try his number again in half an hour.

After retrieving the morning newspaper from the front stoop, she read the rave review of *Magyck!* written by the *Review-Journal*'s entertainment critic. He couldn't find anything wrong with the show. His praise was so effusive that, even reading it by herself, in her own kitchen, she was slightly embarrassed by the effusiveness of the praise.

She ate a light breakfast of grapefruit juice and one English muffin, then went to Danny's room to pack his belongings. When she opened the door, she gasped and halted.

The room was a mess. The airplane models were no longer in the display case; they were strewn across the floor, and a few were broken. Danny's collection of paperbacks had been pulled from the bookcase and tossed into every corner. The tubes of glue, miniature bottles of enamel, and model-crafting tools that had stood on his desk were now on the floor with everything else. A poster of one of the movie monsters had been ripped apart; it hung from the wall in several pieces. The action figures had been knocked off the headboard. The closet doors were open, and all the clothes inside appeared to have been thrown on the floor. The game table had been overturned. The easel lay on the carpet, the chalkboard facing down.

Shaking with rage, Tina slowly crossed the room, carefully stepping through the debris. She stopped at the easel, set it up as it belonged, hesitated, then turned the chalkboard toward her.

NOT DEAD

"Damn!" she said, furious.

Vivienne Neddler had been in to clean last evening, but this wasn't the kind of thing that Vivienne would be capable of doing. If the mess had been here when Vivienne arrived, the old woman would have cleaned it up and would have left a note about what she'd found. Clearly, the intruder had come in after Mrs. Neddler had left.

Fuming, Tina went through the house, meticulously checking every window and door. She could find no sign of forced entry.

In the kitchen again, she phoned Michael. He still didn't answer. She slammed down the handset.

She pulled the telephone directory from a drawer and leafed through the Yellow Pages until she found the advertisements for locksmiths. She chose the company with the largest ad.

"Anderlingen Lock and Security."

"Your ad in the Yellow Pages says you can have a man here to change my locks in one hour."

"That's our emergency service. It costs more."

"I don't care what it costs," Tina said.

"But if you just put your name on our work list, we'll most likely have a man there by four o'clock this afternoon, tomorrow morning at the latest. And the regular service is forty percent cheaper than an emergency job."

"Vandals were in my house last night," Tina said.

"What a world we live in," said the woman at Anderlingen.

"They wrecked a lot of stuff—"

"Oh, I'm sorry to hear that."

"—so I want the locks changed immediately."

"Of course."

"And I want good locks installed. The best you've got."

"Just give me your name and address, and I'll send a man out right away."

A couple of minutes later, having completed the call, Tina went back to Danny's room to survey the damage again. As she looked over the wreckage, she said, "What the hell do you want from me, Mike?"

She doubted that he would be able to answer that question even if he were present to hear it. What possible excuse could he have? What twisted logic could justify this sort of sick behavior? It was crazy, hateful.

She shivered.

TINA ARRIVED AT BALLY'S HOTEL AT TEN MINUTES till two, Wednesday afternoon, leaving her Honda with a valet parking attendant.

Bally's, formerly the MGM Grand, was getting to be one of the older establishments on the continuously rejuvenating Las Vegas Strip, but it was still one of the most popular hotels in town, and on this last day of the year it was packed. At least two or three thousand people were in the casino, which was larger than a football field. Hundreds of gamblers—pretty young women, sweet-faced grandmothers, men in jeans and decoratively stitched Western shirts, retirement-age men in expensive but tacky leisure outfits, a few guys in three-piece suits, salesmen, doctors, mechanics, secretaries, Americans from all of the Western states, junketeers from the East Coast, Japanese tourists, a few Arab men—sat at the semielliptical blackjack tables, pushing money and chips forward, sometimes taking back their winnings, eagerly grabbing the cards that were dealt from the five-deck shoes, each reacting in one of several predictable ways: Some players squealed with delight; some grumbled; others smiled ruefully and shook their heads; some teased the dealers, pleading half seriously for better cards; and still others were silent, polite, attentive, and businesslike, as though they thought they were engaged in some reasonable form of investment planning. Hundreds of other people stood close behind the players, watching impatiently, waiting for a seat to open. At the craps tables, the crowds, primarily men, were more boisterous than the blackjack aficionados; they screamed, howled, cheered, groaned, encouraged the shooter, and prayed loudly to the dice. On the left, slot machines ran the entire length of the casino, bank after nerve-jangling bank of them, brightly and colorfully lighted, attended by gamblers who were more vocal than the card players but not as loud as the craps shooters. On the right, beyond the craps tables, halfway down the long room, elevated from the main floor, the white-marble and brass baccarat pit catered to a more affluent and sedate group of gamblers; at baccarat, the pit boss, the floorman, and the dealers wore tuxedos. And everywhere in the gigantic casino, there were cocktail waitresses in brief costumes, revealing long legs and cleavage; they bustled here and there, back and forth, as if they were the threads that bound the crowd together.

Tina pressed through the milling onlookers who filled the wide center aisle, and she located Michael almost at once. He was dealing blackjack at one of the first tables. The game minimum was a five-dollar bet, and all seven seats were taken. Michael was grinning, chatting amicably with the players. Some dealers were cold and uncommunicative, but Michael felt the day went faster when he was friendly with people. Not unexpectedly, he received considerably more tips than most dealers did.

Michael was lean and blond, with eyes nearly as blue as Tina's. He somewhat resembled Robert Redford, almost too pretty. It was no surprise that women players tipped him more often and more generously than did men.

When Tina squeezed into the narrow gap between the tables and caught Michael's attention, his reaction was far different from what she had expected. She'd thought the sight of her would wipe the smile off his face. Instead, his smile broadened, and there seemed to be genuine delight in his eyes.

He was shuffling cards when he saw her, and he continued to shuffle while he spoke. "Hey, hello there. You look terrific, Tina. A sight for sore eyes."

She wasn't prepared for this pleasantness, nonplussed by the warmth of his greeting.

He said, "That's a nice sweater. I like it. You always looked good in blue."

She smiled uneasily and tried to remember that she had come here to accuse him of cruelly harassing her. "Michael, I have to talk to you."

He glanced at his watch. "I've got a break coming up in five minutes."

"Where should I meet you?"

"Why don't you wait right where you are? You can watch these nice people beat me out of a lot of money."

Every player at the table groaned, and they all had comments to make about the unlikely possibility that they might win anything from this dealer.

Michael grinned and winked at Tina.

She smiled woodenly.

She waited impatiently as the five minutes crawled by; she was never comfortable in a casino when it was busy.

The frantic activity and the unrelenting excitement, which bordered on hysteria at times, abraded her nerves.

The huge room was so noisy that the blend of sounds seemed to coalesce into a visible substance—like a humid yellow haze in the air. Slot machines rang and beeped and whistled and buzzed. Balls clattered around spinning roulette wheels. A five-piece band hammered out wildly amplified pop music from the small stage in the open cocktail lounge beyond and slightly above the slot machines. The paging system blared names. Ice rattled in glasses as gamblers drank while they played. And everyone seemed to be talking at once.

When Michael's break time arrived, a replacement dealer took over the table, and Michael stepped out of the blackjack pit, into the center aisle. "You want to talk?"

"Not here," she said, half-shouting. "I can't hear myself think."

"Let's go down to the arcade."

"Okay."

To reach the escalators that would carry them down to the shopping arcade on the lower level, they had to cross the entire casino. Michael led the way, gently pushing and elbowing through the holiday crowd, and Tina followed quickly in his wake, before the path that he made could close up again.

Halfway across the long room, they stopped at a clearing where a middle-aged man lay on his back, unconscious, in front of a blackjack table. He was wearing a beige suit, a dark brown shirt, and a beige-patterned tie. An overturned stool lay beside him, and approximately five hundred dollars' worth of green chips were scattered on the carpet. Two uniformed security men were performing first aid on the unconscious man, loosening his tie and collar, taking his pulse, while a third guard was keeping curious customers out of the way.

Michael said, "Heart attack, Pete?"

The third guard said, "Hi, Mike. Nah, I don't think it's his heart. Probably a combination of blackjack blackout and bingo bladder. He was sitting here for eight hours straight."

On the floor, the man in the beige suit groaned. His eyelids fluttered.

Shaking his head, obviously amused, Michael moved around the clearing and into the crowd again.

When at last they reached the end of the casino and were on the escalators, heading down toward the shopping arcade, Tina said, "What is blackjack blackout?"

"It's stupid is what it is," Michael said, still amused. "The guy sits down to play cards and gets so involved he loses track of time, which is, of course, exactly what the management wants him to do. That's why there aren't any windows or clocks in the casino. But once in a while, a guy *really* loses track, doesn't get up for hours and hours, just keeps on playing like a zombie. Meanwhile, he's drinking too much. When he *does* finally stand up, he moves too fast. The blood drains from his head—*bang!*—and he faints dead away. Blackjack blackout."

"Ah."

"We see it all the time."

"Bingo bladder?"

"Sometimes a player gets so interested in the game that he's virtually hypnotized by it. He's been drinking pretty regularly, but he's so deep in a trance that he can completely ignore the call of nature until—bingo!—he has a bladder spasm. If it's really a bad one, he finds out his pipes have blocked up. He can't relieve himself, and he has to be taken to the hospital and catheterized."

"My God, are you serious?"

"Yep."

They stepped off the escalator, into the bustling shopping arcade. Crowds surged past the souvenir shops, art galleries, jewelry stores, clothing stores, and other retail businesses, but they were neither shoulder-to-shoulder nor as insistent as they were upstairs in the casino.

"I still don't see any place where we can talk privately," Tina said.

"Let's walk down to the ice-cream parlor and get a couple of pistachio cones. What do you say? You always liked pistachio."

"I don't want any ice cream, Michael."

She had lost the momentum occasioned by her anger, and now she was afraid of losing the sense of purpose that had driven her to confront him. He was trying so hard to be nice, which wasn't like Michael at all. At least it wasn't like the Michael Evans she had known for the past couple of years. When they were first married, he'd been fun, charming, easygoing, but he had not been that way with her in a long time.

"No ice cream," she repeated. "Just some talk."

"Well, if you don't want some pistachio, I certainly do. I'll get a cone, and then we can go outside, walk around the parking lot. It's a fairly warm day."

"How long is your break?"

"Twenty minutes. But I'm tight with the pit boss. He'll cover for me if I don't get back in time."

The ice-cream parlor was at the far end of the arcade. As they walked, Michael continued to try to amuse her by telling her about other unusual maladies to which gamblers were prone.

"There's what we call 'jackpot attack,'" Michael said. "For years people go home from Vegas and tell all their friends that they came out ahead of the game. Lying their heads off. Everyone pretends to be a winner. And when all of a sudden someone *does* hit it big, especially on a slot machine where it can happen in a flash, they're so surprised they pass out. Heart attacks are more frequent around the slot machines than anywhere else in the casino, and a lot of the victims are people who've just lined up three bars and won a bundle.

"Then there's 'Vegas syndrome.' Someone gets so carried away with gambling and running from show to show that he forgets to eat for a whole day or longer. He or she—it happens to women nearly as often as men. Anyway, when he finally gets hungry and realizes he hasn't eaten, he gulps down a huge meal, and the blood rushes from his head to his stomach, and he passes out in the middle of the restaurant. It's not usually dangerous, except if he has a mouthful of food when he faints, because then he might choke to death.

"But my favorite is what we call the 'time-warp syndrome.' People come here from a lot of dull places, and Vegas is like an adult Disneyland. There's so much going on, so much to see and do, constant excitement, so people get out of their normal rhythms. They go to bed at dawn, get up in the afternoon, and they lose track of what day it is. When the excitement wears off a little, they go to check out of the hotel, and they discover their three-day weekend somehow turned into five days. They can't believe it. They think they're being overcharged, and they argue with the desk clerks. When someone shows them a calendar and a daily newspaper, they're really shocked. They've been through a time warp and lost a couple of days. Isn't that weird?"

Michael kept up the friendly patter while he got his cone of ice cream. Then, as they stepped out of the rear entrance of the hotel and walked along the edge of the parking lot in the seventy-degree winter sunshine, he said, "So what did you want to talk about?"

Tina wasn't sure how to begin. Her original intention had been to accuse him of ripping apart Danny's room; she had been prepared to come on strong, so that even if he didn't want her to know he'd done it, he might be rattled enough to reveal his guilt. But now, if she started making nasty accusations after he'd been so pleasant to her, she would seem to be a hysterical harpy, and if she still had any advantage left, she would quickly lose it.

At last she said, "Some strange things have been happening at the house."

"Strange? Like what?"

"I think someone broke in."

"You *think?*"

"Well . . . I'm sure of it."

"When did this happen?"

Remembering the two words on the chalkboard, she said, "Three times in the past week."

He stopped walking and stared at her. "Three times?"

"Yes. Last evening was the latest."

"What do the police say?"

"I haven't called them."

He frowned. "Why not?"

"For one thing, nothing was taken."

"Somebody broke in three times but didn't steal anything?"

If he was faking innocence, he was a much better actor than she thought he was, and she thought she knew him well indeed. After all, she'd lived with him for a long time, through years of happiness and years of misery, and she'd come to know the limits of his talent for deception and duplicity. She'd always known when he was lying. She didn't think he was lying now. There was something peculiar in his eyes, a speculative look, but it wasn't guile. He truly seemed unaware of what had happened at the house. Perhaps he'd had nothing to do with it.

But if Michael hadn't torn up Danny's room, if Michael hadn't written those words on the chalkboard, then who had?

"Why would someone break in and leave without taking anything?" Michael asked.

"I think they were just trying to upset me, scare me."

"Who would want to scare you?" He seemed genuinely concerned.

She didn't know what to say.

"You've never been the kind of person who makes enemies," he said. "You're a damn hard woman to hate."

"You managed," she said, and that was as close as she could come to accusing him of anything.

He blinked in surprise. "Oh, no. No, no, Tina. I never hated you. I was disappointed by the changes in you. I was angry with you. Angry and hurt. I'll admit that, all right. There was a lot of bitterness on my part. Definitely. But it was never as bad as hatred."

She sighed.

Michael hadn't wrecked Danny's room. She was absolutely sure of that now.

"Tina?"

"I'm sorry. I shouldn't have bothered you with this. I'm not really sure why I did," she lied. "I ought to have called the police right away."

He licked his ice-cream cone, studied her, and then he smiled. "I understand. It's hard for you to get around to it. You don't know how to begin. So you come to me with this story."

"Story?"

"It's okay."

"Michael, it's not just a story."

"Don't be embarrassed."

"I'm not embarrassed. Why should I be embarrassed?"

"Relax. It's all right, Tina," he said gently.

"Someone *has* been breaking into the house."

"I understand how you feel." His smile changed; it was smug now.

"Michael—"

"I really do understand, Tina." His voice was reassuring, but his tone was condescending. "You don't need an excuse to ask me what you've come here to ask. Honey, you don't need a story about someone breaking into the house. I understand, and I'm with you. I really am. So go ahead. Don't feel awkward about it. Just get right down to it. Go ahead and say it."

She was perplexed. "Say what?"

"We let the marriage go off the rails. But there at first, for a good many years, we had a great thing going. We can have it again if we really want to try for it."

She was stunned. "Are you serious?"

"I've been thinking about it the past few days. When I saw you walk into the casino a while ago, I knew I was right. As soon as I saw you, I knew everything was going to turn out exactly like I had it figured."

"You *are* serious."

"Sure." He mistook her astonishment for surprised delight. "Now that you've had your fling as a producer, you're ready to settle down. That makes a lot of sense, Tina."

Fling! she thought angrily.

He still persisted in regarding her as a flighty woman who wanted to take a fling at being a Vegas producer. The insufferable bastard! She was furious, but she said nothing; she didn't trust herself to speak, afraid that she would start screaming at him the instant she opened her mouth.

"There's more to life than just having a flashy career," Michael said pontifically. "Home life counts for something. Home and family. That has to be a part of life too. Maybe it's the most important part." He nodded sanctimoniously. "Family. These last few days, as your show's been getting ready to open, I've had the feeling you might finally realize you need something more in life, something a lot more emotionally satisfying than whatever it is you can get out of just producing stage shows."

Tina's ambition was, in part, what had led to the dissolution of their marriage. Well, not her ambition as much as Michael's childish attitude toward it. He was happy being a blackjack dealer; his salary and his good tips were enough for him, and he was content to coast through the years. But merely drifting along in the currents of life wasn't enough for Tina. As she had struggled to move up from dancer to costumer to choreographer to lounge-revue coordinator to producer, Michael had been displeased with her commitment to work. She had never neglected him and Danny. She had been determined that neither of them would have reason to feel that his importance in her life had diminished. Danny had been wonderful; Danny had understood. Michael couldn't or wouldn't. Gradually Michael's displeasure over her desire to succeed was complicated by a darker emotion: He grew jealous of her smallest achievements. She had tried to encourage him to seek advances in his own career—from dealer to floorman to pit boss to higher casino management—but he had no interest in climbing that ladder. He became waspish, petulant. Eventually he started seeing other women. She was shocked by his reaction, then confused, and at last deeply saddened. The only way she could have held on to her husband would have been to abandon her new career, and she had refused to do that.

In time Michael had made it clear to her that he hadn't actually ever loved the real Christina. He didn't tell her directly, but his behavior said as much. He had adored only the showgirl, the dancer, the cute little thing that other men coveted, the pretty woman whose presence at his side had inflated his ego. As long as she remained a dancer, as long as she devoted her life to him, as long as she hung on his arm and looked delicious, he approved of her. But the moment that she wanted to be something more than a trophy wife, he rebelled.

Badly hurt by that discovery, she had given him the freedom that he wanted.

And now he actually thought that she was going to crawl back to him. That was why he'd smiled when he'd seen her at his blackjack table. That was why he had been so charming. The size of his ego astounded her.

Standing before her in the sunshine, his white shirt

shimmering with squiggles of reflected light that bounced off the parked cars, he favored her with that self-satisfied, superior smile that made her feel as cold as this winter day ought to have been.

Once, long ago, she had loved him very much. Now she couldn't imagine how or why she had ever cared.

"Michael, in case you haven't heard, *Magyck!* is a hit. A big hit. Huge."

"Sure," he said. "I know that, baby. And I'm happy for you. I'm happy for you *and* me. Now that you've proved whatever you needed to prove, you can relax."

"Michael, I intend to continue working as a producer. I'm not going to—"

"Oh, I don't expect you to give it up," he said magnanimously.

"You don't, huh?"

"No, no. Of course not. It's good for you to have something to dabble in. I see that now. I get the message. But with *Magyck!* running successfully, you won't have all that much to do. It won't be like before."

"Michael—" she began, intending to tell him that she was going to stage another show within the next year, that she didn't want to be represented by only one production at a time, and that she even had distant designs on New York and Broadway, where the return of Busby Berkeley–style musicals might be greeted with cheers.

But he was so involved with his fantasy that he wasn't aware that she had no desire to be a part of it. He interrupted her before she'd said more than his name. "We can do it, Tina. It was good for us once, those early years. It can be good again. We're still young. We have time to start another family. Maybe even two boys and two girls. That's what I've always wanted."

When he paused to lick his ice-cream cone, she said, "Michael, that's not the way it's going to be."

"Well, maybe you're right. Maybe a large family isn't such a wise idea these days, what with the economy in trouble and all the turmoil in the world. But we can take care of two easily enough, and maybe we'll get lucky and have one boy and one girl. Of course we'll wait a year or so. I'm sure there's a lot of work to do on a show like *Magyck!* even after it opens. We'll wait until it's running smoothly, until it doesn't need much of your time. Then we can—"

"Michael, stop it!" she said harshly.

He flinched as if she'd slapped him.

"I'm not feeling unfulfilled these days," she said. "I'm not pining for the domestic life. You don't understand me one bit better now than you did when we divorced."

His expression of surprise slowly settled into a frown.

She said, "I didn't make up that story about someone breaking into the house just so you could play the strong, reliable man to my weak, frightened female. Someone really *did* break in. I came to you because I thought . . . I believed . . . Well, that doesn't matter anymore."

She turned away from him and started toward the rear entrance of the hotel, out of which they'd come a few minutes ago.

"Wait!" Michael said. "Tina, wait!"

She stopped and regarded him with contempt and sorrow.

He hurried to her. "I'm sorry. It's my fault, Tina. I botched it. Jesus, I was babbling like an idiot, wasn't I? I didn't let you do it your way. I knew what you wanted to say, but I should have let you say it at your own speed. I was wrong. It's just—I was excited, Tina. That's all. I should've shut up and let *you* get around to it first. I'm sorry, baby." His ingratiating, boyish grin was back. "Don't get mad at me, okay? We both want the same thing—a home life, a good family life. Let's not throw away this chance."

She glared at him. "Yes, you're right, I do want a home life, a satisfying family life. You're right about that. But you're wrong about everything else. I don't want to be a producer merely because I need a sideline to dabble in. *Dabble!* Michael, that's stupid. No one gets a show like *Magyck!* off the ground by dabbling. I can't believe you said that! It wasn't a fling. It was a mentally and physically debilitating experience—it was *hard*—and I loved every minute of it! God willing, I'm going to do it again. And again and again. I'm going to produce shows that'll make *Magyck!* look amateurish by comparison. Some day I may also be a mother again. And I'll be a damn good mother too. A good mother and a good producer. I have the intelligence and the talent to be more than just one thing. And I certainly can be more than just your trinket and your housekeeper."

"Now, wait a minute," he said, beginning to get angry. "Wait just a damn minute. You don't—"

She interrupted him. For years she had been filled with hurt and bitterness. She had never vented any of her black anger because, initially, she'd wanted to hide it from Danny; she hadn't wanted to turn him against his father. Later, after Danny was dead, she'd repressed her feelings because she'd known that Michael had been truly suffering from the loss of his child, and she hadn't wanted to add to his misery. But now she vented some of the acid that had been eating at her for so long, cutting him off in midsentence.

"You were wrong to think I'd come crawling back. Why

on earth would I? What do you have to give me that I can't get elsewhere? You've never been much of a giver anyway, Michael. You only give when you're sure of getting back twice as much. You're basically a taker. And before you give me any more of that treacly talk about your great love of family, let me remind you that it wasn't *me* who tore our family apart. It wasn't me who jumped from bed to bed."

"Now, wait—"

"You were the one who started fucking anything that breathed, and then you flaunted each cheap little affair to hurt me. It was *you* who didn't come home at night. It was you who went away for weekends with your girlfriends. And those bed-hopping weekends broke my heart, Michael, broke my heart—which is what you hoped to do, so that was all right with you. But did you ever stop to realize what effect your absences had on Danny? If you loved family life so much, why didn't you spend all those weekends with your son?"

His face was flushed, and there was a familiar meanness in his eyes. "So I'm not a giver, huh? Then who gave you the house you're living in? Huh? Who was it had to move into an apartment when we separated, and who was it kept the house?"

He was trying desperately to deflect her and change the course of the argument. She could see what he was up to, and she was not going to be distracted from her main intention.

She said, "Don't be pathetic, Michael. You know damn well the down payment for the house came out of my earnings. You always spent your money on fast cars, good clothes. I paid every loan installment. You know that. And

I never asked for alimony. Anyway, all of that's beside the point. We were talking about family life, about Danny."

"Now, you listen to me—"

"No. It's your turn to listen. After all these years it's finally your turn to listen. If you know how. You could have taken Danny away for the weekend if you didn't want to be near me. You could have gone camping with him. You could have taken him down to Disneyland for a couple days. Or to the Colorado River to do some fishing. But you were too busy using all those women to hurt me and to prove to yourself what a stud you were. You could have enjoyed that time with your son. He missed you. You could have had that precious time with him. But you didn't want it. And as it turned out, Danny didn't have much time left."

Michael was milk-white, trembling. His eyes were dark with rage. "You're the same goddamn bitch you always were."

She sighed and sagged. She was exhausted. Finished telling him off, she felt pleasantly wrung out, as if some evil, nervous energy had been drained from her.

"You're the same ball-breaking bitch," Michael said.

"I don't want to fight with you, Michael. I'm even sorry if some of what I said about Danny hurt you, although, God knows, you deserve to hear it. I don't really want to hurt you. Oddly enough, I don't really hate you anymore. I don't feel anything for you. Not anything at all."

Turning away, she left him in the sunshine, with the ice cream melting down the cone and onto his hand.

She walked back through the shopping arcade, rode the escalator up to the casino, and made her way through the noisy crowd to the front doors. One of the valet-parking attendants brought her car, and she drove down the hotel's steeply slanted exit drive.

She headed toward the Golden Pyramid, where she had an office, and where work was waiting to be done.

After she had driven only a block, she was forced to pull to the side of the road. She couldn't see where she was going, because hot tears streamed down her face. She put the car in park. Surprising herself, she sobbed loudly.

At first she wasn't sure what she was crying about. She just surrendered to the racking grief that swept through her and did not question it.

After a while she decided that she was crying for Danny. Poor, sweet Danny. He'd hardly begun to live. It wasn't fair. And she was crying for herself too, and for Michael. She was crying for all the things that might have been, and for what could never be again.

In a few minutes she got control of herself. She dried her eyes and blew her nose.

She had to stop being so gloomy. She'd had enough gloom in her life. A whole hell of a lot of gloom.

"Think positive," she said aloud. "Maybe the past wasn't so great, but the future seems pretty damn good."

She inspected her face in the rearview mirror to see how much damage the crying jag had done. She looked better than she expected. Her eyes were red, but she wouldn't pass for Dracula. She opened her purse, found her makeup, and covered the tear stains as best she could.

She pulled the Honda back into traffic and headed for the Pyramid again.

A block farther, as she waited at a red light, she realized that she still had a mystery on her hands. She was positive that Michael had not done the damage in Danny's bedroom.

But then, who *had* done it? No one else had a key. Only a skilled burglar could have broken in without leaving a trace. And why would a first-rate burglar leave without taking anything? Why break in merely to write on Danny's chalkboard and to wreck the dead boy's things?

Weird.

When she had suspected Michael of doing the dirty work, she had been disturbed and distressed, but she hadn't been frightened. If some *stranger* wanted her to feel more pain over the loss of her child, however, that was definitely unsettling. That was scary because it didn't make sense. A stranger? It must be. Michael was the only person who had ever blamed her for Danny's death. Not one other relative or acquaintance had ever suggested that she was even indirectly responsible. Yet the taunting words on the chalkboard and the destruction in the bedroom seemed to be the work of someone who felt that she should be held accountable for the accident. Which meant it had to be someone she didn't even know. Why would a stranger harbor such passionate feelings about Danny's death?

The red traffic light changed.

A horn tooted behind her.

As she drove across the intersection and into the entrance drive that led to the Golden Pyramid Hotel, Tina couldn't shake the creepy feeling that she was being watched by someone who meant to harm her. She checked the rearview mirror to see if she was being followed. As far as she could tell, no one was tailing her.

12

THE THIRD FLOOR OF THE GOLDEN PYRAMID HO-
tel was occupied by management and clerical personnel.
Here, there was no flash, no Vegas glamour. This was where
the work got done. The third floor housed the machinery
that supported the walls of fantasy, beyond which the
tourists gamboled.

Tina's office was large, paneled in whitewashed pine,
with comfortable contemporary upholstery. One wall was
covered by heavy drapes that blocked out the fierce desert
sun. The windows behind the drapes faced the Las Vegas
Strip.

At night the fabled Strip was a dazzling sight, a surg-
ing river of light: red, blue, green, yellow, purple, pink,
turquoise—every color within the visual spectrum of the
human eye; incandescent and neon, fiberoptics and lasers,
flashing and rippling. Hundred-foot-long signs—*five*-
hundred-foot-long signs—towered five or even ten stories
above the street, glittering, winking, thousands of miles of
bright glass tubing filled with glowing gas, blinking, swirling, hundreds of thousands of bulbs, spelling out hotel

names, forming pictures with light. Computer-controlled designs ebbed and flowed, a riotous and mad—but curiously beautiful—excess of energy consumption.

During the day, however, the merciless sun was unkind to the Strip. In the hard light the enormous architectural confections were not always appealing; at times, in spite of the billions of dollars of value that it represented, the Strip looked grubby.

The view of the legendary boulevard was wasted on Tina; she didn't often make use of it. Because she was seldom in her office at night, the drapes were rarely open. This afternoon, as usual, the drapes were closed. The office was shadowy, and she was at her desk in a pool of soft light.

As Tina pored over a final bill for carpentry work on some of the *Magyck!* sets, Angela, her secretary, stepped in from the outer office. "Is there anything more you need before I leave?"

Tina glanced at her watch. "It's only a quarter to four."

"I know. But we get off at four today—New Year's Eve."

"Oh, of course," Tina said. "I completely forgot about the holiday."

"If you want me to, I could stay a little longer."

"No, no, no," Tina said. "You go home at four with the others."

"So is there anything more you need?"

Leaning back in her chair, Tina said, "Yes. In fact, there is something. A lot of our regular junketeers and high rollers couldn't make it to the VIP opening of *Magyck!* I'd like you to get their names from the computer, plus a list of the wedding anniversaries of those who're married."

"Can do," Angela said. "What've you got in mind?"

"During the year, I'm going to send special invitations to

the married ones, asking them to spend their anniversaries here, with everything comped for three days. We'll sell it this way: 'Spend the magic night of your anniversary in the magic world of *Magyck!*' Something like that. We'll make it very romantic. We'll serve them champagne at the show. It'll be a great promotion, don't you think?" She raised her hands, as if framing her next words, "The Golden Pyramid—a *Magyck!* place for lovers."

"The hotel ought to be happy," Angela said. "We'll get lots of favorable media coverage."

"The casino bosses will like it too, 'cause a lot of our high rollers will probably make an extra trip this year. The average gambler won't cancel other planned trips to Vegas. He'll just add on an extra trip for his anniversary. And I'll be happy because the whole stunt will generate more talk about the show."

"It's a great idea," Angela said. "I'll get the list."

Tina returned to her inspection of the carpenter's bill, and Angela was back at five minutes past four with thirty pages of data.

"Thank you," Tina said.

"No trouble."

"Are you shivering?"

"Yeah," Angela said, hugging herself. "Must be a problem with the air conditioning. The last few minutes—my office got chilly."

"It's warm enough in here," Tina said.

"Maybe it's just me. Maybe I'm coming down with something. I sure hope not. I've got big plans tonight."

"Party?"

"Yeah. Big bash over on Rancho Circle."

"Millionaire's Row?"

"My boyfriend's boss lives over there. Anyway . . . happy new year, Tina."

"Happy new year."

"See you Monday."

"Oh? Oh, yeah, that's right. It's a four-day weekend. Well, just watch out for that hangover."

Angela grinned. "There's at least one out there with my name on it."

Tina finished checking the carpenter's bill and approved it for payment.

Alone now on the third floor, she sat in the pool of amber light at her desk, surrounded by shadows, yawning. She'd work for another hour, until five o'clock, and then go home. She'd need two hours to get ready for her date with Elliot Stryker.

She smiled when she thought of him, then picked up the sheaf of papers that Angela had given her, anxious to finish her work.

The hotel possessed an amazing wealth of information about its most favored customers. If she needed to know how much money each of these people earned in a year, the computer could tell her. It could tell her each man's preferred brand of liquor, each wife's favorite flower and perfume, the make of car they drove, the names and ages of their children, the nature of any illnesses or other medical conditions they might have, their favorite foods, their favorite colors, their tastes in music, their political affiliations, and scores of other facts both important and trivial. These were customers to whom the hotel was especially anxious to cater, and the more the Pyramid knew about them, the better it could serve them. Although the hotel collected this data with, for the most part, the customers' happiness in mind, Tina wondered how pleased these people would be to learn that the Golden Pyramid maintained fat dossiers on them.

She scanned the list of VIP customers who hadn't attended the opening of *Magyck!* Using a red pencil, she circled those names that were followed by anniversary dates, trying to ascertain how large a promotion she was proposing. She had counted only twenty-two names when she came to an incredible message that the computer had inserted in the list.

Her chest tightened. She couldn't breathe.

She stared at what the computer had printed, and fear welled in her—dark, cold, oily fear.

Between the names of two high rollers were five lines of type that had nothing to do with the information she had requested:

NOT DEAD
NOT DEAD
NOT DEAD
NOT DEAD
NOT DEAD

The paper rattled as her hands began to shake.

First at home. In Danny's bedroom. Now here. Who was doing this to her?

Angela?

No. Absurd.

Angela was a sweet kid. She wasn't capable of anything as vicious as this. Angela hadn't noticed this interruption in the printout because she hadn't had time to scan it.

Besides, Angela couldn't have broken into the house. Angela wasn't a master burglar, for God's sake.

Tina quickly shuffled through the pages, seeking more of the sick prankster's work. She found it after another twenty-six names.

> DANNY ALIVE
> DANNY ALIVE
> HELP
> HELP
> HELP ME

Her heart seemed to be pumping a refrigerant instead of blood, and an iciness radiated from it.

Suddenly she was aware of how alone she was. More likely than not, she was the only person on the entire third floor.

She thought of the man in her nightmare, the man in black whose face had been lumpy with maggots, and the shadows in the corner of her office seemed darker and deeper than they had been a moment ago.

She scanned another forty names and cringed when she saw what else the computer had printed.

> I'M AFRAID
> I'M AFRAID
> GET ME OUT
> GET ME OUT OF HERE
> PLEASE . . . PLEASE
> HELPHELPHELPHELP

That was the last disturbing insertion. The remainder of the list was as it should be.

Tina threw the printout on the floor and went into the outer office.

Angela had turned the light off. Tina turned it on.

She went to Angela's desk, sat in her chair, and switched on the computer. The screen filled with a soft blue light.

In the locked center drawer of the desk was a book with the code numbers that permitted access to the sensitive information stored not on diskette but only in the central memory. Tina paged through the book until she found the code that she needed to call up the list of the hotel's best customers. The number was 1001012, identified as the access for "Comps," which meant "complimentary guests," a euphemism for "big losers," who were never asked to pay their room charges or restaurant bills because they routinely dropped small fortunes in the casino.

Tina typed her personal access number—E013331555. Because so much material in the hotel's files was extremely confidential information about high rollers, and because the Pyramid's list of favored customers would be of enormous value to competitors, only approved people could obtain this data, and a record was kept of everyone who accessed it. After a moment's hesitation the computer asked for her name; she entered that, and the computer matched her number and name. Then:

CLEARED

She typed in the code for the list of complimentary guests, and the machine responded at once.

PROCEED

Her fingers were damp. She wiped them on her slacks and then quickly tapped out her request. She asked the computer for the same information that Angela had requested a while ago. The names and addresses of VIP customers who had missed the opening of *Magyck!*—along with the wedding anniversaries of those who were married—began to appear on the screen, scrolling upward. Simultaneously the laser printer began to churn out the same data.

Tina snatched each page from the printer tray as it arrived. The laser whispered through twenty names, forty, sixty, seventy, without producing the lines about Danny that had been on the first printout. Tina waited until at least a hundred names had been listed before she decided that the system had been programmed to print the lines about Danny only one time, only on her office's first data request of the afternoon, and on no later call-up.

She canceled this data request and closed out the file. The printer stopped.

Just a couple of hours ago she had concluded that the person behind this harassment had to be a stranger. But how could any stranger so easily gain entrance to both her house and the hotel computer? Didn't he, after all, have to be someone she knew?

But who?

And *why?*

What stranger could possibly hate her so much?

Fear, like an uncoiling snake, twisted and slithered inside of her, and she shivered.

Then she realized it wasn't only fear that made her quiver. The air was chilly.

She remembered the complaint that Angela had made earlier. It hadn't seemed important at the time.

But the room had been warm when Tina had first come in to use the computer, and now it was cool. How could the temperature have dropped so far in such a short time? She listened for the sound of the air conditioner, but the telltale whisper wasn't issuing from the wall vents. Nevertheless, the room was much cooler than it had been only minutes ago.

With a sharp, loud, electronic snap that startled Tina, the computer abruptly began to churn out additional data, although she hadn't requested any. She glanced at the printer, then at the words that flickered across the screen.

NOT DEAD NOT DEAD
NOT DEAD NOT DEAD
NOT IN THE GROUND
NOT DEAD
GET ME OUT OF HERE
GET ME OUT OUT OUT

The message blinked and vanished from the screen. The printer fell silent.

The room was growing colder by the second.

Or was it her imagination?

She had the crazy feeling that she wasn't alone. The man in black. Even though he was only a creature from a nightmare, and even though it was utterly impossible for him to be here in the flesh, she couldn't shake the heart-clenching feeling that he was in the room. The man in black. The man with the evil, fiery eyes. The yellow-toothed grin. Behind her. Reaching toward her with a hand that would be cold and damp. She spun around in her chair, but no one had come into the room.

Of course. He was only a nightmare monster. How stupid of her.

Yet she felt that she was not alone.

She didn't want to look at the screen again, but she did. She had to.

The words still burned there.

Then they disappeared.

She managed to break the grip of fear that had paralyzed her, and she put her fingers on the keyboard. She intended to determine if the words about Danny had been previously programmed to print out on her machine or if they had been sent to her just seconds ago by someone at another computer in another office in the hotel's elaborately networked series of workstations.

She had an almost psychic sense that the perpetrator of this viciousness was in the building *now*, perhaps on the third floor with her. She imagined herself leaving her office, walking down the long hallway, opening doors, peering into silent, deserted offices, until at last she found a man sitting at another terminal. He would turn toward her, surprised, and she would finally know who he was.

And then what?

Would he harm her? Kill her?

This was a new thought: the possibility that his ultimate goal was to do something worse than torment and scare her.

She hesitated, fingers on the keyboard, not certain if she should proceed. She probably wouldn't get the answers she needed, and she would only be acknowledging her presence to whomever might be out there at another workstation. Then she realized that, if he really was nearby, he already knew she was in her office, alone. She had nothing to lose by trying to follow the data chain. But when she attempted to type in her instruction, the keyboard was locked; the keys wouldn't depress.

The printer hummed.

The room was positively arctic.

On the screen, scrolling up:

> I'M COLD AND I HURT
> MOM? CAN YOU HEAR?
> I'M SO COLD
> I HURT BAD
> GET ME OUT OF HERE
> PLEASE PLEASE PLEASE
> NOT DEAD NOT DEAD

The screen glowed with those words—then went blank.

Again, she tried to feed in her questions. But the keyboard remained frozen.

She was still aware of another presence in the room. Indeed the feeling of invisible and dangerous companionship was growing stronger as the room grew colder.

How could he make the room colder without using the air conditioner? Whoever he was, he could override her computer from another terminal in the building; she could accept that. But how could he possibly make the air grow so cold so fast?

Suddenly, as the screen began to fill with the same seven-line message that had just been wiped from it, Tina had enough. She switched the machine off, and the blue glow faded from the screen.

As she was getting up from the low chair, the terminal switched itself on.

I'M COLD AND I HURT
GET ME OUT OF HERE
PLEASE PLEASE PLEASE

"Get you out of where?" she demanded. "The *grave?*"

GET ME OUT OUT OUT

She had to get a grip on herself. She had just spoken to the computer as if she actually thought she was talking to Danny. It wasn't Danny tapping out those words. Goddamn it, *Danny was dead!*

She snapped the computer off.

It turned itself on.

A hot welling of tears blurred her vision, and she struggled to repress them. She had to be losing her mind. The damned thing *couldn't* be switching itself on.

She hurried around the desk, banging her hip against one corner, heading for the wall socket as the printer hummed with the production of more hateful words.

GET ME OUT OF HERE
GET ME OUT OUT
OUT
OUT

Tina stooped beside the wall outlet from which the computer received its electrical power and its data feed. She took hold of the two lines—one heavy cable and one ordinary insulated wire—and they seemed to come alive in her hands, like a pair of snakes, resisting her. She jerked on them and pulled both plugs.

The monitor went dark.

It remained dark.

Immediately, rapidly, the room began to grow warmer.

"Thank God," she said shakily.

She started around Angela's desk, wanting nothing more at the moment than to get off her rubbery legs and onto a chair—and suddenly the door to the hall opened, and she cried out in alarm.

The man in black?

Elliot Stryker halted on the threshold, surprised by her scream, and for an instant she was relieved to see him.

"Tina? What's wrong? Are you all right?"

She took a step toward him, but then she realized that he might have come here straight from a computer in one of the other third-floor offices. Could he be the man who'd been harassing her?

"Tina? My God, you're white as a ghost!"

He moved toward her.

She said, "Stop! Wait!"

He halted, perplexed.

Voice quavery, she said, "What are you doing here?"

He blinked. "I was in the hotel on business. I wondered if you might still be at your desk. I stopped in to see. I just wanted to say hello."

"Were you playing around with one of the other computers?"

"What?" he asked, obviously baffled by her question.

"What were you doing on the third floor?" she demanded. "Who could you possibly have been seeing? They've all gone home. I'm the only one here."

Still puzzled but beginning to get impatient with her, Elliot said, "My business wasn't on the third floor. I had a meeting with Charlie Mainway over coffee, downstairs in the restaurant. When we finished our work a couple minutes ago, I came up to see if you were here. What's wrong with you?"

She stared at him intently.

"Tina? What's happened?"

She searched his face for any sign that he was lying, but his bewilderment seemed genuine. And if he were lying, he wouldn't have told her the story about Charlie and coffee, for that could be substantiated or disproved with only a minimum of effort; he would have come up with a better alibi if he really needed one. He was telling the truth.

She said, "I'm sorry. I just . . . I had . . . an . . . an experience here . . . a weird . . ."

He went to her. "What was it?"

As he drew near, he opened his arms, as if it was the most natural thing in the world for him to hold and comfort her, as if he had held her many times before, and she leaned against him in the same spirit of familiarity. She was no longer alone.

13

Tina kept a well-stocked bar in one corner of her office for those infrequent occasions when a business associate needed a drink after a long work session. This was the first time she'd ever had the need to tap those stores for herself.

At her request, Elliot poured Rémy Martin into two snifters and gave one glass to her. She couldn't pour for them because her hands were shaking too badly.

They sat on the beige sofa, more in the shadows than in the glow from the lamps. She was forced to hold her brandy snifter in both hands to keep it steady.

"I don't know where to begin. I guess I ought to start with Danny. Do you know about Danny?"

"Your son?" he asked.

"Yes."

"Helen Mainway told me he died a little over a year ago."

"Did she tell you how it happened?"

"He was one of the Jaborski group. Front page of the papers."

Bill Jaborski had been a wilderness expert and a scoutmaster. Every winter for sixteen years, he had taken a group of scouts to northern Nevada, beyond Reno, into the High Sierras, on a seven-day wilderness survival excursion.

"It was supposed to build character," Tina said. "And the boys competed hard all year for the chance to be one of those selected to go on the trip. It was supposed to be perfectly safe. Bill Jaborski was supposed to be one of the ten top winter-survival experts in the country. That's what everyone said. And the other adult who went along, Tom Lincoln—he was supposed to be almost as good as Bill. Supposed to be." Her voice had grown thin and bitter. "I believed them, thought it was safe."

"You can't blame yourself for that. All those years they'd taken kids into the mountains, nobody was even scratched."

Tina swallowed some cognac. It was hot in her throat, but it didn't burn away the chill at the center of her.

A year ago Jaborski's excursion had included fourteen boys between the ages of twelve and eighteen. All of them were top-notch scouts—and all of them died along with Jaborski and Tom Lincoln.

"Have the authorities ever figured out exactly why it happened?" Elliot asked.

"Not why. They never will. All they know is *how*. The group went into the mountains in a four-wheel-drive mini-bus built for use on back roads in the winter. Huge tires. Chains. Even a snowplow on the front. They weren't supposed to go into the true heart of the wilderness. Just into the fringes. No one in his right mind would take boys as young as twelve into the deepest parts of the Sierras, no matter how well prepared, supplied, and trained they were, no matter how strong, no matter how many big brothers were there to look out for them."

Jaborski had intended to drive the minibus off the main highway, onto an old logging trail, if conditions permitted. From there they were going to hike for three days with snowshoes and backpacks, making a wide circle around the bus, coming back to it at the end of the week.

"They had the best wilderness clothing and the best down-lined sleeping bags, the best winter tents, plenty of charcoal and other heat sources, plenty of food, and two wilderness experts to guide them. Perfectly safe, everyone said. Absolutely, perfectly safe. So what the fuck went wrong?"

Tina could no longer sit still. She got up and began to pace, taking another swallow of cognac.

Elliot said nothing. He seemed to know that she had to go through the whole story to get it off her mind.

"Something sure as hell went wrong," she said. "Somehow, for some reason, they drove the bus more than *four* miles off the main highway, four miles off and a hell of a long way *up*, right up to the damn clouds. They drove up a steep, abandoned logging trail, a deteriorated dirt road so treacherous, so choked with snow, so icy that only a fool would have attempted to negotiate it any way but on foot."

The bus had run off the road. There were no guardrails in the wilderness, no wide shoulders at the roadside with gentle slopes beyond. The vehicle skidded, then dropped a hundred feet straight onto rocks. The fuel tank exploded. The bus opened like a tin can and rolled another hundred feet into the trees.

"The kids . . . everyone . . . killed." The bitterness in her voice dismayed her because it revealed how little she had healed. "Why? Why did a man like Bill Jaborski do something so stupid as that?"

Still sitting on the couch, Elliot shook his head and stared down at his cognac.

She didn't expect him to answer. She wasn't actually asking the question of him; if she was asking anyone, she was asking God.

"Why? Jaborski was the best. The very best. He was so good that he could safely take young boys into the Sierras for sixteen years, a challenge a lot of other winter survival experts wouldn't touch. Bill Jaborski was smart, tough, clever, and filled with respect for the danger in what he did. He wasn't foolhardy. Why would he do something so dumb, so reckless, as to drive that far along that road in those conditions?"

Elliot looked up at her. Kindness marked his eyes, a deep sympathy. "You'll probably never learn the answer. I understand how hard it must be never to know why."

"Hard," she said. "Very hard."

She returned to the couch.

He took her glass out of her hand. It was empty. She didn't remember finishing her cognac. He went to the bar.

"No more for me," she said. "I don't want to get drunk."

"Nonsense," he said. "In your condition, throwing off all that nervous energy the way you are, two small brandies won't affect you in the slightest."

He returned from the bar with more Rémy Martin. This time she was able to hold the glass in one hand.

"Thank you, Elliot."

"Just don't ask for a mixed drink," he said. "I'm the world's worst bartender. I can pour anything straight or over ice, but I can't even mix vodka and orange juice properly."

"I wasn't thanking you for the drink. I was thanking you for . . . being a good listener."

"Most attorneys talk too much."

For a moment they sat in silence, sipping cognac.

Tina was still tense, but she no longer felt cold inside.

Elliot said, "Losing a child like that . . . devastating. But it wasn't any recollection of your son that had you so upset when I walked in a little while ago."

"In a way it was."

"But something more."

She told him about the bizarre things that had been happening to her lately: the messages on Danny's chalkboard; the wreckage she'd found in the boy's room; the hateful, taunting words that appeared in the computer lists and on the monitor.

Elliot studied the printouts, and together they examined the computer in Angela's office. They plugged it in and tried to get it to repeat what it had done earlier, but they had no luck; the machine behaved exactly as it was meant to behave.

"Someone could have programmed it to spew out this stuff about Danny," Elliot said. "But I don't see how he could make the terminal switch itself on."

"It happened," she said.

"I don't doubt you. I just don't understand."

"And the air . . . so cold . . ."

"Could the temperature change have been subjective?"

Tina frowned. "Are you asking me if I imagined it?"

"You were frightened—"

"But I'm sure I didn't imagine it. Angela felt the chill first, when she got the initial printout with those lines about Danny. It isn't likely Angela and I *both* just imagined it."

"True." He stared thoughtfully at the computer. "Come on."

"Where?"

"Back in your office. I left my drink there. Need to lubricate my thoughts."

She followed him into the wood-paneled inner sanctum.

He picked up his brandy snifter from the low table in front of the sofa, and he sat on the edge of her desk. "Who? Who could be doing it to you?"

"I haven't a clue."

"You must have somebody in mind."

"I wish I did."

"Obviously, it's somebody who at the very least dislikes you, if he doesn't actually hate you. Someone who wants you to suffer. He blames you for Danny's death . . . and it's apparently a personal loss to him, so it can hardly be a stranger."

Tina was disturbed by his analysis because it matched her own, and it led her into the same blind alley that she'd traveled before. She paced between the desk and the drapery-covered windows. "This afternoon I decided it *has* to be a stranger. I can't think of anyone I know who'd be capable of this sort of thing even if they did hate me enough to contemplate it. And I don't know of anyone but Michael who places any of the blame for Danny's death on me."

Elliot raised his eyebrows. "Michael's your ex-husband?"

"Yes."

"And he blames you for Danny's death?"

"He says I never should have let him go with Jaborski. But this isn't Michael's dirty work."

"He sounds like an excellent candidate to me."

"No."

"Are you certain?"

"Absolutely. It's someone else."

Elliot tasted his cognac. "You'll probably need professional help to catch him in one of his tricks."

"You mean the police?"

"I don't think the police would be much help. They probably won't think it's serious enough to waste their time. After all, you haven't been threatened."

"There's an implicit threat in all of this."

"Oh, yeah, I agree. It's scary. But the cops are a literal bunch, not much impressed by implied threats. Besides, to properly watch your house . . . that alone will require a lot more manpower than the police can spare for anything except a murder case, a hot kidnapping, or maybe a narcotics investigation."

She stopped pacing. "Then what did you mean when you said I'd probably need professional help to catch this creep?"

"Private detectives."

"Isn't that melodramatic?"

He smiled sourly. "Well, the person who's harassing you has a melodramatic streak a mile wide."

She sighed and sipped some cognac and sat on the edge of the couch. "I don't know . . . Maybe I'd hire private detectives, and they wouldn't catch anyone but me."

"Send that one by me again."

She had to take another small sip of cognac before she was able to say what was on her mind, and she realized that he had been right about the liquor having little effect on her. She felt more relaxed than she'd been ten minutes ago, but she wasn't even slightly tipsy. "It's occurred to me . . . maybe *I* wrote those words on the chalkboard. Maybe *I* wrecked Danny's room."

"You've lost me."

"Could have done it in my sleep."

"That's ridiculous, Tina."

"Is it? I thought I'd begun to get over Danny's death back in September. I started sleeping well then. I didn't dwell on it when I was alone, like I'd done for so long. I thought I'd put the worst pain behind me. But a month ago I started dreaming about Danny again. The first week, it happened twice. The second week, four nights. And the past two weeks, I've dreamed about him every night without fail. The dreams get worse all the time. They're full-fledged nightmares now."

Elliot returned to the couch and sat beside her. "What are they like?"

"I dream he's alive, trapped somewhere, usually in a deep pit or a gorge or a well, someplace underground. He's calling to me, begging me to save him. But I can't. I'm never able to reach him. Then the earth starts closing in around him, and I wake up screaming, soaked with sweat. And I . . . I always have this powerful feeling that Danny isn't really dead. It never lasts for long, but when I first wake up, I'm sure he's alive somewhere. You see, I've convinced my conscious mind that my boy is dead, but when I'm asleep it's my subconscious mind that's in charge; and my subconscious just isn't convinced that Danny's gone."

"So you think you're—what, sleepwalking? In your sleep, you're writing a rejection of Danny's death on his chalkboard?"

"Don't you believe that's possible?"

"No. Well . . . maybe. I guess it is," Elliot said. "I'm no psychologist. But I don't buy it. I'll admit I don't know you all that well yet, but I think I know you well enough to say you wouldn't react that way. You're a person who meets problems head-on. If your inability to accept Danny's death was a serious problem, you wouldn't push it down into your subconscious. You'd learn to deal with it."

She smiled. "You have a pretty high opinion of me."

"Yes," he said. "I do. Besides, if it was you who wrote on the chalkboard and smashed things in the boy's room, then it was also you who came in here during the night and programmed the hotel computer to spew out that stuff about Danny. Do you really think you're so far gone that you could do something like that and not remember it? Do you think you've got multiple personalities and one doesn't know what the others are up to?"

She sank back on the sofa, slouched down. "No."

"Good."

"So where does that leave us?"

"Don't despair. We're making progress."

"We are?"

"Sure," he said. "We're eliminating possibilities. We've just crossed you off the list of suspects. And Michael. And I'm positive it can't be a stranger, which rules out most of the world."

"And I'm just as positive it isn't a friend or a relative. So you know where that leaves me?"

"Where?"

She leaned forward, put her brandy snifter on the table, and for a moment sat with her face in her hands.

"Tina?"

She lifted her head. "I'm just trying to think how best to phrase what's on my mind. It's a wild idea. Ludicrous. Probably even sick."

"I'm not going to think you're nuts," Elliot assured her. "What is it? Tell me."

She hesitated, trying to hear how it was going to sound before she said it, wondering if she really believed it enough even to give voice to it. The possibility of what she was going to suggest was remote.

At last she just plunged into it: "What I'm thinking . . . maybe Danny *is* alive."

Elliot cocked his head, studied her with those probing, dark eyes. "Alive?"

"I never saw his body."

"You didn't? Why not?"

"The coroner and undertaker said it was in terrible condition, horribly mutilated. They didn't think it was a good idea for me or Michael to see it. Neither of us would have been anxious to view the body even if it had been in perfect shape, so we accepted the mortician's recommendations. It was a closed-coffin funeral."

"How did the authorities identify the body?"

"They asked for pictures of Danny. But mainly I think they used dental records."

"Dental records are almost as good as fingerprints."

"Almost. But maybe Danny didn't die in that accident. Maybe he survived. Maybe someone out there knows where he is. Maybe that someone is trying to tell me that Danny is alive. Maybe there isn't any threat in these strange things happening to me. Maybe someone's just dropping a series of hints, trying to wake me up to the fact that Danny isn't dead."

"Too many *maybes*," he said.

"Maybe not."

Elliot put his hand on her shoulder and squeezed gently.

"Tina, you know this theory doesn't make sense. Danny is dead."

"See? You *do* think I'm crazy."

"No. I think you're distraught, and that's understandable."

"Won't you even consider the possibility that he's alive?"

"How could he be?"

"I don't know."

"How could he have survived the accident you described?" Elliot asked.

"I don't know."

"And where would he have been all this time if not . . . in the grave?"

"I don't know that, either."

"If he were alive," Elliot said patiently, "someone would simply come and tell you. They wouldn't be this mysterious about it, would they?"

"Maybe."

Aware that her answer had disappointed him, she looked down at her hands, which were laced together so tightly that her knuckles were white.

Elliot touched her face, turning it gently toward him.

His beautiful, expressive eyes seemed to be filled with concern for her.

"Tina, you know there isn't any *maybe* about it. You know better than that. If Danny were alive, and if someone were trying to get that news to you, it wouldn't be done like this, not with all these dramatic hints. Am I right?"

"Probably."

"Danny is gone."

She said nothing.

"If you convince yourself he's alive," Elliot said, "you're only setting yourself up for another fall."

She stared deeply into his eyes. Eventually she sighed and nodded. "You're right."

"Danny's gone."

"Yes," she said thinly.

"You're really convinced of that?"

"Yes."

"Good."

Tina got up from the couch, went to the window, and pulled open the drapes. She had a sudden urge to see the Strip. After so much talk about death, she needed a glimpse of movement, action, life; and although the Strip sometimes was grubby in the flat glare of the desert sun, the boulevard was always, day or night, bustling and filled with life.

Now the early winter dusk settled over the city. In waves of dazzling color, millions of lights winked on in the enormous signs. Hundreds of cars progressed sluggishly through the busy street, taxicabs darting in and out, recklessly seeking any small advantage. Crowds streamed along the sidewalks, on their way from this casino to that casino, from one lounge to another, from one show to the next.

Tina turned to Elliot again. "You know what I want to do?"

"What?"

"Reopen the grave."

"Have Danny's body exhumed?"

"Yes. I never saw him. That's why I'm having such a hard time accepting that he's gone. That's why I'm having nightmares. If I'd seen the body, then I'd have known for sure. I wouldn't be able to fantasize about Danny still being alive."

"But the condition of the corpse . . ."

"I don't care," she said.

Elliot frowned, not convinced of the wisdom of exhumation. "The body's in an airtight casket, but it'll be even more deteriorated now than it was a year ago when they recommended you not look at it."

"I've got to *see.*"

"You'd be letting yourself in for a horrible—"

"That's the idea," she said quickly. "Shock. A powerful shock treatment that'll finally blow away all my lingering doubts. If I see Danny's . . . remains, I won't be able to entertain any more doubts. The nightmares will stop."

"Perhaps. Or perhaps you'll wind up with even worse dreams."

She shook her head. "Nothing could be worse than the ones I'm having now."

"Of course," he said, "exhumation of the body won't answer the main question. It won't help you discover who's been harassing you."

"It might," Tina said. "Whoever the creep is, whatever his motivations are, he's not well-balanced. He's one sort of sickie or another. Right? Who knows what might make a person like that reveal himself? If he finds out there's going to be an exhumation, maybe he'll react strongly, give himself away. Anything's possible."

"I suppose you could be right."

"Anyway," she said, "even if reopening the grave doesn't help me find who's responsible for these sick jokes—or whatever the hell they are—at least it'll settle my mind about Danny. That'll improve my psychological condition for sure, and I'll be better able to deal with the creep, whoever he is. So it'll work out for the best either way." She returned from the window, sat on the couch again, beside Elliot. "I'll need an attorney to handle this, won't I?"

"The exhumation? Yeah."

"Will you represent me?"

He didn't hesitate. "Sure."

"How difficult will it be?"

"Well, there's no urgent legal reason to have the body exhumed. I mean, there isn't any doubt about the cause of death, no court trial hinging on a new coroner's report. If that were the situation, we'd have the grave opened very quickly. But even so, this shouldn't be terribly difficult. I'll play up the mother-suffering-distress angle, and the court ought to be sympathetic."

"Have you ever handled anything like this before?"

"In fact, I have," Elliot said. "Five years ago. This eight-year-old girl died unexpectedly of a congenital kidney disease. Both kidneys failed virtually overnight. One day she was a happy, normal kid. The next day she seemed to have a touch of flu, and the third day she was dead. Her mother was shattered, couldn't bear to view the body, though the daughter hadn't suffered substantial physical damage, the way Danny did. The mother wasn't even able to attend the service. A couple weeks after the little girl was buried, the mother started feeling guilty about not paying her last respects."

Remembering her own ordeal, Tina said, "I know. Oh, I know how it is."

"The guilt eventually developed into serious emotional problems. Because the mother hadn't seen the body in the funeral home, she just couldn't bring herself to believe her daughter was really dead. Her inability to accept the truth was a lot worse than yours. She was hysterical most of the time, in a slow-motion breakdown. I arranged to have the grave reopened. In the course of preparing the exhumation request for the authorities, I discovered that my client's reaction was typical. Apparently, when a child dies, one of the worst things a parent can do is refuse to look at the body while it's lying in a casket. You need to spend time with the deceased, enough to accept that the body is never going to be animated again."

"Was your client helped by exhumation?"

"Oh, yes. Enormously."

"You see?"

"But don't forget," Elliot said, "her daughter's body wasn't mutilated."

Tina nodded grimly.

"And we reopened the grave only two months after the funeral, not a whole year later. The body was still in pretty good condition. But with Danny . . . it won't be that way."

"I'm aware of that," she said. "God knows, I'm not happy about this, but I'm convinced it's something I've got to do."

"Okay. I'll take care of it."

"How long will you need?" she asked.

"Will your husband contest it?"

She recalled the hatred in Michael's face when she'd left him a few hours ago. "Yes. He probably will."

Elliot carried their empty brandy glasses to the bar in the corner and switched on the light above the sink. "If your husband's likely to cause trouble, then we'll move fast and without fanfare. If we're clever, he won't know what we're doing until the exhumation is a *fait accompli*. Tomorrow's a holiday, so we can't get anything done officially until Friday."

"Probably not even then, what with the four-day week-end."

Elliot found the bottle of liquid soap and the dishcloth that were stored under the sink. "Ordinarily I'd say we'd have to wait until Monday. But it happens I know a very reasonable judge. Harold Kennebeck. We served in Army Intelligence together. He was my senior officer. If I—"

"Army Intelligence? You were a spy?"

"Nothing as grand as that. No trench coats. No skulking about in dark alleys."

"Karate, cyanide capsules, that sort of stuff?" she asked.

"Well, I've had a lot of martial arts training. I still work at that a couple of days a week because it's a good way to keep in shape. Really, though, it wasn't like what you see in the movies. No James Bond cars with machine guns hidden behind the headlights. It was mostly dull information gathering."

"Somehow," she said, "I get the feeling it was considerably more . . . interesting than you make it out to be."

"Nope. Document analysis, tedious interpretation of satellite reconnaissance photographs, that sort of thing. Boring as hell most of the time. Anyway, Judge Kennebeck and I go back a long way. We respect each other, and I'm sure he'll do something for me if he can. I'll be seeing him tomorrow afternoon at a New Year's Day party. I'll discuss the situation with him. Maybe he'll be willing to slip into the courthouse long enough on Friday to review my exhumation request and rule on it. He'd only need a few minutes. Then we could open the grave early Saturday."

Tina went to the bar and sat on one of the three stools, across the counter from Elliot. "The sooner the better. Now that I've made up my mind to do it, I'm anxious to get it over with."

"That's understandable. And there's another advantage in doing it this weekend. If we move fast, it isn't likely Michael will find out what we're up to. Even if he does somehow get a whiff of it, he'll have to locate another judge who'll be willing to stay or vacate the exhumation order."

"You think he'll be able to do that?"

"No. That's my point. There won't be many judges around over the holiday. Those on duty will be swamped with arraignments and bail hearings for drunken drivers and for people involved in drunken assaults. Most likely, Michael won't be able to get hold of a judge until Monday morning, and by then it'll be too late."

"Sneaky."

"That's my middle name." He finished washing the first brandy snifter, rinsed it in hot water, and put it in the drainage rack to dry.

"Elliot Sneaky Stryker," she said.

He smiled. "At your service."

"I'm glad you're my attorney."

"Well, let's see if I can actually pull it off."

"You can. You're the kind of person who meets every problem head-on."

"You have a pretty high opinion of me," he said, repeating what she had said to him earlier.

She smiled. "Yes, I do."

All the talk about death and fear and madness and pain seemed to have taken place further back in the past than a mere few seconds ago. They wanted to have a little fun during the evening that lay ahead, and now they began putting themselves in the mood for it.

As Elliot rinsed the second snifter and placed it in the rack, Tina said, "You do that very well."

"But I don't wash windows."

"I like to see a man being domestic."

"Then you should see me cook."

"You cook?"

"Like a dream."

"What's your best dish?"

"Everything I make."

"Obviously, you don't make humble pie."

"Every great chef must be an egomaniac when it comes to his culinary art. He must be totally secure in his estimation of his talents if he is to function well in the kitchen."

"What if you cooked something for me, and I didn't like it?"

"Then I'd eat your serving as well as mine."

"And what would I eat?"

"Your heart out."

After so many months of sorrow, how good it felt to be sharing an evening with an attractive and amusing man.

Elliot put away the dishwashing liquid and the wet dishcloth. As he dried his hands on the towel, he said, "Why don't we forget about going out to dinner? Let me cook for you instead."

"On such short notice?"

"I don't need much time to plan a meal. I'm a whiz. Besides, you can help by doing the drudgery, like cleaning the vegetables and chopping the onions."

"I should go home and freshen up," she said.

"You're already too fresh for me."

"My car—"

"You can drive it. Follow me to my place."

They turned out the lights and left the room, closing the door after them.

As they crossed the reception area on their way toward the hall, Tina glanced nervously at Angela's computer. She was afraid it was going to click on again, all by itself.

But she and Elliot left the outer office, flicking off the lights as they went, and the computer remained dark and silent.

14

ELLIOT STRYKER LIVED IN A LARGE, PLEASANT, contemporary house overlooking the golf course at the Las Vegas Country Club. The rooms were warm, inviting, decorated in earth tones, with J. Robert Scott furniture complemented by a few antique pieces, and richly textured Edward Fields carpets. He owned a fine collection of paintings by Eyvind Earle, Jason Williamson, Larry W. Dyke, Charlotte Armstrong, Carl J. Smith, and other artists who made their homes in the western United States and who usually took their subject matter from either the old or the new West.

As he showed her through the house, he was eager to hear her reaction to it, and she didn't make him wait long.

"It's beautiful," she said. "Stunning. Who was your interior decorator?"

"You're looking at him."

"Really?"

"When I was poor, I looked forward to the day when I'd have a lovely home full of beautiful things, all arranged by the very best interior decorator. Then, when I had the money, I didn't want some stranger furnishing it for me. I wanted to have all the fun myself. Nancy, my late wife, and I decorated our first home. The project became a vocation for her, and I spent nearly as much time on it as I did on my legal practice. The two of us haunted furniture stores from Vegas to Los Angeles to San Francisco, antique shops, galleries, everything from flea markets to the most expensive stores we could find. We had a damn good time. And when she died . . . I discovered I couldn't learn to cope with the loss if I stayed in a place that was so crowded with memories of her. For five or six months I was an emotional wreck because every object in the house reminded me of Nancy. Finally I took a few mementos, a dozen pieces by which I'll always remember her, and I moved out, sold the house, bought this one, and started decorating all over again."

"I didn't realize you'd lost your wife," Tina said. "I mean, I thought it must have been a divorce or something."

"She passed away three years ago."

"What happened?"

"Cancer."

"I'm so sorry, Elliot."

"At least it was fast. Pancreatic cancer, exceedingly virulent. She was gone two months after they diagnosed it."

"Were you married long?"

"Twelve years."

She put a hand on his arm. "Twelve years leaves a big hole in the heart."

He realized they had even more in common than he had thought. "That's right. You had Danny for nearly twelve years."

"With me, of course, it's only been little more than a year

since I've been alone. With you, it's been three years. Maybe you can tell me . . ."

"What?"

"Does it ever stop?" she asked.

"The hurting?"

"Yes."

"So far it hasn't. Maybe it will after four years. Or five. Or ten. It doesn't hurt as bad now as it once did. And the ache isn't constant anymore. But still there are moments when . . ."

He showed her through the rest of the house, which she wanted to see. Her ability to create a stylish stage show was not a fluke; she had taste and a sharp eye that instantly knew the difference between prettiness and genuine beauty, between cleverness and art. He enjoyed discussing antiques and paintings with her, and an hour passed in what seemed to be only ten minutes.

The tour ended in the enormous kitchen, which boasted a copper ceiling, a Santa Fe tile floor, and restaurant-quality equipment. She checked the walk-in cooler, inspected the yard-square grill, the griddle, the two Wolf ranges, the microwave, and the array of labor-saving appliances. "You've spent a small fortune here. I guess your law practice isn't just another Vegas divorce mill."

Elliot grinned. "I'm one of the founding partners of Stryker, West, Dwyer, Coffey, and Nichols. We're one of the largest law firms in town. I can't take a whole lot of credit for that. We were lucky. We were in the right place at the right time. Owen West and I opened for business in a cheap storefront office twelve years ago, right at the start of the biggest boom this town has ever seen. We represented some people no one else would touch, entrepreneurs who had a lot of good ideas but not much money for start-up legal fees. Some of our clients made smart moves and were carried right to the top by the explosive growth of the gaming industry and the Vegas real-estate market, and we just sort of shot up there along with them, hanging on to their coattails."

"Interesting," Tina said.

"It is?"

"You are."

"I am?"

"You're so modest about having built a splendid law practice, yet you're an egomaniac when it comes to your cooking."

He laughed. "That's because I'm a better cook than attorney. Listen, why don't you mix us a couple of drinks while I change out of this suit. I'll be back in five minutes, and then you'll see how a true culinary genius operates."

"If it doesn't work out, we can always jump in the car and go to McDonald's for a hamburger."

"Philistine."

"Their hamburgers are hard to beat."

"I'll make you eat crow."

"How do you cook it?"

"Very funny."

"Well, if you cook it very funny, I don't know if I want to eat it."

"If I *did* cook crow," he said, "it would be delicious. You would eat every scrap of it, lick your fingers, and beg for more."

Her smile was so lovely that he could have stood there all evening, just staring at the sweet curve of her lips.

• • •

Elliot was amused by the effect that Tina had on him. He could not remember ever having been half so clumsy in the kitchen as he was this evening. He dropped spoons. He knocked over cans and bottles of spices. He forgot to watch a pot, and it boiled over. He made a mistake blending the salad dressing and had to begin again from scratch. She flustered him, and he loved it.

"Elliot, are you sure you aren't feeling those cognacs we had at my office?"

"Absolutely not."

"Then the drink you've been sipping on here."

"No. This is just my kitchen style."

"Spilling things is your style?"

"It gives the kitchen a pleasant *used* look."

"Are you sure you don't want to go to McDonald's?"

"Do *they* bother to give their kitchen a pleasant *used* look?"

"They not only have good hamburgers—"

"Their hamburgers have a pleasant *used* look."

"—their French fries are terrific."

"So I spill things," he said. "A cook doesn't have to be graceful to be a good cook."

"Does he have to have a good memory?"

"Huh?"

"That mustard powder you're just about to put into the salad dressing."

"What about it?"

"You already put it in a minute ago."

"I did? Thanks. I wouldn't want to have to mix this damn stuff *three* times."

She had a throaty laugh that was not unlike Nancy's had been.

Although she was different from Nancy in many ways, being with her was like being with Nancy. She was easy to talk to—bright, funny, sensitive.

Perhaps it was too soon to tell for sure, but he was beginning to think that fate, in an uncharacteristic flush of generosity, had given him a second chance at happiness.

• • •

When he and Tina finished dessert, Elliot poured second cups of coffee. "Still want to go to McDonald's for a hamburger?"

The mushroom salad, the fettuccine Alfredo, and the zabaglione had been excellent. "You really *can* cook."

"Would I lie to you?"

"I guess I'll have to eat that crow now."

"I believe you just did."

"And I didn't even notice the feathers."

While Tina and Elliot had been joking in the kitchen, even before dinner had been completely prepared, she had begun to think they might go to bed together. By the time they finished eating dinner, she *knew* they would. Elliot wasn't pushing her. For that matter, she wasn't pushing him, either. They were both being driven by natural forces. Like the rush of water downstream. Like the relentless building of a storm wind and then the lightning. They both realized that they were in need of each other, physically and mentally and emotionally, and that whatever happened between them would be good.

It was fast but right, inevitable.

At the start of the evening, the undercurrent of sexual tension made her nervous. She hadn't been to bed with any man but Michael in the past fourteen years, since she was nineteen. She hadn't been to bed with *anyone at all* for almost two years. Suddenly it seemed to her that she had done a mad, stupid thing when she'd hidden away like a nun for two years. Of course, during the first of those two years, she'd still been married to Michael and had felt compelled to remain faithful to him, even though a separation and then a divorce had been in the works, and even though he had not felt constrained by any similar moral sense. Later, with the stage show to produce and with poor Danny's death weighing heavily on her, she hadn't been in the mood for romance. Now she felt like an inexperienced girl. She wondered if she would know what to *do*. She was afraid that she would be inept, clumsy, ridiculous, foolish in bed. She told herself that sex was just like riding a bicycle, impossible to *un*learn, but the frivolousness of that analogy didn't increase her self-confidence.

Gradually, however, as she and Elliot went through the standard rites of courtship, the indirect sexual thrusts and parries of a budding relationship, albeit at an accelerated pace, the familiarity of the games reassured her. Amazing that it should be so familiar. Maybe it really was a bit like riding a bicycle.

After dinner they adjourned to the den, where Elliot built a fire in the black-granite fireplace. Although winter days in the desert were often as warm as springtime elsewhere, winter nights were always cool, sometimes downright bitter. With a chilly night wind moaning at the windows and howling incessantly under the eaves, the blazing fire was welcome.

Tina kicked off her shoes.

They sat side by side on the sofa in front of the fireplace, watching the flames and the occasional bursts of orange sparks, listening to music, and talking, talking, talking. Tina felt as if they had talked without pause all evening, speaking with quiet urgency, as if each had a vast quantity of earthshakingly important information that he must pass on to the other before they parted. The more they talked, the more they found in common. As an hour passed in front of the fire, and then another hour, Tina discovered that she liked Elliot Stryker more with each new thing she learned about him.

She never was sure who initiated the first kiss. He may have leaned toward her, or perhaps she tilted toward him. But before she realized what was happening, their lips met softly, briefly. Then again. And a third time. And then he began planting small kisses on her forehead, on her eyes, on her cheeks, her nose, the corners of her mouth, her chin. He kissed her ears, her eyes again, and left a chain of kisses along her neck, and when at last he returned to her mouth, he kissed her more deeply than before, and she responded at once, opening her mouth to him.

His hands moved over her, testing the firmness and resilience of her, and she touched him too, gently squeezing his shoulders, his arms, the hard muscles of his back. Nothing had ever felt better to her than he felt at that moment.

As if drifting in a dream, they left the den and went into the bedroom. He switched on a small lamp that stood upon the dresser, and he turned down the sheets.

During the minute that he was away from her, she was afraid the spell was broken. But when he returned, she kissed him tentatively, found that nothing had changed, and pressed against him once more.

She felt as if the two of them had been here, like this, locked in an embrace, many times before.

"We hardly know each other," she said.

"Is that the way you feel?"

"No."

"Me, neither."

"I know you so well."

"For ages."

"Yet it's only been two days."

"Too fast?" he asked.

"What do you think?"

"Not too fast for me."

"Not too fast at all," she agreed.

"Sure?"

"Positive."

"You're lovely."

"Love me."

He was not a particularly large man, but he picked her up in his arms as if she were a child.

She clung to him. She saw a longing and a need in his dark eyes, a powerful wanting that was only partly sex, and she knew the same need to be loved and valued must be in her eyes for him to see.

He carried her to the bed, put her down, and urged her to lie back. Without haste, with a breathless anticipation that lit up his face, he undressed her.

He quickly stripped off his own clothes and joined her on the bed, took her in his arms.

He explored her body slowly, deliberately, first with his eyes, then with his loving hands, then with his lips and tongue.

Tina realized that she had been wrong to think that

celibacy should be a part of her period of mourning. Just the opposite was true. Good, healthy lovemaking with a man who cared for her would have helped her recover much faster than she had done, for sex was the antithesis of death, a joyous celebration of life, a denial of the tomb's existence.

The amber light molded to his muscles.

He lowered his face to hers. They kissed.

She slid a hand between them, squeezed and stroked him.

She felt wanton, shameless, insatiable.

As he entered her, she let her hands travel over his body, along his lean flanks.

"You're so sweet," he said.

He began the age-old rhythm of love. For a long, long time, they forgot that death existed, and they explored the delicious, silken surfaces of love, and it seemed to them, in those shining hours, that they would both live forever.

THURSDAY,

JANUARY 1

15

Tina stayed the night with Elliot, and he realized that he had forgotten how pleasant it could be to share his bed with someone for whom he truly cared. He'd had other women in this bed during the past two years, and a few had stayed the night, but not one of those other lovers had made him feel content merely by the fact of her presence, as Tina did. With her, sex was a delightful bonus, a lagniappe, but it wasn't the main reason he wanted her beside him. She was an excellent lover—silken, smooth, and uninhibited in the pursuit of her own pleasure—but she was also vulnerable and kind. The vague, shadowy shape of her under the covers, in the darkness, was a talisman to ward off loneliness.

Eventually he fell asleep, but at four o'clock in the morning, he was awakened by cries of distress.

She sat straight up, the sheets knotted in her fists, catapulted out of a nightmare. She was quaking, gasping about a man dressed all in black, the monstrous figure from her dream.

Elliot switched on the bedside lamp to prove to her that they were alone in the room.

She had told him about the dreams, but he hadn't realized, until now, how terrible they were. The exhumation of Danny's body would be good for her, regardless of the horror that she might have to confront when the coffin lid was raised. If seeing the remains would put an end to these bloodcurdling nightmares, she would gain an advantage from the grim experience.

He switched off the bedside lamp and persuaded her to lie down again. He held her until she stopped shuddering.

To his surprise, her fear rapidly changed to desire. They fell easily into the pace and rhythm that had earlier best pleased them. Afterward, they slipped into sleep again.

•   •   •

Over breakfast he asked her to go with him to the afternoon party at which he was going to corner Judge Kennebeck to ask about the exhumation. But Tina wanted to go back to her place and clean out Danny's room. She felt up to the challenge now, and she intended to finish the task before she lost her nerve again.

"We'll see each other tonight, won't we?" he asked.

"Yes."

"I'll cook for you again."

She smiled lasciviously. "In what sense do you mean that?"

She rose out of her chair, leaned across the table, kissed him.

The smell of her, the vibrant blue of her eyes, the feel of her supple skin as he put a hand to her face—those things generated waves of affection and longing within him.

He walked her to her Honda in the driveway and leaned

in the window after she was behind the wheel, delaying her for another fifteen minutes while he planned, to her satisfaction, every dish of this evening's dinner.

When at last she drove away, he watched her car until it turned the corner and disappeared, and when she was gone he knew why he had not wanted to let her go. He'd been trying to postpone her departure because he was afraid that he would never see her again after she drove off.

He had no rational reason to entertain such dark thoughts. Certainly, the unknown person who was harassing Tina might have violent intentions. But Tina herself didn't think there was any serious danger, and Elliot tended to agree with her. The malicious tormentor wanted her to suffer mental anguish and spiritual pain; but he didn't want her to die, because that would spoil his fun.

The fear Elliot felt at her departure was purely superstitious. He was convinced that, with her arrival on the scene, he had been granted too much happiness, too fast, too soon, too easily. He had an awful suspicion that fate was setting him up for another hard fall. He was afraid Tina Evans would be taken away from him just as Nancy had been.

Unsuccessfully trying to shrug off the grim premonition, he went into the house.

He spent an hour and a half in his library, paging through legal casebooks, boning up on precedents for the exhumation of a body that, as the court had put it, "was to be disinterred in the absence of a pressing legal need, solely for humane reasons, in consideration of certain survivors of the deceased." Elliot didn't think Harold Kennebeck would give him any trouble, and he didn't expect the judge to request a list of precedents for something as relatively simple and harmless as reopening Danny's grave, but he intended to be well prepared. In Army Intelligence, Kennebeck had been a fair but always demanding superior officer.

At one o'clock Elliot drove his silver Mercedes S600 sports coupe to the New Year's Day party on Sunrise Mountain. The sky was cerulean blue and clear, and he wished he had time to take the Cessna up for a few hours. This was perfect weather for flying, one of those crystalline days when being above the earth would make him feel clean and free.

On Sunday, when the exhumation was out of the way, maybe he would fly Tina to Arizona or to Los Angeles for the day.

On Sunrise Mountain most of the big, expensive houses featured natural landscaping—which meant rocks, colored stones, and artfully arranged cacti instead of grass, shrubs, and trees—in acknowledgment that man's grip on this portion of the desert was new and perhaps tenuous. At night the view of Las Vegas from the mountainside was undeniably spectacular, but Elliot couldn't understand what other reasons anyone could possibly have for choosing to live here rather than in the city's older, greener neighborhoods. On hot summer days these barren, sandy slopes seemed godforsaken, and they would not be made lush and green for another ten years at least. On the brown hills, the huge houses thrust like the bleak monuments of an ancient, dead religion. The residents of Sunrise Mountain could expect to share their patios and decks and pool aprons with occasional visiting scorpions, tarantulas, and rattlesnakes. On windy days the dust was as thick as fog, and it pushed its dirty little cat feet under doors, around windows, and through attic vents.

The party was at a large Tuscan-style house, halfway up

the slopes. A three-sided, fan-shaped tent had been erected on the back lawn, to one side of the sixty-foot pool, with the open side facing the house. An eighteen-piece orchestra performed at the rear of the gaily striped canvas structure. Approximately two hundred guests danced or milled about behind the house, and another hundred partied within its twenty rooms.

Many of the faces were familiar to Elliot. Half of the guests were attorneys and their wives. Although a judicial purist might have disapproved, prosecutors and public defenders and tax attorneys and criminal lawyers and corporate counsel were mingling and getting pleasantly drunk with the judges before whom they argued cases most every week. Las Vegas had a judicial style and standards of its own.

After twenty minutes of diligent mixing, Elliot found Harold Kennebeck. The judge was a tall, dour-looking man with curly white hair. He greeted Elliot warmly, and they talked about their mutual interests: cooking, flying, and river-rafting.

Elliot didn't want to ask Kennebeck for a favor within hearing of a dozen lawyers, and today there was nowhere in the house where they could be assured of privacy. They went outside and strolled down the street, past the party-goers' cars, which ran the gamut from Rolls-Royces to Range Rovers.

Kennebeck listened with interest to Elliot's unofficial feeler about the chances of getting Danny's grave reopened. Elliot didn't tell the judge about the malicious prankster, for that seemed like an unnecessary complication; he still believed that once the fact of Danny's death was established by the exhumation, the quickest and surest way of dealing with the harassment was to hire a first-rate firm of private investigators to track down the perpetrator. Now, for the judge's benefit, and to explain why an exhumation had suddenly become such a vital matter, Elliot exaggerated the anguish and confusion that Tina had undergone as a direct consequence of never having seen the body of her child.

Harry Kennebeck had a poker face that also *looked* like a poker—hard and plain, dark—and it was difficult to tell if he had any sympathy whatsoever for Tina's plight. As he and Elliot ambled along the sun-splashed street, Kennebeck mulled over the problem in silence for almost a minute. At last he said, "What about the father?"

"I was hoping you wouldn't ask."

"Ah," Kennebeck said.

"The father will protest."

"You're positive?"

"Yes."

"On religious grounds?"

"No. There was a bitter divorce shortly before the boy died. Michael Evans hates his ex-wife."

"Ah. So he'd contest the exhumation for no other reason but to cause her grief?"

"That's right," Elliot said. "No other reason. No legitimate reason."

"Still, I've got to consider the father's wishes."

"As long as there aren't any religious objections, the law requires the permission of only one parent in a case like this," Elliot said.

"Nevertheless, I have a duty to protect everyone's interests in the matter."

"If the father has a chance to protest," Elliot said, "we'll probably get involved in a knock-down-drag-out legal battle. It'll tie up a hell of a lot of the court's time."

"I wouldn't like that," Kennebeck said thoughtfully. "The court's calendar is overloaded now. We simply don't have enough judges or enough money. The system's creaking and groaning."

"And when the dust finally settled," Elliot said, "my client would win the right to exhume the body anyway."

"Probably."

"Definitely," Elliot said. "Her husband would be engaged in nothing more than spiteful obstructionism. In the process of trying to hurt his ex-wife, he'd waste several days of the court's time, and the end result would be exactly the same as if he'd never been given a chance to protest."

"Ah," Kennebeck said, frowning slightly.

They stopped at the end of the next block. Kennebeck stood with his eyes closed and his face turned up to the warm winter sun.

At last the judge said, "You're asking me to cut corners."

"Not really. Simply issue an exhumation order on the mother's request. The law allows it."

"You want the order right away, I assume."

"Tomorrow morning if possible."

"And you'll have the grave reopened by tomorrow afternoon."

"Saturday at the latest."

"Before the father can get a restraining order from another judge," Kennebeck said.

"If there's no hitch, maybe the father won't ever find out about the exhumation."

"Ah."

"Everyone benefits. The court saves a lot of time and

effort. My client is spared a great deal of unnecessary anguish. And her husband saves a bundle in attorney's fees that he'd just be throwing away in a hopeless attempt to stop us."

"Ah," Kennebeck said.

In silence they walked back to the house, where the party was getting louder by the minute.

In the middle of the block, Kennebeck finally said, "I'll have to chew on it for a while, Elliot."

"How long?"

"Ah. Will you be here all afternoon?"

"I doubt it. With all these attorneys, it's sort of a busman's holiday, don't you think?"

"Going home from here?" Kennebeck asked.

"Yes."

"Ah." He pushed a curly strand of white hair back from his forehead. "Then I'll call you at home this evening."

"Can you at least tell me how you're leaning?"

"In your favor, I suppose."

"You know I'm right, Harry."

Kennebeck smiled. "I've heard your argument, counselor. Let's leave it at that for now. I'll call you this evening, after I've had a chance to think about it."

At least Kennebeck hadn't refused the request; nevertheless, Elliot had expected a quicker and more satisfying response. He wasn't asking the judge for much of a favor. Besides, the two of them went back a long way indeed. He knew that Kennebeck was a cautious man, but usually not excessively so. The judge's hesitation in this relatively simple matter struck Elliot as odd, but he said nothing more. He had no choice but to wait for Kennebeck's call.

As they approached the house, they talked about the

delights of pasta served with a thin, light sauce of olive oil, garlic, and sweet basil.

* * *

Elliot remained at the party only two hours. There were too many attorneys and not enough civilians to make the bash interesting. Everywhere he went, he heard talk about torts, writs, briefs, suits, countersuits, motions for continuation, appeals, plea bargaining, and the latest tax shelters. The conversations were like those in which he was involved at work, eight or ten hours a day, five days a week, and he didn't intend to spend a holiday nattering about the same damned things.

By four o'clock he was home again, working in the kitchen. Tina was supposed to arrive at six. He had a few chores to finish before she came, so they wouldn't have to spend a lot of time doing galley labor as they had done last night. Standing at the sink, he peeled and chopped a small onion, cleaned six stalks of celery, and peeled several slender carrots. He had just opened a bottle of balsamic vinegar and poured four ounces into a measuring cup when he heard movement behind him.

Turning, he saw a strange man enter the kitchen from the dining room. The guy was about five feet eight with a narrow face and a neatly trimmed blond beard. He wore a dark blue suit, white shirt, and blue tie, and he carried a physician's bag. He was nervous.

"What the hell?" Elliot said.

A second man appeared behind the first. He was considerably more formidable than his associate: tall, rough-edged, with large, big-knuckled, leathery hands—like something that had escaped from a recombinant DNA lab experimenting in the crossbreeding of human beings with bears. In freshly pressed slacks, a crisp blue shirt, a patterned tie, and a gray sports jacket, he might have been a professional hitman uncomfortably gotten up for the baptism of his Mafia don's grandchild. But he didn't appear to be nervous at all.

"What is this?" Elliot demanded.

Both intruders stopped near the refrigerator, twelve or fourteen feet from Elliot. The small man fidgeted, and the tall man smiled.

"How'd you get in here?"

"A lock-release gun," the tall man said, smiling cordially and nodding. "Bob here"—he indicated the smaller man—"has the neatest set of tools. Makes things easier."

"What the hell is this about?"

"Relax," said the tall man.

"I don't keep a lot of money here."

"No, no," the tall man said. "It's not money."

Bob shook his head in agreement, frowning, as if he was dismayed to think that he could be mistaken for a common thief.

"Just relax," the tall man repeated.

"You've got the wrong guy," Elliot assured them.

"You're the one, all right."

"Yes," Bob said. "You're the one. There's no mistake."

The conversation had the disorienting quality of the off-kilter exchanges between Alice and the scrawny denizens of Wonderland.

Putting down the vinegar bottle and picking up the knife, Elliot said, "Get the fuck out of here."

"Calm down, Mr. Stryker," the tall one said.

"Yes," Bob said. "Please calm down."

Elliot took a step toward them.

The tall man pulled a silencer-equipped pistol out of a shoulder holster that was concealed under his gray sports jacket. "Easy. Just you take it real nice and easy."

Elliot backed up against the sink.

"That's better," the tall man said.

"Much better," Bob said.

"Put the knife down, and we'll all be happy."

"Let's keep this happy," Bob agreed.

"Yeah, nice and happy."

The Mad Hatter would be along any minute now.

"Down with the knife," said the tall man. "Come on, come on."

Finally Elliot put it down.

"Push it across the counter, out of reach."

Elliot did as he was told. "Who are you guys?"

"As long as you cooperate, you won't get hurt," the tall man assured him.

Bob said, "Let's get on with it, Vince."

Vince, the tall man, said, "We'll use the breakfast area over there in the corner."

Bob went to the round maple table. He put down the black, physician's bag, opened it, and withdrew a compact cassette tape recorder. He removed other things from the bag too: a length of flexible rubber tubing, a sphygmomanometer for monitoring blood pressure, two small bottles of amber-colored fluid, and a packet of disposable hypodermic syringes.

Elliot's mind raced through a list of cases that his law firm was currently handling, searching for some connection with these two intruders, but he couldn't think of one.

The tall man gestured with the gun. "Go over to the table and sit down."

"Not until you tell me what this is all about."

"I'm giving the orders here."

"But I'm not taking them."

"I'll put a hole in you if you don't move."

"No. You won't do that," Elliot said, wishing that he felt as confident as he sounded. "You've got something else in mind, and shooting me would ruin it."

"Move your ass over to that table."

"Not until you explain yourself."

Vince glared at him.

Elliot met the stranger's eyes and didn't look away.

At last Vince said, "Be reasonable. We've just got to ask you some questions."

Determined not to let them see that he was frightened, aware that any sign of fear would be taken as proof of weakness, Elliot said, "Well, you've got one hell of a weird approach for someone who's just taking a public opinion survey."

"Move."

"What are the hypodermic needles for?"

"Move."

"What are they for?"

Vince sighed. "We gotta be sure you tell us the truth."

"The entire truth," said Bob.

"Drugs?" Elliot asked.

"They're effective and reliable," said Bob.

"And when you've finished, I'll have a brain the consistency of grape jelly."

"No, no," Bob said. "These drugs won't do any lasting physical or mental damage."

"What sort of questions?" Elliot asked.

"I'm losing my patience with you," Vince said.

"It's mutual," Elliot assured him.

"Move."

Elliot didn't move an inch. He refused to look at the muzzle of the pistol. He wanted them to think that guns didn't scare him. Inside, he was vibrating like a tuning fork.

"You son of a bitch, *move!*"

"What sort of questions do you want to ask me?"

The big man scowled.

Bob said, "For Christ's sake, Vince, tell him. He's going to hear the questions anyway when he finally sits down. Let's get this over with and split."

Vince scratched his concrete-block chin with his shovel of a hand and then reached inside his jacket. From an inner pocket, he withdrew a few sheets of folded typing paper.

The gun wavered, but it didn't move off target far enough to give Elliot a chance.

"I'm supposed to ask you every question on this list," Vince said, shaking the folded paper at Elliot. "It's a lot, thirty or forty questions altogether, but it won't take long if you just sit down over there and cooperate."

"Questions about what?" Elliot insisted.

"Christina Evans."

This was the last thing Elliot expected. He was dumbfounded. "Tina Evans? What about her?"

"Got to know why she wants her little boy's grave reopened."

Elliot stared at him, amazed. "How do you know about that?"

"Never mind," Vince said.

"Yeah," Bob said. "Never mind *how* we know. The important thing is we *do* know."

"Are you the bastards who've been harassing Tina?"

"Huh?"

"Are you the ones who keep sending her messages?"

"What messages?" Bob asked.

"Are you the ones who wrecked the boy's room?"

"What are you talking about?" Vince asked. "We haven't heard anything about this."

"Someone's sending messages about the kid?" Bob asked.

They appeared to be genuinely surprised by this news, and Elliot was pretty sure they weren't the people who had been trying to scare Tina. Besides, though they both struck him as slightly wacky, they didn't seem to be merely hoaxers or borderline psychopaths who got their kicks by scaring defenseless women. They looked and acted like organization men, even though the big one was rough enough at the edges to pass for a common thug. A silencer-equipped pistol, lock-release gun, truth serums— their apparatus indicated that these guys were part of a sophisticated outfit with substantial resources.

"What about the messages she's been getting?" Vince asked, still watching Elliot closely.

"I guess that's just one more question you're not going to get an answer for," Elliot said.

"We'll get the answer," Vince said coldly.

"We'll get all the answers," Bob agreed.

"Now," Vince said, "counselor, are you going to walk over to the table and sit your ass down, or am I going to have to motivate you with this?" He gestured with his pistol again.

"Kennebeck!" Elliot said, startled by a sudden insight. "The only way you could have found out about the exhumation so quickly is if Kennebeck told you."

The two men glanced at each other. They were unhappy to hear the judge's name.

"Who?" Vince asked, but it was too late to cover the revealing look they had exchanged.

"That's why he stalled me," Elliot said. "He wanted to give you time to get to me. Why in the hell should Kennebeck care whether or not Danny's grave is reopened? Why should *you* care? Who the hell are you people?"

The Ursine escapee from the island of Dr. Moreau was no longer merely impatient; he was angry. "Listen, you stupid fuck, I'm not gonna humor you any longer. I'm not gonna answer any more questions, but I *am* gonna put a bullet in your crotch if you don't move over to the table and sit down."

Elliot pretended not to have heard the threat. The pistol still frightened him, but he was now thinking of something else that scared him more than the gun. A chill spread from the base of his spine, up his back, as he realized what the presence of these men implied about the accident that had killed Danny.

"There's something about Danny's death . . . something strange about the way all those scouts died. The truth of it isn't anything like the version everyone's been told. The bus accident . . . that's a lie, isn't it?"

Neither man answered him.

"The truth is a lot worse," Elliot said. "Something so terrible that some powerful people want to hush it up. Kennebeck . . . once an agent, always an agent. Which set of letters do you guys work for? Not the FBI. They're all Ivy Leaguers these days, polished, educated. Same for the CIA. You're too crude. Not the CID, for sure; there's no military discipline about you. Let me guess. You work for some set of letters the public hasn't even heard about yet. Something secret and dirty."

Vince's face darkened like a slab of Spam on a hot griddle. "Goddamn it, I said *you* were going to answer the questions from now on."

"Relax," Elliot said. "I've played your game. I was in Army Intelligence back when. I'm not exactly an outsider. I know how it works—the rules, the moves. You don't have to be so hard-assed with me. Open up. Give me a break, and I'll give you a break."

Evidently sensing Vince's onrushing blowup and aware that it wouldn't help them accomplish their mission, Bob quickly said, "Listen, Stryker, we can't answer most of your questions because we don't know. Yes, we work for a government agency. Yes, it's one you've never heard of and probably never will. But we don't know why this Danny Evans kid is so important. We haven't been told the details, not even half of them. And we don't *want* to know all of it, either. You understand what I'm saying—the less a guy knows, the less he can be nailed for later. Christ, we're not big shots in this outfit. We're strictly hired help. They only tell us as much as we need to know. So will you cool it? Just come over here, sit down, let me inject you, give us a few answers, and we can all get on with our lives. We can't just stand here forever."

"If you're working for a government intelligence agency, then go away and come back with the legal papers," Elliot said. "Show me search warrants and subpoenas."

"You know better than that," Vince said harshly.

"The agency we work for doesn't officially exist," Bob said. "So how can an agency that doesn't exist go to court for a subpoena? Get serious, Mr. Stryker."

"If I do submit to the drug, what happens to me after you've got your answers?" Elliot asked.

"Nothing," Vince said.

"Nothing at all," Bob said.

"How can I be sure?"

At this indication of imminent surrender, the tall man relaxed slightly, although his lumpish face was still flushed with anger. "I told you. When we've got what we want, we'll leave. We just have to find out exactly why the Evans woman wants the grave reopened. We have to know if someone's ratted to her. If someone has, then we gotta spike his ass to a barn door. But we don't have anything against you. Not personally, you know. After we find out what we want to know, we'll leave."

"And let me go to the police?" Elliot asked.

"Cops don't scare us," Vince said arrogantly. "Hell, you won't be able to tell them who we were or where they can start looking for us. They won't get anywhere. Nowhere. Zip. And if they *do* pick up our trail somehow, we can put pressure on them to drop it fast. This is national security business, pal, the biggest of the big time. The government is allowed to bend the rules if it wants. After all, it makes them."

"That's not quite the way they explained the system in law school," Elliot said.

"Yeah, well, that's ivory tower stuff," Bob said, nervously straightening his tie.

"Right," Vince said. "And this is real life. Now sit down at the table like a good boy."

"Please, Mr. Stryker," Bob said.

"No."

When they got their answers, they would kill him. If they

had intended to let him live, they wouldn't have used their real names in front of him. And they wouldn't have wasted so much time coaxing him to cooperate; they would have used force without hesitation. They wanted to gain his cooperation without violence because they were reluctant to mark him; their intention was that his death should appear to be an accident or a suicide. The scenario was obvious. Probably a suicide. While he was still under the influence of the drug, they might be able to make him write a suicide note and sign it in a legible, identifiable script. Then they would carry him out to the garage, prop him up in his little Mercedes, put the seat belt snugly around him, and start the engine without opening the garage door. He would be too drugged to move, and the carbon monoxide would do the rest. In a day or two someone would find him out there, his face blue-green-gray, his tongue dark and lolling, his eyes bulging in their sockets as he stared through the windshield as if on a drive to Hell. If there were no unusual marks on his body, no injuries incompatible with the coroner's determination of suicide, the police would be quickly satisfied.

"No," he said again, louder this time. "If you bastards want me to sit down at that table, you're going to have to drag me there."

16

TINA RESOLUTELY CLEANED UP THE MESS IN Danny's room and packed his belongings. She intended to donate everything to Goodwill Industries.

Several times she was on the verge of tears as the sight of one object or another released a flood of memories. She gritted her teeth, however, and restrained the urge to leave the room with the job uncompleted.

Not much remained to be done: The contents of three cartons in the back of the deep closet had to be sorted. She tried to lift one of them, but it was too heavy. She dragged it into the bedroom, across the carpet, into the shafts of reddish-gold afternoon sunlight that filtered through the sheltering trees outside and then through the dust-filmed window.

When she opened the carton, she saw that it contained part of Danny's collection of comic books and graphic novels. They were mostly horror comics.

She'd never been able to understand this morbid streak in him. Monster movies. Horror comics. Vampire novels. Scary stories of every kind, in every medium. Initially his growing fascination with the macabre had not seemed entirely healthy to her, but she had never denied him the freedom to pursue it. Most of his friends had shared his avid interest in ghosts and ghouls; besides, the grotesque hadn't been his *only* interest, so she had decided not to worry about it.

In the carton were two stacks of comic books, and the two issues on top sported gruesome, full-color covers. On the first, a black carriage, drawn by four black horses with evil glaring eyes, rushed along a night highway, beneath a gibbous moon, and a headless man held the reins, urging the frenzied horses forward. Bright blood streamed from the ragged stump of the coachman's neck, and gelatinous clots of blood clung to his white, ruffled shirt. His grisly head stood on the driver's seat beside him, grinning fiendishly, filled with malevolent life even though it had been brutally severed from his body.

Tina grimaced. If this was what Danny had read before going to bed at night, how had he been able to sleep so well? He'd always been a deep, unmoving sleeper, never troubled by bad dreams.

She dragged another carton out of the closet. It was as heavy as the first, and she figured it contained more comic books, but she opened it to be sure.

She gasped in shock.

He was glaring up at her from inside the box. From the cover of a graphic novel. *Him.* The man dressed all in black. That same face. Mostly skull and withered flesh. Prominent sockets of bone, and the menacing, inhuman crimson eyes staring out with intense hatred. The cluster of maggots squirming on his cheek, at the corner of one eye. The rotten, yellow-toothed grin. In every repulsive detail, he was precisely like the hideous creature that stalked her nightmares.

How could she have dreamed about this hideous creature just last night and then find it waiting for her here, today, only hours later?

She stepped back from the cardboard box.

The burning, scarlet eyes of the monstrous figure in the drawing seemed to follow her.

She must have seen this lurid cover illustration when Danny had first brought the magazine into the house. The memory of it was fixed in her subconscious, festering, until she eventually incorporated it into her nightmares.

That seemed to be the only logical explanation.

But she knew it wasn't true.

She had never seen this drawing before. When Danny had first begun collecting horror comics with his allowance, she had closely examined those books to decide whether or not they were harmful to him. But after she had made up her mind to let him read such stuff, she never thereafter even glanced at his purchases.

Yet she had dreamed about the man in black.

And here he was. Grinning at her.

Curious about the story from which the illustration had been taken, Tina stepped to the box again to pluck out the graphic novel. It was thicker than a comic book and printed on slick paper.

As her fingers touched the glossy cover, a bell rang.

She flinched and gasped.

The bell rang again, and she realized that someone was at the front door.

Heart thumping, she went to the foyer.

Through the fish-eye lens in the door, she saw a young,

clean-cut man wearing a blue cap with an unidentifiable emblem on it. He was smiling, waiting to be acknowledged.

She didn't open the door. "What do you want?"

"Gas-company repair. We need to check our lines where they come into your house."

Tina frowned. "On New Year's Day?"

"Emergency crew," the repairman said through the closed door. "We're investigating a possible gas leak in the neighborhood."

She hesitated, but then opened the door without removing the heavy-duty security chain. She studied him through the narrow gap. "Gas leak?"

He smiled reassuringly. "There probably isn't any danger. We've lost some pressure in our lines, and we're trying to find the cause of it. No reason to evacuate people or panic or anything. But we're trying to check every house. Do you have a gas stove in the kitchen?"

"No. Electric."

"What about the heating system?"

"Yes. There's a gas furnace."

"Yeah. I think all the houses in this area have gas furnaces. I'd better have a look at it, check the fittings, the incoming feed, all that."

She looked him over carefully. He was wearing a gas-company uniform, and he was carrying a large tool kit with the gas-company emblem on it.

She said, "Can I see some identification?"

"Sure." From his shirt pocket, he withdrew a laminated ID card with the gas-company seal, his picture, his name, and his physical statistics.

Feeling slightly foolish, like an easily spooked old

woman, Tina said, "I'm sorry. It's not that you strike me as a dangerous person or anything. I just—"

"Hey, it's okay. Don't apologize. You did the right thing, asking for an ID. These days, you're crazy if you open your door without knowing exactly who's on the other side of it."

She closed the door long enough to slip off the security chain. Then she opened it again and stepped back. "Come in."

"Where's the furnace? In the garage?"

Few Vegas houses had basements. "Yes. The garage."

"If you want, I could just go in through the garage door."

"No. That's all right. Come in."

He stepped across the threshold.

She closed and locked the door.

"Nice place you've got here."

"Thank you."

"Cozy. Good sense of color. All these earth tones. I like that. It's a little bit like our house. My wife has a real good sense of color."

"It's relaxing," Tina said.

"Isn't it? So nice and natural."

"The garage is this way," she said.

He followed her past the kitchen, into the short hall, into the laundry room, and from there into the garage.

Tina switched on the light. The darkness was dispelled, but shadows remained along the walls and in the corners.

The garage was slightly musty, but Tina wasn't able to detect the odor of gas.

"Doesn't smell like there's trouble here," she said.

"You're probably right. But you never can tell. It could be an underground break on your property. Gas might be leaking under the concrete slab and building up down there, in which case it's possible you wouldn't detect it right away, but you'd still be sitting on top of a bomb."

"What a lovely thought."

"Makes life interesting."

"It's a good thing you're not working in the gas company's public relations department."

He laughed. "Don't worry. If I really believed there was even the tiniest chance of anything like that, would I be standing here so cheerful?"

"I guess not."

"You can bet on it. Really. Don't worry. This is just going to be a routine check."

He went to the furnace, put his heavy tool kit on the floor, and hunkered down. He opened a hinged plate, exposing the furnace's workings. A ring of brilliant, pulsing flame was visible in there, and it bathed his face in an eerie blue light.

"Well?" she said.

He looked up at her. "This will take me maybe fifteen or twenty minutes."

"Oh. I thought it was just a simple thing."

"It's best to be thorough in a situation like this."

"By all means, be thorough."

"Hey, if you've got something to do, feel free to go ahead with it. I won't be needing anything."

Tina thought of the graphic novel with the man in black on its cover. She was curious about the story out of which that creature had stepped, for she had the peculiar feeling that, in some way, it would be similar to the story of Danny's death. This was a bizarre notion, and she didn't know where it had come from, but she couldn't dispel it.

"Well," she said, "I *was* cleaning the back room. If you're sure—"

"Oh, certainly," he said. "Go ahead. Don't let me interrupt your housework."

She left him there in the shadowy garage, his face painted by shimmering blue light, his eyes gleaming with twin reflections of fire.

WHEN ELLIOT REFUSED TO MOVE AWAY FROM THE sink to the breakfast table in the far corner of the big kitchen, Bob, the smaller of the two men, hesitated, then reluctantly took a step toward him.

"Wait," Vince said.

Bob stopped, obviously relieved that his hulking accomplice was going to deal with Elliot.

"Don't get in my way," Vince advised. He tucked the sheaf of typewritten questions into his coat pocket. "Let me handle this bastard."

Bob retreated to the table, and Elliot turned his attention to the larger intruder.

Vince held the pistol in his right hand and made a fist with his left. "You really think you want to tangle with me, little man? Hell, my fist is just about as big as your head. You know what this fist is going to feel like when it hits, little man?"

Elliot had a pretty good idea of what it would feel like, and he was sweating under his arms and in the small of his back, but he didn't move, and he didn't respond to the stranger's taunting.

"It's going to feel like a freight train ramming straight through you," Vince said. "So stop being so damn stubborn."

They were going to great lengths to avoid using violence, which confirmed Elliot's suspicion that they wanted to leave him unmarked, so that later his body would bear no cuts or bruises incompatible with suicide.

The bear-who-would-be-a-man shambled toward him. "You want to change your mind, be cooperative?"

Elliot held his ground.

"One good punch in the belly," Vince said, "and you'll be puking your guts out on your shoes."

Another step.

"And when you're done puking your guts out," Vince said, "I'm going to grab you by your balls and drag you over to the table."

One more step.

Then the big man stopped.

They were only an arm's length apart.

Elliot glanced at Bob, who was still standing at the breakfast table, the packet of syringes in his hand.

"Last chance to do it the easy way," Vince said.

In one smooth lightning-fast movement, Elliot seized the measuring cup into which he had poured four ounces of vinegar a few minutes ago, and he threw the contents in Vince's face. The big man cried out in surprise and pain, temporarily blinded. Elliot dropped the measuring cup and seized the gun, but Vince reflexively squeezed off a shot that breezed past Elliot's face and smashed the window behind the sink. Elliot ducked a wild roundhouse punch, stepped in close, still holding on to the pistol that the other man wouldn't surrender. He swung one arm around, slamming his bent elbow into Vince's throat. The big man's head snapped back, and Elliot chopped the exposed Adam's apple with the flat blade of his hand. He rammed his knee into his adversary's crotch and tore the gun out of the bear-paw hand as those clutching fingers went slack. Vince bent forward, gagging, and Elliot slammed the butt of the gun against the side of his head, with a sound like stone meeting stone.

Elliot stepped back.

Vince dropped to his knees, then onto his face. He stayed there, tongue-kissing the floor tiles.

The entire battle had taken less than ten seconds.

The big man had been overconfident, certain that his six-inch advantage in height and his extra eighty pounds of muscle made him unbeatable. He had been wrong.

Elliot swung toward the other intruder, pointing the confiscated pistol.

Bob was already out of the kitchen, in the dining room, running toward the front of the house. Evidently he wasn't carrying a gun, and he was impressed by the speed and ease with which his partner had been taken out of action.

Elliot went after him but was slowed by the dining-room chairs, which the fleeing man had overturned in his wake. In the living room, other furniture was knocked over, and books were strewn on the floor. The route to the entrance foyer was an obstacle course.

By the time Elliot reached the front door and rushed out of the house, Bob had run the length of the driveway and crossed the street. He was climbing into a dark-green, unmarked Chevy sedan. Elliot got to the street in time to watch the Chevy pull away, tires squealing, engine roaring.

He couldn't get the license number. The plates were smeared with mud.

He hurried back to the house.

The man in the kitchen was still unconscious and would probably remain that way for another ten or fifteen minutes. Elliot checked his pulse and pulled back one of his eyelids. Vince would survive, although he might need hospitalization, and he wouldn't be able to swallow without pain for days to come.

Elliot went through the thug's pockets. He found some small change, a comb, a wallet, and the sheaf of papers on which were typed the questions that Elliot had been expected to answer.

He folded the pages and stuffed them into his hip pocket.

Vince's wallet contained ninety-two dollars, no credit cards, no driver's license, no identification of any kind. Definitely not FBI. Bureau men carried the proper credentials. Not CIA, either. CIA operatives were loaded with ID, even if it was in a phony name. As far as Elliot was concerned, the absence of ID was more sinister than a collection of patently false papers would have been, because this absolute anonymity smacked of a secret police organization.

Secret police. Such a possibility scared the hell out of Elliot. Not in the good old U. S. of A. Surely not. In China, in the new Russia, in Iran or Iraq—yes. In a South American banana republic—yes. In half the countries in the world, there were secret police, modern gestapos, and citizens lived in fear of a late-night knock on the door. But not in America, damn it.

Even if the government had established a secret police

force, however, why was it so anxious to cover up the true facts of Danny's death? What were they trying to hide about the Sierra tragedy? What *really* had happened up in those mountains?

Tina.

Suddenly he realized she was in as much danger as he was. If these people were determined to kill him just to stop the exhumation, they would *have* to kill Tina. In fact, she must be their primary target.

He ran to the kitchen phone, snatched up the handset, and realized that he didn't know her number. He quickly leafed through the telephone directory. But there was no listing for Christina Evans.

He would never be able to con an unlisted number out of the directory-assistance operator. By the time he called the police and managed to explain the situation, they might be too late to help Tina.

Briefly he stood in terrible indecision, incapacitated by the prospect of losing Tina. He thought of her slightly crooked smile, her eyes as quick and deep and cool and blue as a pure mountain stream. The pressure in his chest grew so great that he couldn't get his breath.

Then he remembered her address. She had given it to him two nights ago, at the party after the premiere of *Magyck!* She didn't live far from him. He could be at her place in five minutes.

He still had the silencer-equipped pistol in his hand, and he decided to keep it.

He ran to the car in the driveway.

18

TINA LEFT THE REPAIRMAN FROM THE GAS COMPANY in the garage and returned to Danny's room. She took the graphic novel out of the carton and sat on the edge of the bed in the tarnished-copper sunlight that fell like a shower of pennies through the window.

The magazine contained half a dozen illustrated horror stories. The one from which the cover painting had been drawn was sixteen pages long. In letters that were supposed to look as if they had been formed from rotting shroud cloth, the artist had emblazoned the title across the top of the first page, above a somber, well-detailed scene of a rain-swept graveyard. Tina stared at those words in shocked disbelief.

THE BOY WHO WAS NOT DEAD

She thought of the words on the chalkboard and on the computer printout: *Not dead, not dead, not dead. . . .*

Her hands shook. She had trouble holding the magazine steady enough to read.

The story was set in the mid-nineteenth century, when a

physician's perception of the thin line between life and death was often cloudy. It was the tale of a boy, Kevin, who fell off a roof and took a bad knock on the head, thereafter slipping into a deep coma. The boy's vital signs were undetectable to the medical technology of that era. The doctor pronounced him dead, and his grieving parents committed Kevin to the grave. In those days the corpse was not embalmed; therefore, the boy was buried while still alive. Kevin's parents went away from the city immediately after the funeral, intending to spend a month at their summer house in the country, where they could be free from the press of business and social duties, the better to mourn their lost child. But the first night in the country, the mother received a vision in which Kevin was buried alive and calling for her. The vision was so vivid, so disturbing, that she and her husband raced back to the city that very night to have the grave reopened at dawn. But Death decided that Kevin belonged to him, because the funeral had been held already and because the grave had been closed. Death was determined that the parents would not reach the cemetery in time to save their son. Most of the story dealt with Death's attempts to stop the mother and father on their desperate night journey; they were assaulted by every form of the walking dead, every manner of living corpse and vampire and ghoul and zombie and ghost, but they triumphed. They arrived at the grave by dawn, had it opened, and found their son alive, released from his coma. The last panel of the illustrated story showed the parents and the boy walking out of the graveyard while Death watched them leave. Death was saying, "Only a temporary victory. You'll all be mine sooner or later. You'll be back some day. I'll be waiting for you."

Tina was dry-mouthed, weak.

She didn't know what to make of the damned thing.

This was just a silly comic book, an absurd horror story. Yet . . . strange parallels existed between this gruesome tale and the recent ugliness in her own life.

She put the magazine aside, cover-down, so she wouldn't have to meet Death's wormy, red-eyed gaze.

The Boy Who Was Not Dead.

It was weird.

She had dreamed that Danny was buried alive. Into her dream she incorporated a grisly character from an old issue of a horror-comics magazine that was in Danny's collection. The lead story in this issue was about a boy, approximately Danny's age, mistakenly pronounced dead, then buried alive, and then exhumed.

Coincidence?

Yeah, sure, just about as coincidental as sunrise following sunset.

Crazily, Tina felt as if her nightmare had not come from within her, but from without, as if some person or force had projected the dream into her mind in an effort to—

To what?

To tell her that Danny had been buried alive?

Impossible. He could not have been buried alive. The boy had been battered, burned, frozen, horribly mutilated in the crash, dead beyond any shadow of a doubt. That's what both the authorities and the mortician had told her. Furthermore, this was not the mid-nineteenth century; these days, doctors could detect even the vaguest heartbeat, the shallowest respiration, the dimmest traces of brain-wave activity.

Danny certainly had been dead when they had buried him.

And if, by some million-to-one chance, the boy *had* been alive when he'd been buried, why would it take an entire year for her to receive a vision from the spirit world?

This last thought profoundly shocked her. The spirit world? Visions? Clairvoyant experiences? She didn't believe in any of that psychic, supernatural stuff. At least she'd always thought she didn't believe in it. Yet now she was seriously considering the possibility that her dreams had some otherworldly significance. This was sheer claptrap. Utter nonsense. The roots of all dreams were to be found in the store of experiences in the psyche; dreams were not sent like ethereal telegrams from spirits or gods or demons. Her sudden gullibility dismayed and alarmed her, because it indicated that the decision to have Danny's body exhumed was not having the stabilizing effect on her emotions that she had hoped it would.

Tina got up from the bed, went to the window, and gazed at the quiet street, the palms, the olive trees.

She had to concentrate on the indisputable facts. Rule out all of this nonsense about the dream having been sent by some outside force. It was *her* dream, entirely of *her* making.

But what about the horror comic?

As far as she could see, only one rational explanation presented itself. She *must* have glimpsed the grotesque figure of Death on the cover of the magazine when Danny first brought the issue home from the newsstand.

Except that she knew she hadn't.

And even if she had seen the color illustration before, she knew damned well that she hadn't read the story—*The Boy Who Was Not Dead*. She had paged through only two of the magazines Danny had bought, the first two, when she had been trying to make up her mind whether such unusual reading material could have any harmful effects on him. From the date on its cover, she knew that the issue containing *The Boy Who Was Not Dead* couldn't be one of the first pieces in Danny's collection. It had been published only two years ago, long after she had decided that horror comics were harmless.

She was back where she'd started.

Her dream had been patterned after the images in the illustrated horror story. That seemed indisputable.

But she hadn't read the story until a few minutes ago. That was a fact as well.

Frustrated and angry at herself for her inability to solve the puzzle, she turned from the window. She went back to the bed to have another look at the magazine, which she'd left there.

The gas company workman called from the front of the house, startling Tina.

She found him waiting by the front door.

"I'm finished," he said. "I just wanted to let you know I was going, so you could lock the door behind me."

"Everything all right?"

"Oh, yeah. Sure. Everything here is in great shape. If there's a gas leak in this neighborhood, it's not anywhere on your property."

She thanked him, and he said he was only doing his job. They both said "Have a nice day," and she locked the door after he left.

She returned to Danny's room and picked up the lurid magazine. Death glared hungrily at her from the cover.

Sitting on the edge of the bed, she read the story again,

hoping to see something important in it that she had overlooked in the first reading.

Three or four minutes later the doorbell rang—one, two, three, four times, insistently.

Carrying the magazine, she went to answer the bell. It rang three more times during the ten seconds that she took to reach the front door.

"Don't be so damn impatient," she muttered.

To her surprise, through the fish-eye lens, she saw Elliot on the stoop.

When she opened the door, he came in fast, almost in a crouch, glancing past her, left and right, toward the living room, then toward the dining area, speaking rapidly, urgently. "Are you okay? Are you all right?"

"I'm fine. What's wrong with you?"

"Are you alone?"

"Not now that you're here."

He closed the door, locked it. "Pack a suitcase."

"What?"

"I don't think it's safe for you to stay here."

"Elliot, is that a gun?"

"Yeah. I was—"

"A real gun?"

"Yeah. I took it off the guy who tried to kill me."

She was more able to believe that he was joking than that he had really been in danger. "What man? When?"

"A few minutes ago. At my place."

"But—"

"Listen, Tina, they wanted to kill me just because I was going to help you get Danny's body exhumed."

She gaped at him. "What are you talking about?"

"Murder. Conspiracy. Something damn strange. They probably intend to kill you too."

"But that's—"

"Crazy," he said. "I know. But it's true."

"Elliot—"

"Can you pack a suitcase fast?"

At first she half believed that he was trying to be funny, playing a game to amuse her, and she was going to tell him that none of this struck her as funny. But she stared into his dark, expressive eyes, and she knew that he'd meant every word he said.

"My God, Elliot, did someone really try to kill you?"

"I'll tell you about it later."

"Are you hurt?"

"No, no. But we ought to lie low until we can figure this out."

"Did you call the police?"

"I'm not sure that's a good idea."

"Why not?"

"Maybe they're part of it somehow."

"Part of it? The *cops?*"

"Where do you keep your suitcases?"

She felt dizzy. "Where are we going?"

"I don't know yet."

"But—"

"Come on. Hurry. Let's get you packed and the hell out of here before any more of these guys show up."

"I have suitcases in my bedroom closet."

He put a hand against her back, gently but firmly urging her out of the foyer.

She headed for the master bedroom, confused and beginning to be frightened.

He followed close behind her. "Has anyone been around here this afternoon?"

"Just me."

"I mean, anyone snooping around? Anyone at the door?"

"No."

"I can't figure why they'd come for me first."

"Well, there was the gas man," Tina said as she hurried down the short hall toward the master bedroom.

"The what?"

"The repairman from the gas company."

Elliot put a hand on her shoulder, stopped her, and turned her around just as they entered the bedroom. "A gas company workman?"

"Yes. Don't worry. I asked to see his credentials."

Elliot frowned. "But it's a holiday."

"He was an emergency crewman."

"What emergency?"

"They've lost some pressure in the gas lines. They think there might be a leak in this neighborhood."

The furrows in Elliot's brow grew deeper. "What did this workman need to see you for?"

"He wanted to check my furnace, make sure there wasn't any gas escaping."

"You didn't let him in?"

"Sure. He had a photo ID card from the gas company. He checked the furnace, and it was okay."

"When was this?"

"He left just a couple minutes before you came in."

"How long was he here?"

"Fifteen, twenty minutes."

"It took him that long to check out the furnace?"

"He wanted to be thorough. He said—"

"Were you with him the whole time?"

"No. I was cleaning out Danny's room."

"Where's your furnace?"

"In the garage."

"Show me."

"What about the suitcases?"

"There may not be time," he said.

He was pale. Fine beads of sweat had popped out along his hairline.

She felt the blood drain from her face.

She said, "My God, you don't think—"

"The furnace!"

"This way."

Still carrying the magazine, she rushed through the house, past the kitchen, into the laundry room. A door stood at the far end of this narrow, rectangular work area. As she reached for the knob, she smelled the gas in the garage.

"Don't open that door!" Elliot warned.

She snatched her hand off the knob as if she had almost picked up a tarantula.

"The latch might cause a spark," Elliot said. "Let's get the hell out. The front door. Come on. *Fast!*"

They hurried back the way they had come.

Tina passed a leafy green plant, a four-foot-high schefflera that she had owned since it was only one-fourth as tall as it was now, and she had the insane urge to stop and risk getting caught in the coming explosion just long enough to pick up the plant and take it with her. But an image of crimson eyes, yellow skin—the leering face of death— flashed through her mind, and she kept moving.

She tightened her grip on the horror-comics magazine in her left hand. It was important that she not lose it.

In the foyer, Elliot jerked open the front door, pushed her through ahead of him, and they both plunged into the golden late-afternoon sunshine.

"Into the street!" Elliot urged.

A blood-freezing image rose at the back of her mind: the house torn apart by a colossal blast, shrapnel of wood and glass and metal whistling toward her, hundreds of sharp fragments piercing her from head to foot.

The flagstone walk that led across her front lawn seemed to be one of those treadmill pathways in a dream, stretching out farther in front of her the harder that she ran, but at last she reached the end of it and dashed into the street. Elliot's Mercedes was parked at the far curb, and she was six or eight feet from the car when the sudden outward-sweeping shock of the explosion shoved her forward. She stumbled and fell into the side of the sports car, banging her knee painfully.

Twisting around in terror, she called Elliot's name. He was safe, close behind her, knocked off balance by the force of the shock wave, staggering forward, but unhurt.

The garage had gone up first, the big door ripping from its hinges and splintering into the driveway, the roof dissolving in a confetti-shower of shake shingles and flaming debris. But even as Tina looked from Elliot to the fire, before all of the shingles had fallen back to earth, a second explosion slammed through the house, and a billowing cloud of flame roared from one end of the structure to the other, bursting those few windows that had miraculously survived the first blast.

Tina watched, stunned, as flames leaped from a window of the house and ignited dry palm fronds on a nearby tree.

Elliot pushed her away from the Mercedes so he could open the door on the passenger side. "Get in. Quick!"

"But my house is on fire!"

"You can't save it now."

"We have to wait for the fire company."

"The longer we stand here, the better targets we make."

He grabbed her arm, swung her away from the burning house, the sight of which affected her as much as if it had been a hypnotist's slowly swinging pocket watch.

"For God's sake, Tina, get in the car, and let's go before the shooting starts."

Frightened, dazed by the incredible speed at which her world had begun to disintegrate, she did as he said.

When she was in the car, he shut her door, ran to the driver's side, and climbed in behind the steering wheel.

"Are you all right?" he asked.

She nodded dumbly.

"At least we're still alive," he said.

He put the pistol on his lap, the muzzle facing toward his door, away from Tina. The keys were in the ignition. He started the car. His hands were shaking.

Tina looked out the side window, watching in disbelief as the flames spread from the shattered garage roof to the main roof of the house, long tongues of lambent fire, licking, licking, hungry, bloodred in the last orange light of the afternoon.

As Elliot drove away from the burning house, his instinctual sense of danger was as sensitive as it had been in his military days. He was on the thin line that separated animal alertness from nervous frenzy.

He glanced at the rearview mirror and saw a black van pull away from the curb, half a block behind them.

"We're being followed," he said.

Tina had been looking back at her house. Now she turned all the way around and stared through the rear window of the sports car. "I'll bet the bastard who rigged my furnace is in that truck."

"Probably."

"If I could get my hands on the son of a bitch, I'd gouge his eyes out."

Her fury surprised and pleased Elliot. Stupefied by the unexpected violence, by the loss of her house, and by her close brush with death, she had seemed to be in a trance; now she had snapped out of it. He was encouraged by her resilience.

"Put on your seat belt," he said. "We'll be moving fast and loose."

She faced front and buckled up. "Are you going to try to lose them?"

"I'm not just going to *try*."

In this residential neighborhood the speed limit was twenty-five miles an hour. Elliot tramped on the accelerator, and the low, sleek, two-seat Mercedes jumped forward.

Behind them the van dwindled rapidly, until it was a block and a half away. Then it stopped dwindling as it also accelerated.

"He can't catch up with us," Elliot said. "The best he can hope to do is avoid losing more ground."

Along the street, people came out of their houses, seeking the source of the explosion. Their heads turned as the Mercedes rocketed past.

When Elliot rounded the corner two blocks later, he braked from sixty miles an hour to make the turn. The tires squealed, and the car slid sideways, but the superb suspension and responsive steering held the Mercedes firmly on four wheels all the way through the arc.

"You don't think they'll actually start shooting at us?" Tina asked.

"Hell if I know. They wanted it to appear as if you'd died in an accidental gas explosion. And I think they had a fake suicide planned for me. But now that they know we're on to them, they might panic, might do anything. I don't know. The only thing I *do* know is they can't let us just walk away."

"But who—"

"I'll tell you what I know, but later."

"What do they have to do with Danny?"

"Later," he said impatiently.

"But it's all so crazy."

"You're telling *me?*"

He wheeled around another corner, and then another, trying to disappear from the men in the van long enough to leave them with so many choices of streets to follow that they would have to give up the chase in confusion. Too late, he saw the sign at the fourth intersection—NOT A THROUGH STREET—but they were already around the corner and headed down the narrow dead end, with nothing but a row of ten modest stucco houses on each side.

"Damn!"

"Better back out," she said.

"And run right into them."

"You've got the gun."

"There's probably more than one of them, and they'll be armed."

At the fifth house on the left, the garage door was open, and there wasn't a car inside.

"We've got to get off the street and out of sight," Elliot said.

He drove into the open garage as boldly as if it were his own. He switched off the engine, scrambled out of the car, and ran to the big door. It wouldn't come down. He struggled with it for a moment, and then he realized that it was equipped with an automatic system.

Behind him, Tina said, "Stand back."

She had gotten out of the car and had located the control button on the garage wall.

He glanced outside, up the street. He couldn't see the van.

The door rumbled down, concealing them from anyone who might drive past.

Elliot went to her. "That was close."

She took his hand in hers, squeezed it. Her hand was cold, but her grip was firm.

"So who the hell are they?" she asked.

"I saw Harold Kennebeck, the judge I mentioned. He—"

The door that connected the garage to the house opened without warning, but with a sharp, dry squeak of unoiled hinges.

An imposing, barrel-chested man in rumpled chinos and a white T-shirt snapped on the garage light and peered curiously at them. He had meaty arms; the circumference of one of them almost equaled the circumference of Elliot's thigh. And there wasn't a shirt made that could be buttoned easily around his thick, muscular neck. He appeared formidable, even with his beer belly, which bulged over the waistband of his trousers.

First Vince and now this specimen. It was the Day of the Giants.

"Who're you?" the pituitary-challenged behemoth asked in a soft, gentle voice that didn't equate with his appearance.

Elliot had the awful feeling that this guy would reach for the button Tina had pushed less than a minute ago, and that the garage door would lift just as the black van was rolling slowly by in the street.

Stalling for time, he said, "Oh, hi. My name's Elliot, and this is Tina."

"Tom," the big man said. "Tom Polumby."

Tom Polumby didn't appear to be worried by their

presence in his garage; he seemed merely perplexed. A man of his size probably wasn't frightened any more easily than Godzilla confronted by the pathetic bazooka-wielding soldiers surrounding doomed Tokyo.

"Nice car," Tom said with an unmistakable trace of reverence in his voice. He gazed covetously at the S600.

Elliot almost laughed. *Nice car!* They pulled into this guy's garage, parked, closed the door bold as you please, and all he had to say was *Nice car!*

"Very nice little number," Tom said, nodding, licking his lips as he studied the Mercedes.

Apparently Tom couldn't conceive that burglars, psychopathic killers, and other low-lifes were permitted to purchase a Mercedes-Benz if they had the money for it. To him, evidently, anyone who drove a Mercedes had to be the right kind of people.

Elliot wondered how Tom would have reacted if they had shrieked into his garage in an old battered Chevy.

Pulling his covetous gaze from the car, Tom said, "What're you doing here?" There was still neither suspicion nor belligerence in his voice.

"We're expected," Elliot said.

"Huh? I wasn't expecting nobody."

"We're here . . . about the boat," Elliot said, not even knowing where he was going to go with that line, ready to say anything to keep Tom from putting up the garage door and throwing them out.

Tom blinked. "What boat?"

"The twenty-footer."

"I don't own a twenty-footer."

"The one with the Evinrude motor."

"Nothing like that here."

"You must be mistaken," Elliot said.

"I figure you've got the wrong place," Tom said, stepping out of the doorway, into the garage, reaching for the button that would raise the big door.

Tina said, "Mr. Polumby, wait. There must be some mistake, really. This is definitely the right place."

Tom's hand stopped short of the button.

Tina continued: "You're just not the man we were supposed to see, that's all. He probably forgot to tell you about the boat."

Elliot blinked at her, amazed by her natural facility for deception.

"Who's this guy you're supposed to see?" Tom asked, frowning.

Appearing to be somewhat amazed herself, Tina hesitated not at all before she said, "Sol Fitzpatrick."

"Nobody here by that name."

"But this is the address he gave us. He said the garage door would be open and that we were to pull right inside."

Elliot wanted to hug her. "Yeah. Sol said we were to pull in, out of the driveway, so that he'd have a place to put the boat when he got here with it."

Tom scratched his head, then pulled on one ear. "Fitzpatrick?"

"Yeah."

"Never heard of him," Tom said. "What's he bringing a boat here for, anyway?"

"We're buying it from him," Tina said.

Tom shook his head. "No. I mean, why *here*?"

"Well," Elliot said, "the way we understood it, this was where he lived."

"But he doesn't," Tom said. "I live here. Me and my wife and our little girl. They're out right now, and there's nobody ever been here named Fitzpatrick."

"Well, why would he tell us this was his address?" Tina asked, scowling.

"Lady," Tom said, "I don't have the foggiest. Unless maybe . . . Did you already pay him for the boat?"

"Well . . ."

"Maybe just a down payment?" Tom asked.

"We did give him two thousand on deposit," Elliot said.

Tina said, "It was a refundable deposit."

"Yeah. Just to hold the boat until we could see it and make up our minds."

Smiling, Tom said, "I think the deposit might not turn out to be as refundable as you thought."

Pretending surprise, Tina said, "You don't mean Mr. Fitzpatrick would cheat us?"

Obviously it pleased Tom to think that people who could afford a Mercedes were not so smart after all. "If you gave him a deposit, and if he gave you this address and claimed he lived here, then it's not very likely this Sol Fitzpatrick even owns any boat in the first place."

"Damn," Elliot said.

"We were swindled?" Tina asked, feigning shock, buying time.

Grinning broadly now, Tom said, "Well, you can look at it that way if you want. Or you can think of it as an important lesson this here Fitzpatrick fella taught you."

"Swindled," Tina said, shaking her head.

"Sure as the sun will come up tomorrow," Tom said.

Tina turned to Elliot. "What do you think?"

Elliot glanced at the garage door, then at his watch. He said, "I think it's safe to leave."

"Safe?" Tom asked.

Tina stepped lightly past Tom Polumby and pressed the button that raised the garage door. She smiled at her bewildered host and went to the passenger side of the car while Elliot opened the driver's door.

Polumby looked from Elliot to Tina to Elliot, puzzled. "Safe?"

Elliot said, "I sure hope it is, Tom. Thanks for your help." He got in the car and backed it out of the garage.

Any amusement he felt at the way they had handled Polumby evaporated instantly as he reversed warily out of sanctuary, down the driveway, and into the street. He sat stiffly behind the wheel, clenching his teeth, wondering if a bullet would crack through the windshield and shatter his face.

He wasn't accustomed to this tension. Physically, he was still hard, tough; but mentally and emotionally, he was softer than he had been in his prime. A long time had passed since his years in military intelligence, since the nights of fear in the Persian Gulf and in countless cities scattered around the Mideast and Asia. Then, he'd had the resiliency of youth and had been less burdened with respect for death than he was now. In those days it had been easy to play the hunter. He had taken pleasure in stalking human prey; hell, there had even been a measure of joy in *being* stalked, for it gave him the opportunity to prove himself by outwitting the hunter on his trail. Much had changed. He was soft. A successful, civilized attorney. Living the good life. He had never expected to play that game again. But once more, incredibly, he was being hunted, and he wondered how long he could survive.

Tina glanced both ways along the street as Elliot swung the car out of the driveway. "No black van," she said.

"So far."

Several blocks to the north, an ugly column of smoke rose into the twilight sky from what was left of Tina's house, roiling, night-black, the upper reaches tinted around the edges by the last pinkish rays of the setting sun.

As he drove from one residential street to another, steadily heading away from the smoke, working toward a major thoroughfare, Elliot expected to encounter the black van at every intersection.

Tina appeared to be no less pessimistic about their hope of escape than he was. Each time he glanced at her, she was either crouched forward, squinting at every new street they entered, or twisted halfway around in her seat, looking out the rear window. Her face was drawn, and she was biting her lower lip.

However, by the time they reached Charleston Boulevard—via Maryland Parkway, Sahara Avenue, and Las Vegas Boulevard—they began to relax. They were far from Tina's neighborhood now. No matter who was searching for them, no matter how large the organization pitted against them, this city was too big to harbor danger for them in every nook and crevice. With more than a million full-time residents, with more than twenty million tourists a year, and with a vast desert on which to sprawl, Vegas offered thousands of dark, quiet corners where two people on the run could safely stop to catch their breath and settle upon a course of action.

At least that was what Elliot wanted to believe.

"Where to?" Tina asked as Elliot turned west on Charleston Boulevard.

"Let's ride out this way for a few miles and talk. We've got a lot to discuss. Plans to make."

"What plans?"

"How to stay alive."

WHILE ELLIOT DROVE, HE TOLD TINA WHAT HAD happened at his house: the two thugs, their interest in the possibility of Danny's grave being reopened, their admission that they worked for some government agency, the hypodermic syringes. . . .

She said, "Maybe we should go back to your place. If this Vince is still there, we should use those drugs on him. Even if he really doesn't know why his organization is interested in the exhumation, he'll at least know who his bosses are. We'll get names. There's bound to be a lot we can learn from him."

They stopped at a red traffic light. Elliot took her hand. The contact gave him strength. "I'd sure like to interrogate Vince, but we can't. He probably isn't at my place anymore. He'll have come to his senses and scrammed by now. And even if he was deeper under than I thought, some of his people probably went in there and pulled him out while I was rushing off to you. Besides, if we go back to my house, we'll just be walking into the dragon's jaws. They'll be watching the place."

The traffic light changed to green, and Elliot reluctantly let go of her hand.

"The only way these people are going to get us," he said, "is if we just give ourselves over to them. No matter who they are, they're not omniscient. We can hide from them for a long time if we have to. If they can't find us, they can't kill us."

As they continued west on Charleston Boulevard, Tina said, "Earlier you told me we couldn't go to the police with this."

"Right."

"Why can't we?"

"The cops might be a part of it, at least to the extent that Vince's bosses can put pressure on them. Besides, we're dealing with a government agency, and government agencies tend to cooperate with one another."

"It's all so paranoid."

"Eyes everywhere. If they have a judge in their pocket, why not a few cops?"

"But you told me you respected Kennebeck. You said he was a good judge."

"He is. He's well versed in the law, and he's fair."

"Why would he cooperate with these killers? Why would he violate his oath of office?"

"Once an agent, always an agent," Elliot said. "That's the wisdom of the service, not mine, but in many cases it's true. For some of them, it's the only loyalty they'll ever be capable of. Kennebeck held several jobs in different intelligence organizations. He was deeply involved in that world for thirty years. After he retired about ten years ago, he was still a young man, fifty-three, and he needed something else to occupy his time. He had his law degree, but he didn't want the hassle of a day-to-day legal practice. So he ran for an elective position on the court, and he won. I think he takes his job seriously. Nevertheless, he was an intelligence agent a hell of a lot longer than he's been a judge, and I guess breeding tells. Or maybe he never actually retired at all. Maybe he's still on the payroll of some spook shop, and maybe the whole plan was for him to pretend to retire and then get elected as a judge here in Vegas, so his bosses would have a friendly courtroom in town."

"Is that likely? I mean, how could they be sure he'd win the election?"

"Maybe they fixed it."

"You're serious, aren't you?"

"Remember maybe ten years ago when that Texas elections official revealed how Lyndon Johnson's first local election was fixed? The guy said he was just trying to clear his conscience after all those years. He might as well have saved his breath. Hardly anyone raised an eyebrow. It happens now and then. And in a small local election like the one Kennebeck won, stacking the deck would be easy if you had enough money and government muscle behind you."

"But why would they want Kennebeck on a Vegas court instead of in Washington or New York or someplace more important?"

"Oh, Vegas is a *very* important town," Elliot said. "If you want to launder dirty money, this is by far the easiest place to do it. If you want to purchase a false passport, a counterfeit driver's license, or anything of that nature, you can pick and choose from several of the best document-forgery artists in the world, because this is where a lot of them live. If you're looking for a freelance hit man, someone who deals in carload lots of illegal weapons, maybe a mercenary who can put together a small expeditionary force for an overseas operation—you can find all of them here. Nevada has fewer state laws on the books than any state in the nation. Its tax rates are low. There's no state income tax at all. Regulations on banks and real estate agents and on everyone else—except casino owners—are less troublesome here than in other states, which takes a burden off everybody, but which is especially attractive to people trying to spend and invest dirty cash. Nevada offers more personal freedom than anywhere in the country, and that's good, by my way of thinking. But wherever there's a great deal of personal freedom, there's also an element that takes more than fair advantage of the liberal legal structure. Vegas is an important field office for any American spook shop."

"So there really are eyes everywhere."

"In a sense, yes."

"But even if Kennebeck's bosses have a lot of influence with the Vegas police, would the cops let us be killed? Would they really let it go that far?"

"They probably couldn't provide enough protection to stop it."

"What kind of government agency would have the authority to circumvent the law like this? What kind of agency would be empowered to kill innocent civilians who got in its way?"

"I'm still trying to figure that one. It scares the hell out of me."

They stopped at another red traffic light.

"So what are you saying?" Tina asked. "That we'll have to handle this all by ourselves?"

"At least for the time being."

"But that's hopeless! How can we?"

"It isn't hopeless."

"Just two ordinary people against *them*?"

Elliot glanced in the rearview mirror, as he had been doing every minute or two since they'd turned onto Charleston Boulevard. No one was following them, but he kept checking.

"It isn't hopeless," he said again. "We just need time to think about it, time to work out a plan. Maybe we'll come up with someone who can help us."

"Like who?"

The traffic light turned green.

"Like the newspapers, for one," Elliot said, accelerating across the intersection, glancing in the rearview mirror. "We've got proof that something unusual is happening: the silencer-equipped pistol I took off Vince, your house blowing up. . . . I'm pretty sure we can find a reporter who'll go with that much and write a story about how a bunch of nameless, faceless people want to keep us from reopening Danny's grave, how maybe something truly strange lies at the bottom of the Sierra tragedy. Then a lot of people are going to be pushing for an exhumation of *all* those boys. There'll be a demand for new autopsies, investigations. Kennebeck's bosses want to stop us before we sow any seeds of doubt about the official explanation. But once those seeds are sown, once the parents of the other scouts and the entire city are clamoring for an investigation, Kennebeck's buddies won't have anything to gain by eliminating us. It isn't hopeless, Tina, and it's not like you to give up so easily."

She sighed. "I'm not giving up."

"Good."

"I won't stop until I know what really happened to Danny."

"That's better. That sounds more like the Christina Evans I know."

Dusk was sliding into night. Elliot turned on the headlights.

Tina said, "It's just that . . . for the past year I've been struggling to adjust to the fact that Danny died in that stupid, pointless accident. And now, just when I'm beginning to think I can face up to it and put it behind me, I discover he might not have died accidentally after all. Suddenly everything's up in the air again."

"It'll come down."

"Will it?"

"Yes. We'll get to the bottom of this."

He glanced in the rearview mirror.

Nothing suspicious.

He was aware of her watching him, and after a while she said, "You know what?"

"What?"

"I think . . . in a way . . . you're actually enjoying this."

"Enjoying what?"

"The chase."

"Oh, no. I don't enjoy taking guns away from men half again as big as I am."

"I'm sure you don't. That isn't what I said."

"And I sure wouldn't *choose* to have my nice, peaceful, quiet life turned upside down. I'd rather be a comfortable, upstanding, boring citizen than a fugitive."

"I didn't say anything about what you'd choose if it were up to you. But now that it's happened, now that it's been thrust upon you, you're not entirely unhappy. There's a part of you, deep down, that's responding to the challenge with a degree of pleasure."

"Baloney."

"An animal awareness . . . a new kind of energy you didn't have this morning."

"The only thing new about me is that I wasn't scared stiff this morning, and now I am."

"Being scared—that's part of it," she said. "The danger has struck a chord in you."

He smiled. "The good old days of spies and counterspies? Sorry, but no, I don't long for that at all. I'm not a natural-born man of action. I'm just me, the same old me that I always was."

"Anyway," Tina said, "I'm glad I've got you on my side."

"I like it better when you're on top," he said, and he winked at her.

"Have you always had such a dirty mind?"

"No. I've had to cultivate it."

"Joking in the midst of disaster," she said.

"'Laughter is a balm for the afflicted, the best defense against despair, the only medicine for melancholy.'"

"Who said that?" she asked. "Shakespeare?"

"Groucho Marx, I think."

She leaned forward and picked something up from the floor between her feet. "And then there's this damn thing."

"What did you find?"

"I brought it from my place," she said.

In the rush to get out of her house before the gas explosion leveled it, he hadn't noticed that she'd been carrying anything. He risked a quick look, shifting his attention from the road, but there wasn't enough light in the car for him to see what she held. "I can't make it out."

"It's a horror-comics magazine," she said. "I found it when I was cleaning out Danny's room. It was in a box with a lot of other magazines."

"So?"

"Remember the nightmares I told you about?"

"Yeah, sure."

"The monster in my dreams is on the cover of this magazine. It's him. Detail for detail."

"Then you must have seen the magazine before, and you just—"

"No. That's what I tried to tell myself. But I never saw it until today. I know I didn't. I pored through Danny's collection. When he came home from the newsstand, I never monitored what he'd bought. I never snooped."

"Maybe you—"

"Wait," she said. "I haven't told you the worst part."

The traffic thinned out as they drove farther from the heart of town, closer to the looming black mountains that thrust into the last electric-purple light in the western sky.

Tina told Elliot about *The Boy Who Was Not Dead.*

The similarities between the horror story and their attempt to exhume Danny's body chilled Elliot.

"Now," Tina said, "just like Death tried to stop the parents in the story, someone's trying to stop me from opening *my* son's grave."

They were getting too far out of town. A hungry darkness lay on both sides of the road. The land began to rise toward Mount Charleston where, less than an hour away, pine forests were mantled with snow. Elliot swung the car around and started back toward the lights of the city, which spread like a vast, glowing fungus on the black desert plain.

"There *are* similarities," he said.

"You're damned right there are. Too many."

"There's also one big difference. In the story, the boy was buried alive. But Danny *is* dead. The only thing in doubt is how he died."

"But that's the only difference between the basic plot of this story and what we're going through. And the words *Not Dead* in the title. And the boy in the story being Danny's age. It's just too much," she said.

They rode in silence for a while.

Finally Elliot said, "You're right. It can't be coincidence."

"Then how do you explain it?"

"I don't know."

"Welcome to the club."

A roadside diner stood on the right, and Elliot pulled into the parking lot. A single mercury-vapor pole lamp at the entrance shed fuzzy purple light over the first third of the parking lot. Elliot drove behind the restaurant and tucked the Mercedes into a slot in the deepest shadows, between a Toyota Celica and a small motor home, where it could not be seen from the street.

"Hungry?" he asked.

"Starving. But before we go in, let's check out that list of questions they were going to make you answer."

"Let's look at it in the café," Elliot said. "The light will be better. It doesn't seem to be busy in there. We should be able to talk without being overheard. Bring the magazine too. I want to see that story."

As he got out of the car, his attention was drawn to a window on the side of the motor home next to which he had parked. He squinted through the glass into the perfectly black interior, and he had the disconcerting feeling that someone was hiding in there, staring out at him.

Don't succumb to paranoia, he warned himself.

When he turned from the motor home, his gaze fell on a dense pool of shadows around the trash bin at the back of the restaurant, and again he had the feeling that someone was watching him from concealment.

He had told Tina that Kennebeck's bosses were not omniscient. He must remember that. He and Tina apparently were confronted with a powerful, lawless, dangerous organization hell-bent on keeping the secret of the Sierra tragedy. But any organization was composed of ordinary men and women, none of whom had the all-seeing gaze of God.

Nevertheless . . .

As he and Tina walked across the parking lot toward the diner, Elliot couldn't shake the feeling that someone or something was watching them. Not necessarily a person. Just . . . something . . . weird, strange. Something both more and less than human. That was a bizarre thought, not at all the sort of notion he'd ordinarily get in his head, and he didn't like it.

Tina stopped when they reached the purple light under the mercury-vapor lamp. She glanced back toward the car, a curious expression on her face.

"What is it?" Elliot asked.

"I don't know. . . ."

"See something?"

"No."

They stared at the shadows.

At length she said, "Do you feel it?"

"Feel what?"

"I've got this . . . prickly feeling."

He didn't say anything.

"You *do* feel it, don't you?" she asked.

"Yes."

"As if we aren't alone."

"It's crazy," he said, "but I feel eyes on me."

She shivered. "But no one's really there."

"No. I don't think anyone is."

They continued to squint at the inky blackness, searching for movement.

She said, "Are we both cracking under the strain?"

"Just jumpy," he said, but he wasn't really convinced that their imagination was to blame.

A soft cool wind sprang up. It carried with it the odor of dry desert weeds and alkaline sand. It hissed through the branches of a nearby date palm.

"It's such a *strong* feeling," she said. "And you know what it reminds me of? It's the same damn feeling I had in Angela's office when that computer terminal started operating on its own. I feel . . . not just as if I'm being watched but . . . something more . . . like a *presence* . . . as if something I can't see is standing right beside me. I can feel the weight of it, a pressure in the air . . . sort of *looming*."

He knew exactly what she meant, but he didn't want to think about it, because there was no way he could make sense of it. He preferred to deal with hard facts, realities; that was why he was such a good attorney, so adept at taking threads of evidence and weaving a good case out of them.

"We're both overwrought," he suggested.

"That doesn't change what I feel."

"Let's get something to eat."

She stayed a moment longer, staring back into the gloom, where the purple mercury-vapor light did not reach.

"Tina . . . ?"

A breath of wind stirred a dry tumbleweed and blew it across the blacktop.

A bird swooped through the darkness overhead. Elliot couldn't see it, but he could hear the beating of its wings.

Tina cleared her throat. "It's as if . . . the night itself is watching us . . . the night, the shadows, the eyes of darkness."

The wind ruffled Elliot's hair. It rattled a loose metal fixture on the trash bin, and the restaurant's big sign creaked between its two standards.

At last he and Tina went into the diner, trying not to look over their shoulders.

21

THE LONG L-SHAPED DINER WAS FILLED WITH glimmering surfaces: chrome, glass, plastic, yellow Formica, and red vinyl. The jukebox played a country tune by Garth Brooks, and the music shared the air with the delicious aromas of fried eggs, bacon, and sausages. True to the rhythm of Vegas life, someone was just beginning his day with a hearty breakfast. Tina's mouth began to water as soon as she stepped through the door.

Eleven customers were clustered at the end of the long arm of the L, near the entrance, five on stools at the counter, six in the red booths. Elliot and Tina sat as far from everyone as possible, in the last booth in the short wing of the restaurant.

Their waitress was a redhead named Elvira. She had a round face, dimples, eyes that twinkled as if they had been waxed, and a Texas drawl. She took their orders for cheeseburgers, French fries, coleslaw, and Coors.

When Elvira left the table and they were alone, Tina said, "Let's see the papers you took off that guy."

Elliot fished the pages out of his hip pocket, unfolded

them, and put them on the table. There were three sheets of paper, each containing ten or twelve typewritten questions.

They leaned in from opposite sides of the booth and read the material silently:

1. How long have you known Christina Evans?
2. Why did Christina Evans ask you, rather than another attorney, to handle the exhumation of her son's body?
3. What reason does she have to doubt the official story of her son's death?
4. Does she have any proof that the official story of her son's death is false?
5. If she has such proof, what is it?
6. Where did she obtain this evidence?
7. Have you ever heard of "Project Pandora"?
8. Have you been given, or has Mrs. Evans been given, any material relating to military research installations in the Sierra Nevada Mountains?

Elliot looked up from the page. "Have you ever heard of Project Pandora?"

"No."

"Secret labs in the High Sierras?"

"Oh, sure. Mrs. Neddler told me all about them."

"Mrs. Neddler?"

"My cleaning woman."

"Jokes again."

"At a time like this."

"Balm for the afflicted, medicine for melancholy."

"Groucho Marx," she said.

"Evidently they think someone from Project Pandora has decided to rat on them."

"Is that who's been in Danny's room? Did someone from Project Pandora write on the chalkboard . . . and then fiddle with the computer at work?"

"Maybe," Elliot said.

"But you don't think so."

"Well, if someone had a guilty conscience, why wouldn't he approach you directly?"

"He could be afraid. Probably has good reason to be."

"Maybe," Elliot said again. "But I think it's more complicated than that. Just a hunch."

They read quickly through the remaining material, but none of it was enlightening. Most of the questions were concerned with how much Tina knew about the true nature of the Sierra accident, how much she had told Elliot, how much she had told Michael, and with how many people she had discussed it. There were no more intriguing tidbits like Project Pandora, no more clues or leads.

Elvira brought two frosted glasses and icy bottles of Coors.

The jukebox began to play a mournful Alan Jackson song.

Elliot sipped his beer and paged through the horror-comics magazine that had belonged to Danny. "Amazing," he said when he finished skimming *The Boy Who Was Not Dead*.

"You'd think it was even more amazing if you'd suffered those nightmares," she said. "So now what do we do?"

"Danny's was a closed-coffin funeral. Was it the same with the other thirteen scouts?"

"About half the others were buried without viewings," Tina said.

"Their parents never saw the bodies?"

"Oh, yes. All the other parents were asked to identify their kids, even though some of the corpses were in such a horrible state they couldn't be cosmetically restored for viewing at a funeral. Michael and I were the only ones who were strongly advised not to look at the remains. Danny was the only one who was too badly . . . mangled."

Even after all this time, when she thought about Danny's last moments on earth—the terror he must have known, the excruciating pain he must have endured, even if it was of brief duration—she began to choke with sorrow and pity. She blinked back tears and took a swallow of beer.

"Damn," Elliot said.

"What?"

"I thought we might make some quick allies out of those other parents. If they hadn't seen their kids' bodies, they might have just gone through a year of doubt like you did, might be easily persuaded to join us in a call for the reopening of *all* the graves. If that many voices were raised, then Vince's bosses couldn't risk silencing all of them, and we'd be safe. But if the other people had a chance to view the bodies, if none of them has had any reason to entertain doubts like yours, then they're all just finally learning to cope with the tragedy. If we go to them now with a wild story about a mysterious conspiracy, they aren't going to be anxious to listen."

"So we're still alone."

"Yeah."

"You said we could go to a reporter, try to get media interest brewing. Do you have anyone in mind?"

"I know a couple of local guys," Elliot said. "But maybe

it's not wise to go to the local press. That might be just what Vince's bosses are expecting us to do. If they're waiting, watching—we'll be dead before we can tell a reporter more than a sentence or two. I think we'll have to take the story out of town, and before we do that, I'd like to have a few more facts."

"I thought you said we had enough to interest a good newsman. The pistol you took off that man . . . my house being blown up . . ."

"That might be enough. Certainly, for the Las Vegas paper, it ought to be sufficient. This city still remembers the Jaborski group, the Sierra accident. It was a local tragedy. But if we go to the press in Los Angeles or New York or some other city, the reporters there aren't going to have a whole lot of interest in it unless they see an aspect of the story that lifts it out of the local-interest category. Maybe we've already got enough to convince them it's big news. I'm not sure. And I want to be *damn* sure before we try to go public with it. Ideally, I'd even like to be able to hand the reporter a neat theory about what really happened to those scouts, something sensational that he can hook his story onto."

"Such as?"

He shook his head. "I don't have anything worked out yet. But it seems to me the most obvious thing we have to consider is that the scouts and their leaders saw something they weren't supposed to see."

"Project Pandora?"

He sipped his beer and used one finger to wipe a trace of foam from his upper lip. "A military secret. I can't see what else would have brought an organization like Vince's so deeply into this. An intelligence outfit of that size and sophistication doesn't waste its time on Mickey Mouse stuff."

"But military secrets . . . that seems so far out."

"In case you didn't know it, since the Cold War ended and California took such a big hit in the defense downsizing, Nevada has more Pentagon-supported industries and installations than any state in the union. And I'm not just talking about the obvious ones like Nellis Air Force Base and the Nuclear Test Site. This state's ideally suited for secret or quasi-secret, high-security weapons research centers. Nevada has thousands of square miles of remote unpopulated land. The deserts. The deeper reaches of the mountains. And most of those remote areas are owned by the federal government. If you put a secret installation in the middle of all that lonely land, you have a pretty easy job maintaining security."

Arms on the table, both hands clasped around her glass of beer, Tina leaned toward Elliot. "You're saying that Mr. Jaborski, Mr. Lincoln, and the boys stumbled across a place like that in the Sierras?"

"It's possible."

"And saw something they weren't supposed to see."

"Maybe."

"And then what? You mean . . . because of what they saw, they were *killed*?"

"It's a theory that ought to excite a good reporter."

She shook her head. "I just can't believe the government would murder a group of little children just because they accidentally got a glimpse of a new weapon or something."

"Wouldn't it? Think of Waco—all those dead children. Ruby Ridge—a fourteen-year-old boy shot in the back by the FBI. Vince Foster found dead in a Washington park and officially declared a suicide even though most of the forensic evidence points to murder. Even a primarily good government, when it's big enough, has some pretty mean sharks swimming in the darker currents. We're living in strange times, Tina."

The rising night wind thrummed against the large pane of glass beside their booth. Beyond the window, out on Charleston Boulevard, traffic sailed murkily through a sudden churning river of dust and paper scraps.

Chilled, Tina said, "But how much could the kids have seen? You're the one who said security was easy to maintain when one of these installations is located in the wilderness. The boys couldn't have gotten very close to such a well-guarded place. Surely they couldn't have managed to get more than a glimpse."

"Maybe a glimpse was enough to condemn them."

"But kids aren't the best observers," she argued. "They're impressionable, excitable, given to exaggeration. If they *had* seen something, they'd have come back with at least a dozen different stories about it, none of them accurate. A group of young boys wouldn't be a threat to the security of a secret installation."

"You're probably right. But a bunch of hard-nosed security men might not have seen it that way."

"Well, they'd have had to be pretty stupid to think murder was the safest way to handle it. Killing all those people and trying to fake an accident—that was a whole lot riskier than letting the kids come back with their half-baked stories about seeing something peculiar in the mountains."

"Remember, there were two adults with those kids. People might have discounted most of what the boys said about it, but they'd have believed Jaborski and Lincoln. Maybe there was so much at stake that the security men at the installation decided Jaborski and Lincoln had to die. Then it became necessary to kill the kids to eliminate witnesses to the first two murders."

"That's . . . diabolical."

"But not unlikely."

Tina looked down at the wet circle that her glass had left on the table. While she thought about what Elliot had said, she dipped one finger in the water and drew a grim mouth, a nose, and a pair of eyes in the circle; she added two horns, transforming the blot of moisture into a little demonic face. Then she wiped it away with the palm of her hand.

"I don't know . . . hidden installations . . . military secrets . . . it all seems just too incredible."

"Not to me," Elliot said. "To me, it sounds plausible if not probable. Anyway, I'm not saying that's what really happened. It's only a theory. But it's the kind of theory that almost any smart, ambitious reporter will go for in a big, big way—if we can come up with enough facts that appear to support it."

"What about Judge Kennebeck?"

"What about him?"

"He could tell us what we want to know."

"We'd be committing suicide if we went to Kennebeck's place," Elliot said. "Vince's friends are sure to be waiting for us there."

"Well, isn't there any way that we could slip past them and get at Kennebeck?"

He shook his head. "Impossible."

She sighed, slumped back in the booth.

"Besides," Elliot said, "Kennebeck probably doesn't

know the whole story. He's just like the two men who came to see me. He's probably been told only what he needs to know."

Elvira arrived with their food. The cheeseburgers were made from juicy ground sirloin. The French fries were crisp, and the coleslaw was tart but not sour.

By unspoken agreement, Tina and Elliot didn't talk about their problems while they ate. In fact they didn't talk much at all. They listened to the country music on the jukebox and watched Charleston Boulevard through the window, where the desert dust storm clouded oncoming headlights and forced the traffic to move slowly. And they thought about those things that neither of them wanted to speak of: murder past and murder present.

When they finished eating, Tina spoke first. "You said we ought to come up with more evidence before we go to the newspapers."

"We have to."

"But how are we supposed to get it? From where? From whom?"

"I've been pondering that. The best thing we could do is get the grave reopened. If the body were exhumed and reexamined by a topnotch pathologist, we'd almost certainly find proof that the cause of death wasn't what the authorities originally said it was."

"But we can't reopen the grave ourselves," Tina said. "We can't sneak into the graveyard in the middle of the night, move a ton of earth with shovels. Besides, it's a private cemetery, surrounded by a high wall, so there must be a security system to deal with vandals."

"And Kennebeck's cronies have almost certainly put a watch on the place. So if we can't examine the body, we'll have to do the next best thing. We'll have to talk to the man who saw it last."

"Huh? Who?"

"Well, I guess . . . the coroner."

"You mean the medical examiner in Reno?"

"Was that where the death certificate was issued?"

"Yes. The bodies were brought out of the mountains, down to Reno."

"On second thought . . . maybe we'll skip the coroner," Elliot said. "He's the one who had to designate it an accidental death. There's a better than even chance he's been co-opted by Kennebeck's crowd. One thing for sure, he's definitely not on our side. Approaching him would be dangerous. We might eventually have to talk to him, but first we should pay a visit to the mortician who handled the body. There might be a lot he can tell us. Is he here in Vegas?"

"No. An undertaker in Reno prepared the body and shipped it here for the funeral. The coffin was sealed when it arrived, and we didn't open it."

Elvira stopped by the table and asked if they wanted anything more. They didn't. She left the check and took away some of the dirty dishes.

To Tina, Elliot said, "Do you remember the name of the mortician in Reno?"

"Yes. Bellicosti. Luciano Bellicosti."

Elliot finished the last swallow of beer in his glass. "Then we'll go to Reno."

"Can't we just call Bellicosti?"

"These days, everyone's phone seems to be tapped. Besides, if we're face-to-face with him, we'll have a better idea of whether or not he's telling the truth. No, it can't be done long-distance. We have to go up there."

Her hand shook when she raised her glass to drink the last of her own Coors.

Elliot said, "What's wrong?"

She wasn't exactly sure. She was filled with a new dread, a fear greater than the one that had burned within her during the past few hours. "I . . . I guess I'm just . . . afraid to go to Reno."

He reached across the table and put his hand over hers. "It's okay. There's less to be frightened of up there than here. It's *here* we've got killers hunting us."

"I know. Sure, I'm scared of those creeps. But more than that, what I'm afraid of . . . is finding out the truth about Danny's death. And I have a strong feeling we'll find it in Reno."

"I thought that was exactly what you wanted to know."

"Oh, I do. But at the same time, I'm afraid of knowing. Because it's going to be bad. The truth is going to be something really terrible."

"Maybe not."

"Yes."

"The only alternative is to give up, to back off and never know what really happened."

"And that's worse," she admitted.

"Anyway, we have to learn what really happened in the Sierras. If we know the truth, we can use it to save ourselves. It's our only hope of survival."

"So when do we leave for Reno?" she asked.

"Tonight. Right now. We'll take my Cessna Skylane. Nice little machine."

"Won't they know about it?"

"Probably not. I only hooked up with you today, so they haven't had time to learn more than the essentials about me. Just the same, we'll approach the airfield with caution."

"If we can use the Cessna, how soon would we get to Reno?"

"A few hours. I think it would be wise for us to stay up there for a couple of days, even after we've talked to Bellicosti, until we can figure a way out of this mess. Everyone'll still be looking for us in Vegas, and we'll breathe a little easier if we aren't here."

"But I didn't get a chance to pack that suitcase," Tina said. "I need a change of clothes, at least a toothbrush and a few other things. Neither one of us has a coat, and it's damn cold in Reno at this time of year."

"We'll buy whatever we need before we leave."

"I don't have any money with me. Not a penny."

"I've got some," Elliot said. "A couple hundred bucks. Plus a wallet filled with credit cards. We could go around the world on the cards alone. They might track us when we use the cards, but not for a couple of days."

"But it's a holiday and—"

"And this is Las Vegas," Elliot said. "There's always a store open somewhere. And the shops in the hotels won't be closed. This is one of their busiest times of the year. We'll be able to find coats and whatever else we need, and we'll find it all in a hurry." He left a generous tip for the waitress and got to his feet. "Come on. The sooner we're out of this town, the safer I'll feel."

She went with him to the cash register, which was near the entrance.

The cashier was a white-haired man, owlish behind a pair of thick spectacles. He smiled and asked Elliot if their dinner had been satisfactory, and Elliot said it had been fine, and the old man began to make change with slow, arthritic fingers.

The rich odor of chili sauce drifted out of the kitchen. Green peppers. Onions. Jalapeños. The distinct aromas of melted cheddar and Monterey Jack.

The long wing of the diner was nearly full of customers now; about forty people were eating dinner or waiting to be served. Some were laughing. A young couple was plotting conspiratorially, leaning toward each other from opposite sides of a booth, their heads almost touching. Nearly everyone was engaged in animated conversations, couples and cozy groups of friends, enjoying themselves, looking forward to the remaining three days of the four-day holiday.

Suddenly Tina felt a pang of envy. She wanted to be one of these fortunate people. She wanted to be enjoying an ordinary meal, on an ordinary evening, in the middle of a blissfully ordinary life, with every reason to expect a long, comfortable, ordinary future. None of these people had to worry about professional killers, bizarre conspiracies, gas-company men who were not gas-company men, silencer-equipped pistols, exhumations. They didn't realize how lucky they were. She felt as if a vast unbridgeable gap separated her from people like these, and she wondered if she ever again would be as relaxed and free from care as these diners were at this moment.

A sharp, cold draft prickled the back of her neck.

She turned to see who had entered the restaurant.

The door was closed. No one had entered.

Yet the air remained cool—*changed.*

On the jukebox, which stood to the left of the door, a currently popular country ballad was playing:

"Baby, baby, baby, I love you still.
Our love will live; I know it will
And one thing on which you can bet
Is that our love is not dead yet.
No, our love is not dead—
   not dead—
   not dead—
   not dead—"

The record stuck.
Tina stared at the jukebox in disbelief.

  "not dead—
  not dead—
  not dead—
  not dead—"

Elliot turned away from the cashier and put a hand on Tina's shoulder. "What the hell . . . ?"
Tina couldn't speak. She couldn't move.
The air temperature was dropping precipitously.
She shuddered.
The other customers stopped talking and turned to stare at the stuttering machine.

  "not dead—
  not dead—
  not dead—
  not dead—"

The image of Death's rotting face flashed into Tina's mind.

"Stop it," she pleaded.

Someone said, "Shoot the piano player."

Someone else said, "Kick the damn thing."

Elliot stepped to the jukebox and shook it gently. The two words stopped repeating. The song proceeded smoothly again—but only for one more line of verse. As Elliot turned away from the machine, the eerily meaningful repetition began again:

> *"not dead—*
> *not dead—*
> *not dead—"*

Tina wanted to walk through the diner and grab each of the customers by the throat, shake and threaten each of them, until she discovered who had rigged the jukebox. At the same time, she knew this wasn't a rational thought; the explanation, whatever it might be, was not that simple. No one here had rigged the machine. Only a moment ago, she had envied these people for the very ordinariness of their lives. It was ludicrous to suspect any of them of being employed by the secret organization that had blown up her house. Ludicrous. Paranoid. They were just ordinary people in a roadside restaurant, having dinner.

> *"not dead—*
> *not dead—*
> *not dead—"*

Elliot shook the jukebox again, but this time to no avail. The air grew colder still. Tina heard some of the customers commenting on it.

Elliot shook the machine harder than he had done the last time, then harder still, but it continued to repeat the two-word message in the voice of the country singer, as if an invisible hand were holding the pick-up stylus or laser-disc reader firmly in place.

The white-haired cashier came out from behind the counter. "I'll take care of it, folks." He called to one of the waitresses: "Jenny, check the thermostat. We're supposed to have heat in here tonight, not air conditioning."

Elliot stepped out of the way as the old man approached.

Although no one was touching the jukebox, the volume increased, and the two words boomed through the diner, thundered, vibrated in the windows, and rattled silverware on the tables.

"NOT DEAD—
NOT DEAD—
NOT DEAD—"

Some people winced and put their hands over their ears.

The old man had to shout to be heard above the explosive voices on the jukebox. "There's a button on the back to reject the record."

Tina wasn't able to cover her ears; her arms hung straight down at her sides, frozen, rigid, hands fisted, and she couldn't find the will or the strength to lift them. She wanted to scream, but she couldn't make a sound.

Colder, colder.

She became aware of the familiar, spiritlike presence that had been in Angela's office when the computer had begun to operate by itself. She had the same feeling of being watched that she'd had in the parking lot a short while ago.

The old man crouched beside the machine, reached behind it, found the button. He pushed it several times.

> "NOT DEAD—
> NOT DEAD—
> NOT DEAD—"

"Have to unplug it!" the old man said.

The volume increased again. The two words blasted out of the speakers in all corners of the diner with such incredible, bone-jarring force that it was difficult to believe that the machine had been built with the capability of pouring out sound with this excessive, unnerving power.

Elliot pulled the jukebox from the wall so the old man could reach the cord.

In that instant Tina realized she had nothing to fear from the presence that lay behind this eerie manifestation. It meant her no harm. Quite the opposite, in fact. In a flash of understanding she saw through to the heart of the mystery. Her hands, which had been curled into tight fists, came open once more. The tension went out of her neck and shoulder muscles. Her heartbeat became less like the pounding of a jackhammer, but it still did not settle into a normal rhythm; now it was affected by excitement rather than terror. If she tried to scream now, she would be able to do so, but she no longer wanted to scream.

As the white-haired cashier grasped the plug in his arthritis-gnarled hands and wiggled it back and forth in the wall socket, trying to free it, Tina almost told him to stop. She wanted to see what would happen next if no one interfered with the presence that had taken control of the jukebox. But before she could think of a way to phrase her odd request, the old man succeeded in unplugging the machine.

Following the monotonous, earsplitting repetition of that two-word message, the silence was stunning.

After a second of surprised relief, everyone in the diner applauded the old fellow.

Jenny, the waitress, called to him from behind the counter. "Hey, Al, I didn't touch the thermostat. It says the heat's on and set at seventy. You better take a look at it."

"You must have done something to it," Al said. "It's getting warm in here again."

"I didn't touch it," Jenny insisted.

Al didn't believe her, but Tina did.

Elliot turned away from the jukebox and looked at Tina with concern. "Are you all right?"

"Yes. God, yes! Better than I've been in a long time."

He frowned, baffled by her smile.

"I know what it is. Elliot, I know exactly what it is! Come on," she said excitedly. "Let's go."

He was confused by the change in her demeanor, but she didn't want to explain things to him here in the diner. She opened the door and went outside.

22

THE WINDSTORM WAS STILL IN PROGRESS, BUT IT was not raging as fiercely as it had been when Elliot and Tina had watched it through the restaurant window. A brisk wind pushed across the city from the east. Laden with dust and with the powdery white sand that had been swept in from the desert, the air abraded their faces and had an unpleasant taste.

They put their heads down and scurried past the front of the diner, around the side, through the purple light under the single mercury-vapor lamp, and into the deep shadows behind the building.

In the Mercedes, in the darkness, with the doors locked, she said, "No wonder we haven't been able to figure it out!"

"Why on earth are you so—"

"We've been looking at this all wrong—"

"—so bubbly when—"

"—approaching it ass-backwards. No wonder we haven't been able to find a solution."

"What are you talking about? Did you see what I saw in there? Did you hear the jukebox? I don't see how that could have cheered you up. It made my blood run cold. It was *weird*."

"Listen," she said excitedly, "we thought someone was sending me messages about Danny being alive just to rub my face in the fact that he was actually dead—or to let me know, in a roundabout fashion, that the *way* he died wasn't anything like what I'd been told. But those messages haven't been coming from a sadist. And they haven't been coming from someone who wants to expose the true story of the Sierra accident. They aren't being sent by a total stranger or by Michael. They are *exactly* what they appear to be!"

Confused, he said, "And to your way of thinking, what do they appear to be?"

"They're cries for help."

"What?"

"They're coming from *Danny!*"

Elliot stared at her with consternation and with pity, his dark eyes reflecting a distant light. "What're you saying— that Danny reached out to you from the grave to cause that excitement in the restaurant? Tina, you really don't think his ghost was haunting a jukebox?"

"No, no, no. I'm saying Danny isn't dead."

"Wait a minute. Wait a minute."

"My Danny is alive! I'm sure of it."

"We've already been through this argument, and we rejected it," he reminded her.

"We were wrong. Jaborski, Lincoln, and all the other boys might have died in the Sierras, but Danny didn't. I know it. I *sense* it. It's like . . . a revelation . . . almost like a vision. Maybe there was an accident, but it wasn't like anything we were told. It was something very different, something exceedingly strange."

"That's already obvious. But—"

"The government had to hide it, and so this organization that Kennebeck works for was given responsibility for the cover-up."

"I'm with you that far," Elliot said. "That's logical. But how do you figure Danny's alive? That doesn't necessarily follow."

"I'm only telling you what I *know*, what I feel," she said. "A tremendous sense of peace, of reassurance, came over me in the diner, just before you finally managed to shut off the jukebox. It wasn't just an inner feeling of peace. It came from outside of me. Like a wave. Oh, hell, I can't really explain it. I only know what I felt. Danny was trying to reassure me, trying to tell me that he was still alive. I *know* it. Danny survived the accident, but they couldn't let him come home because he'd tell everyone the government was responsible for the deaths of the others, and that would blow their secret military installation wide open."

"You're reaching, grasping for straws."

"I'm not, I'm not," she insisted.

"So where *is* Danny?"

"They're keeping him somewhere. I don't know why they didn't kill him. I don't know how long they think they can keep him bottled up like this. But that's what they're doing. That's what's going on. Those might not be the precise circumstances, but they're pretty damn close to the truth."

"Tina—"

She wouldn't let him interrupt. "This secret police force, these people behind Kennebeck . . . they think someone involved with Project Pandora has turned on them and told me what really happened to Danny. They're wrong, of course. It wasn't one of them. It's Danny. Somehow . . . I don't know how . . . but he's reaching out to me." She struggled to explain the understanding that had come to her in the diner. "Somehow . . . some way . . . he's reaching out . . . with his mind, I guess. Danny was the one who wrote those words on the chalkboard. *With his mind.*"

"The only proof of this is what you say you feel . . . this vision you've had."

"Not a vision—"

"Whatever. Anyway, that's no proof at all."

"It's proof enough for me," she said. "And it would be proof enough for you, if you'd had the same experience back there in the diner, if you'd felt what I felt. It was Danny who reached out for me when I was at work . . . found me in the office . . . tried to use the hotel computer to send his message to me. And now the jukebox. He must be . . . psychic. That's it! That's what he is. He's psychic. He has some *power*, and he's reaching out, trying to tell me he's alive, asking me to find him and save him. And the people who're holding him *don't know he's doing it!* They're blaming the leak on one of their own, on someone from Project Pandora."

"Tina, this is a very imaginative theory, but—"

"It might be imaginative, but it's not a theory. It's true. It's fact. I *feel* it deep in my bones. Can you shoot holes through it? Can you prove I'm wrong?"

"First of all," Elliot said, "before he went into the mountains with Jaborski, in all the years you knew him and lived in the same house with him, did Danny ever show any signs of being psychic?"

She frowned. "No."

"Then how come he suddenly has all these amazing powers?"

"Wait. Yeah, I *do* remember some little things he did that were sort of odd."

"Like what?"

"Like the time he wanted to know exactly what his daddy did for a living. He was eight or nine years old, and he was curious about the details of a dealer's job. Michael sat at the kitchen table with him and dealt blackjack. Danny was barely old enough to understand the rules, but he'd never played before. He certainly wasn't old enough to remember all the cards that were dealt and calculate his chances from that, like some of the very best players can do. Yet he won steadily. Michael used a jar full of peanuts to represent casino chips, and Danny won every nut in the jar."

"The game must have been rigged," Elliot said. "Michael was letting him win."

"That's what I thought at first. But Michael swore he wasn't doing that. And he seemed genuinely astonished by Danny's streak of luck. Besides, Michael isn't a card mechanic. He can't handle a deck well enough to stack it while he's shuffling. And then there was Elmer."

"Who's Elmer?"

"He was our dog. A cute little mutt. One day, about two years ago, I was in the kitchen, making an apple pie, and Danny came in to tell me Elmer wasn't anywhere to be found in the yard. Apparently, the pooch slipped out of the gate when the gardeners came around. Danny said he was sure Elmer wasn't going to come back because he'd been hit and killed by a truck. I told him not to worry. I said we'd find Elmer safe and sound. But we never did. We never found him at all."

"Just because you never found him—that's not proof he was killed by a truck."

"It was proof enough for Danny. He mourned for weeks."

Elliot sighed. "Winning a few hands at blackjack—that's luck, just like you said. And predicting that a runaway dog will be killed in traffic—that's just a reasonable assumption to make under the circumstances. And even if those were examples of psychic ability, little tricks like that are light-years from what you're attributing to Danny now."

"I know. Somehow, his abilities have grown a lot stronger. Maybe because of the situation he's in. The fear. The stress."

"If fear and stress could increase the power of his psychic gifts, why didn't he start trying to get in touch with you months ago?"

"Maybe it took a year of stress and fear to develop the ability. I don't know." A flood of unreasonable anger washed through her: "Christ, how could I know the answer to that?"

"Calm down," he said. "You dared me to shoot holes in your theory. That's what I'm doing."

"No," she said. "As far as I can see, you haven't shot one hole in it yet. Danny's alive, being held somewhere, and he's trying to reach me with his mind. Telepathically. No. Not telepathy. He's able to move objects just by thinking about them. What do you call that? Isn't there a name for that ability?"

"Telekinesis," Elliot said.

"Yes! That's it. He's telekinetic. Do you have a better explanation for what happened in the diner?"

"Well . . . no."

"Are you going to tell me it was coincidence that the record stuck on those two words?"

"No," Elliot said. "It wasn't a coincidence. That would be

even more unlikely than the possibility that Danny did it."

"You admit I'm right."

"No," he said. "I can't think of a better explanation, but I'm not ready to accept yours. I've never believed in that psychic crap."

For a minute or two neither of them spoke. They stared out at the dark parking lot and at the fenced storage yard full of fifty-gallon drums that lay beyond the lot. Sheets, puffs, and spinning funnels of vaguely phosphorescent dust moved like specters through the night.

At last Tina said, "I'm *right*, Elliot. I know I am. My theory explains everything. Even the nightmares. That's another way Danny's been trying to reach me. He's been sending me nightmares for the past few weeks. That's why they've been so much different from any dreams I've had before, so much stronger and more vivid."

He seemed to find this new statement more outrageous than what she'd said before. "Wait, wait, wait. Now you're talking about another power besides telekinesis."

"If he has one ability, why not the other?"

"Because pretty soon you'll be saying he's God."

"Just telekinesis and the power to influence my dreams. That explains why I dreamed about the hideous figure of Death in this comic book. If Danny's sending me messages in dreams, it's only natural he'd use images he was familiar with—like a monster out of a favorite horror story."

"But if he can send dreams to you," Elliot said, "why wouldn't he simply transmit a neat, clear message telling you what's happened to him and where he is? Wouldn't that get him the help he wants a lot faster? Why would he be so unclear and indirect? He should send a concise mental message, psychic E-mail from the Twilight Zone, make it a lot easier for you to understand."

"Don't get sarcastic," she said.

"I'm not. I'm merely asking a tough question. It's another hole in your theory."

She would not be deterred. "It's not a hole. There's a good explanation. Obviously, like I told you, Danny isn't telepathic exactly. He's telekinetic, able to move objects with his mind. And he can influence dreams to some extent. But he's not flat-out telepathic. He can't transmit detailed thoughts. He can't send 'concise mental messages' because he doesn't have that much power or control. So he has to try to reach me as best he can."

"Will you listen to us?"

"I've been listening," she said.

"We sound like a couple of prime candidates for a padded cell."

"No. I don't think we do."

"This talk of psychic power . . . it's not exactly level-headed stuff," Elliot said.

"Then explain what happened in the diner."

"I can't. Damn it, I can't," he said, sounding like a priest whose faith had been deeply shaken. The faith that he was beginning to question was not religious, however, but scientific.

"Stop thinking like an attorney," she said. "Stop trying to herd the facts into neat corrals of logic."

"That's exactly what I've been trained to do."

"I know," she said sympathetically. "But the world is full of illogical things that are nonetheless true. And this is one of them."

The wind buffeted the sports car, moaned along the windows, seeking a way in.

Elliot said, "If Danny has this incredible power, why is he sending messages just to you? Why doesn't he at least contact Michael too?"

"Maybe he doesn't feel close enough to Michael to try reaching him. After all, the last couple of years we were married, Michael was running around with a lot of other women, spending most of his time away from home, and Danny felt even more abandoned than I did. I never talked against Michael. I even tried to justify some of his actions, because I didn't want Danny to hate him. But Danny was hurt just the same. I suppose it's natural for him to reach out to me rather than to his father."

A wall of dust fell softly over the car.

"Still think you can shoot my theory full of holes?" she asked.

"No. You argued your case pretty well."

"Thank you, judge."

"I still can't believe you're right. I know some pretty damn intelligent people believe in ESP, but I don't. I can't bring myself to accept this psychic crap. Not yet, anyway. I'm going to keep looking for some less exotic explanation."

"And if you come up with one," Tina said, "I'll give it very serious consideration."

He put a hand on her shoulder. "The reason I've argued with you is . . . I'm worried about you, Tina."

"About my sanity?"

"No, no. This psychic explanation bothers me mainly because it gives you hope that Danny's still alive. And that's dangerous. It seems to me as if you're just setting yourself up for a bad fall, a lot of pain."

"No. Not at all. Because Danny really is alive."

"But what if he isn't?"

"He is."

"If you discover he's dead, it'll be like losing him all over again."

"But he's not dead," she insisted. "I feel it. I sense it. I *know* it, Elliot."

"And if he *is* dead?" Elliot asked, every bit as insistent as she was.

She hesitated. Then: "I'll be able to handle it."

"You're sure?"

"Positive."

In the dim light, where the brightest thing was mauve shadow, he found her eyes, held her with his intent gaze. She felt as if he were not merely looking at her but into her, through her. Finally he leaned over and kissed the corner of her mouth, then her cheek, her eyes.

He said, "I don't want to see your heart broken."

"It won't be."

"I'll do what I can to see it isn't."

"I know."

"But there isn't much I *can* do. It's out of my hands. We just have to flow with events."

She slipped a hand behind his neck, holding his face close. The taste of his lips and his warmth made her inexpressibly happy.

He sighed, leaned back from her, and started the car. "We better get moving. We have some shopping to do. Winter coats. A couple of toothbrushes."

Though Tina continued to be buoyed by the unshakable conviction that Danny was alive, fear crept into her again as they drove onto Charleston Boulevard. She was no longer afraid of facing the awful truth that might be waiting in Reno. What had happened to Danny might still prove to be terrible, shattering, but she didn't think it would be as hard to accept as his "death" had been. The only thing that scared her now was the possibility that they might find Danny—and then be unable to rescue him. In the process of locating the boy, she and Elliot might be killed. If they found Danny and then perished trying to save him, that would be a nasty trick of fate, for sure. She knew from experience that fate had countless nasty tricks up its voluminous sleeve, and *that* was why she was scared shitless.

WILLIS BRUCKSTER STUDIED HIS KENO TICKET,
carefully comparing it to the winning numbers beginning to
flash onto the electronic board that hung from the casino
ceiling. He tried to appear intently interested in the outcome
of this game, but in fact he didn't care. The marked ticket in
his hand was worthless; he hadn't taken it to the betting
window, hadn't wagered any money on it. He was using
keno as a cover.

He didn't want to attract the attention of the omnipresent
casino security men, and the easiest way to escape their
notice was to appear to be the least threatening hick in the
huge room. With that in mind, Bruckster wore a cheap green
polyester leisure suit, black loafers, and white socks. He was
carrying two books of the discount coupons that casinos use
to pull slot-machine players into the house, and he wore a
camera on a strap around his neck. Furthermore, keno was
a game that didn't have any appeal for either smart gamblers
or cheaters, the two types of customers who most interested
the security men. Willis Bruckster was so sure he appeared

dull and ordinary that he wouldn't have been surprised if a guard had looked at him and yawned.

He was determined not to fail on this assignment. It was a career maker—or breaker. The Network badly wanted to eliminate everyone who might press for the exhumation of Danny Evans's body, and the agents targeted against Elliot Stryker and Christina Evans had thus far failed to carry out their orders to terminate the pair. Their ineptitude gave Willis Bruckster a chance to shine. If he made a clean hit here, in the crowded casino, he would be assured of a promotion.

Bruckster stood at the head of the escalator that led from the lower shopping arcade to the casino level of Bally's Hotel. During their periodic breaks from the gaming tables, nursing stiff necks and sore shoulders and leaden arms, the weary dealers retired to a combination lounge and locker room at the bottom—and to the right—of the escalator. A group had gone down a while ago and would be returning for their last stand at the tables before a whole new staff came on duty with the shift change. Bruckster was waiting for one of those dealers: Michael Evans.

He hadn't expected to find the man at work. He had thought Evans might be keeping a vigil at the demolished house, while the firemen sifted through the still-smoldering debris, searching for the remains of the woman they thought might be buried there. But when Bruckster had come into the hotel thirty minutes ago, Evans had been chatting with the players at his blackjack table, cracking jokes, and grinning as if nothing of any importance had happened in his life lately.

Perhaps Evans didn't know about the explosion at his

former house. Or maybe he *did* know and just didn't give a damn about his ex-wife. It might have been a bitter divorce.

Bruckster hadn't been able to get close to Evans when the dealer left the blackjack pit at the beginning of the break. Consequently, he'd stationed himself here, at the head of the escalator, and had pretended to be interested in the keno board. He was confident that he would nail Evans when the man returned from the dealer's lounge in the next few minutes.

The last of the keno numbers flashed onto the board. Willis Bruckster stared at them, then crumpled his game card with obvious disappointment and disgust, as if he had lost a few hard-earned dollars.

He glanced down the escalator. Dealers in black trousers, white shirts, and string ties were ascending.

Bruckster sidled away from the escalator and unfolded his keno card. He compared it once more with the numbers on the electronic board, as if he were praying that he had made a mistake the first time.

Michael Evans was the seventh dealer off the escalator. He was a handsome, easygoing guy who ambled rather than walked. He stopped to have a word with a strikingly pretty cocktail waitress, and she smiled at him. The other dealers streamed by, and when Evans finally turned away from the waitress, he was the last in the procession as it moved toward the blackjack pits.

Bruckster fell in beside and slightly behind his target as they pressed through the teeming mob that jammed the enormous casino. He reached into a pocket of his leisure suit and took out a tiny aerosol can that was only slightly larger than one of those spray-style breath fresheners, small enough to be concealed in Bruckster's hand.

They came to a standstill at a cluster of laughing people. No one in the jolly group seemed to realize that he was obstructing the main aisle. Bruckster took advantage of the pause to tap his quarry on the shoulder.

Evans turned, and Bruckster said, "I think maybe you dropped this back there."

"Huh?"

Bruckster held his hand eighteen inches below Michael Evans's eyes, so that the dealer was forced to glance down to see what was being shown to him.

The fine spray, propelled with tremendous pressure, caught him squarely in the face, across the nose and lips, penetrating swiftly and deeply into the nostrils. Perfect.

Evans reacted as anyone would. He gasped in surprise as he realized he was being squirted.

The gasp drew the deadly mist up his nose, where the active poison—a particularly fast-acting neurotoxin—was instantaneously absorbed through the sinus membranes. In two seconds it was in his bloodstream, and the first seizure hit his heart.

Evans's surprised expression turned to shock. Then a wild, twisted expression of agony wrenched his face as brutal pain slammed through him. He gagged, and a ribbon of foamy saliva unraveled from the corner of his mouth, down his chin. His eyes rolled back in his head, and he fell.

As Bruckster pocketed the miniature aerosol device, he said, "We have a sick man here."

Heads turned toward him.

"Give the man room," Bruckster said. "For God's sake, someone get a doctor!"

No one could have seen the murder. It had been committed in a sheltered space within the crowd, hidden by the killer's and the victim's bodies. Even if someone had been monitoring that area from an overhead camera, there would not have been much for him to see.

Willis Bruckster quickly knelt at Michael Evans's side and took his pulse as if he expected to find one. There was no heartbeat whatsoever, not even a faint lub-dub.

A thin film of moisture covered the victim's nose and lips and chin, but this was only the harmless medium in which the toxin had been suspended. The active poison itself had already penetrated the victim's body, done its work, and begun to break down into a series of naturally occurring chemicals that would raise no alarms when the coroner later studied the results of the usual battery of forensic tests. In a few seconds the medium would evaporate too, leaving nothing unusual to arouse the initial attending physician's suspicion.

A uniformed security guard shouldered through the mob of curious onlookers and stooped next to Bruckster. "Oh, damn, it's Mike Evans. What happened here?"

"I'm no doctor," Bruckster said, "but it sure looks like a heart attack to me, the way he dropped like a stone, same way my uncle Ned went down last Fourth of July right in the middle of the fireworks display."

The guard tried to find a pulse but wasn't able to do so. He began CPR, but then relented. "I think it's hopeless."

"How could it be a heart attack, him being so young?" Bruckster wondered. "Jesus, you just never know, do you?"

"You never know," the guard agreed.

The hotel doctor would call it a heart attack after he had examined the body. So would the coroner. So would the death certificate.

A perfect murder.

Willis Bruckster suppressed a smile.

24

JUDGE HAROLD KENNEBECK BUILT EXQUISITELY detailed ships in bottles. The walls of his den were lined with examples of his hobby. A tiny model of a seventeenth-century Dutch pinnace was perpetually under sail in a small, pale-blue bottle. A large four-masted topsail schooner filled a five-gallon jug. Here was a four-masted barkentine with sails taut in a perpetual wind; and here was a mid-sixteenth-century Swedish kravel. A fifteenth-century Spanish caravel. A British merchantman. A Baltimore clipper. Every ship was created with remarkable care and craftsmanship, and many were in uniquely shaped bottles that made their construction all the more difficult and admirable.

Kennebeck stood before one of the display cases, studying the minutely detailed rigging of a late-eighteenth-century French frigate. As he gazed at the model, he wasn't transported back in time or lost in fantasies of high-seas adventure; rather, he was mulling over the recent developments in the Evans case. His ships, sealed in their glass worlds, relaxed him; he liked to spend time with them when he had a problem to work out or when he was on edge, for they made him feel serene, and that security allowed his mind to function at peak performance.

The longer he thought about it, the less Kennebeck was able to believe that the Evans woman knew the truth about her son. Surely, if someone from Project Pandora had told her what had happened to that busload of scouts, she wouldn't have reacted to the news with equanimity. She would have been frightened, terrified . . . and damned angry. She would have gone straight to the police, the newspapers—or both.

Instead, she had gone to Elliot Stryker.

And that was where the paradox jumped up like a jack-in-the-box. On the one hand, she behaved as if she did not know the truth. But on the other hand, she was working through Stryker to have her son's grave reopened, which seemed to indicate that she knew *something*.

If Stryker could be believed, the woman's motivations were innocent enough. According to the attorney, Mrs. Evans felt guilty about not having had the courage to view the boy's mutilated body prior to the burial. She felt as if she had failed to pay her last respects to the deceased. Her guilt had grown gradually into a serious psychological problem. She was in great distress, and she suffered from horrible dreams that plagued her every night. That was Stryker's story.

Kennebeck tended to believe Stryker. There was an element of coincidence involved, but not all coincidence was meaningful. That was something one tended to forget when he spent his life in the intelligence game. Christina Evans probably hadn't entertained a single doubt about the official explanation of the Sierra accident; she probably hadn't known a damned thing about Pandora when she had requested an exhumation, but her timing couldn't have been worse.

If the woman actually hadn't known anything of the cover-up, then the Network could have used her ex-husband and the legal system to delay the reopening of the grave. In the meantime, Network agents could have located a boy's body in the same state of decay as Danny's corpse would have been if it had been locked in that coffin for the past year. They would have opened the grave secretly, at night, when the cemetery was closed, switching the remains of the fake Danny for the rocks that were currently in the casket. Then the guilt-stricken mother could have been permitted one last, late, ghastly look at the remains of her son.

That would have been a complex operation, fraught with the peril of discovery. The risks would have been acceptable, however, and there wouldn't have been any need to kill anyone.

Unfortunately, George Alexander, chief of the Nevada bureau of the Network, hadn't possessed the patience or the skill to determine the woman's true motives. He had assumed the worst and had acted on that assumption. When Kennebeck informed Alexander of Elliot Stryker's request for an exhumation, the bureau chief responded immediately with extreme force. He planned a suicide for Stryker, an accidental death for the woman, and a heart attack for the woman's husband. Two of those hurriedly organized assassination attempts had failed. Stryker and the woman had disappeared. Now the entire Network was in the soup, *deep* in it.

As Kennebeck turned away from the French frigate, beginning to wonder if he ought to get out from under the Network before it collapsed on him, George Alexander entered the study through the door that opened off the downstairs hallway. The bureau chief was a slim, elegant, distinguished-looking man. He was wearing Gucci loafers, an expensive suit, a handmade silk shirt, and a gold Rolex watch. His stylishly cut brown hair shaded to iron-gray at the temples. His eyes were green, clear, alert, and—if one took the time to study them—menacing. He had a well-formed face with high cheekbones, a narrow straight nose, and thin lips. When he smiled, his mouth turned up slightly at the left corner, giving him a vaguely haughty expression, although at the moment he wasn't smiling.

Kennebeck had known Alexander for five years and had despised him from the day they met. He suspected that the feeling was mutual.

Part of this antagonism between them rose because they had been born into utterly different worlds and were equally proud of their origins—as well as disdainful of all others. Harry Kennebeck had come from a dirt-poor family and, by his own estimation at least, made quite a lot of himself. Alexander, on the other hand, was the scion of a Pennsylvania family that had been wealthy and powerful for a hundred and fifty years, perhaps longer. Kennebeck had lifted himself out of poverty through hard work and steely determination. Alexander knew nothing of hard work; he had ascended to the top of his field as if he were a prince with a divine right to rule.

Kennebeck was also irritated by Alexander's hypocrisy. The whole family was nothing but a bunch of hypocrites. The society-register Alexanders were proud of their history of public service. Many of them had been Presidential appointees, occupying high-level posts in the federal government; a few had served on the President's cabinet, in half a dozen administrations, though none had ever deigned to run for an elective position. The famous Pennsylvania Alexanders had always been prominently associated with the struggle for minority civil rights, the Equal Rights Amendment, the crusade against capital punishment, and social idealisms of every variety. Yet numerous members of the family had secretly rendered service—some of it dirty—to the FBI, the CIA, and various other intelligence and police agencies, often the very same organizations that they publicly criticized and reviled. Now George Alexander was the Nevada bureau chief of the nation's first truly secret police force—a fact that apparently did not weigh heavily on his liberal conscience.

Kennebeck's politics were of the extreme right-wing variety. He was an unreconstructed fascist and not the least bit ashamed of it. When, as a young man, he had first embarked upon a career in the intelligence services, Harry had been surprised to discover that not all of the people in the espionage business shared his ultraconservative political views. He had expected his co-workers to be super-patriotic right-wingers. But all the snoop shops were staffed with leftists too. Eventually Harry realized that the extreme left and the extreme right shared the same two basic goals: They wanted to make society more orderly than it naturally was, and they wanted to centralize control of the population in a strong government. Left-wingers and right-wingers differed about certain details, of course, but their only major point of contention centered on the identity of those who would be permitted to be a part of the privileged ruling class, once the power had been sufficiently centralized.

At least I'm honest about my motives, Kennebeck thought as he watched Alexander cross the study. *My public opinions are the same as those I express privately, and that's a virtue he doesn't possess. I'm not a hypocrite. I'm not at all like Alexander. Jesus, he's such a smug, Janus-faced bastard!*

"I just spoke with the men who're watching Stryker's house," Alexander said. "He hasn't shown up yet."

"I told you he wouldn't go back there."

"Sooner or later he will."

"No. Not until he's absolutely certain the heat is off. Until then he'll hide out."

"He's bound to go to the police at some point, and then we'll have him."

"If he thought he could get any help from the cops, he'd have been there already," Kennebeck said. "But he hasn't shown up. And he won't."

Alexander glanced at his watch. "Well, he still might pop up here. I'm sure he wants to ask you a lot of questions."

"Oh, I'm damn sure he does. He wants my hide," Kennebeck said. "But he won't come. Not tonight. Eventually, yes, but not for a long time. He knows we're waiting for him. He knows how the game is played. Don't forget he used to play it himself."

"That was a long time ago," Alexander said impatiently. "He's been a civilian for fifteen years. He's out of practice. Even if he was a natural then, there's no way he could still be as sharp as he once was."

"But that's what I've been trying to tell you," Kennebeck said, pushing a lock of snow-white hair back from his forehead. "Elliot isn't stupid. He was the best and brightest young officer who ever served under me. He *was* a natural. And that was when he was young and relatively inexperienced. If he's aged as well as he seems to have done, then he might even be sharper these days."

Alexander didn't want to hear it. Although two of the hits he had ordered had gone totally awry, Alexander remained self-assured; he was convinced that he would eventually triumph.

He's always so damned self-confident, Harry Kennebeck thought. *And usually there's no good reason why he should be. If he was aware of his own shortcomings, the son of a bitch would be crushed to death under his collapsing ego.*

Alexander went to the huge maple desk and sat behind it, in Kennebeck's wing chair.

The judge glared at him.

Alexander pretended not to notice Kennebeck's displeasure. "We'll find Stryker and the woman before morning. I've no doubt about that. We're covering all the bases. We've got men checking every hotel and motel—"

"That's a waste of time," Kennebeck said. "Elliot is too smart to waltz into a hotel and leave his name on the register. Besides, there are more hotels and motels in Vegas than in any other city in the world."

"I'm fully aware of the complexity of the task," Alexander said. "But we might get lucky. Meanwhile, we're checking out Stryker's associates in his law firm, his friends, the woman's friends, anyone with whom they might have taken refuge."

"You don't have enough manpower to follow up all those possibilities," the judge said. "Can't you see that? You should use your people more judiciously. You're spreading yourself too thin. What you should be doing—"

"*I'll* make those decisions," Alexander said icily.

"What about the airport?"

"That's taken care of," Alexander assured him. "We've got men going over the passenger lists of every outbound flight." He picked up an ivory-handled letter opener, turned it over and over in his hands. "Anyway, even if we're spread a bit thin, it doesn't matter much. I already know where we're going to nail Stryker. Here. Right here in this house. That's why I'm still hanging around. Oh, I know, I know, you don't think he'll show up. But a long time ago you were Stryker's mentor, the man he respected, the man he learned from, and now you've betrayed him. He'll come here to confront you, even if he knows it's risky. I'm sure he will."

"Ridiculous," Kennebeck said sourly. "Our relationship was never like that. He——"

"I know human nature," Alexander said, though he was one of the least observant and least analytical men that Kennebeck had ever known.

These days cream seldom rose in the intelligence community—but crap still floated.

Angry, frustrated, Kennebeck turned again to the bottle that contained the French frigate. Suddenly he remembered something important about Elliot Stryker. "Ah," he said.

Alexander put down the enameled cigarette box that he had been studying. "What is it?"

"Elliot's a pilot. He owns his own plane."

Alexander frowned.

"Have you been checking small craft leaving the airport?" Kennebeck asked.

"No. Just scheduled airliners and charters."

"Ah."

"He'd have had to take off in the dark," Alexander said. "You think he's licensed for instrument flying? Most businessmen-pilots and hobby pilots aren't certified for anything but daylight."

"Better get hold of your men at the airport," Kennebeck

said. "I already know what they're going to find. I'll bet a hundred bucks to a dime Elliot slipped out of town under your nose."

• • •

The Cessna Turbo Skylane RG knifed through the darkness, two miles above the Nevada desert, with the low clouds under it, wings plated silver by moonlight.

"Elliot?"

"Hmmm?"

"I'm sorry I got you mixed up in this."

"You don't like my company?"

"You know what I mean. I'm really sorry."

"Hey, you didn't get me mixed up in it. You didn't twist my arm. I practically volunteered to help you with the exhumation, and it all just fell apart from there. It's not your fault."

"Still . . . here you are, running for your life, and all because of me."

"Nonsense. You couldn't have known what would happen after I talked to Kennebeck."

"I can't help feeling guilty about involving you."

"If it wasn't me, it would have been some other attorney. And maybe he wouldn't have known how to handle Vince. In which case, both he and you might be dead. So if you look at it that way, it worked out as well as it possibly could."

"You're really something else," she said.

"What else am I?"

"Lots of things."

"Such as?"

"Terrific."

"Not me. What else?"

"Brave."

"Bravery is a virtue of fools."

"Smart."

"Not as smart as I think I am."

"Tough."

"I cry at sad movies. See, I'm not as great as you think I am."

"You can cook."

"Now *that's* true!"

The Cessna hit an air pocket, dropped three hundred feet with a sickening lurch, and then soared to its correct altitude.

"A great cook but a lousy pilot," she said.

"That was God's turbulence. Complain to Him."

"How long till we land in Reno?"

"Eighty minutes."

●   ●   ●

George Alexander hung up the telephone. He was still sitting in Kennebeck's wing chair. "Stryker and the woman took off from McCarran International more than two hours ago. They left in his Cessna. He filed a flight plan for Flagstaff."

The judge stopped pacing. "Arizona?"

"That's the only Flagstaff I know. But why would they go to Arizona, of all places?"

"They probably didn't," Kennebeck said. "I figure Elliot filed a false flight plan to throw you off his trail." He was perversely proud of Stryker's cleverness.

"If they actually headed for Flagstaff," Alexander said, "they ought to have landed by now. I'll call the night manager at the airport down there, pretend to be FBI, see what he can tell me."

Because the Network did not officially exist, it couldn't openly use its authority to gather information. As a result, Network agents routinely posed as FBI men, with counterfeit credentials in the names of actual FBI agents.

While he waited for Alexander to finish with the night manager at the Flagstaff airport, Kennebeck moved from one model ship to another. For the first time in his experience, the sight of this bottled fleet didn't calm him.

Fifteen minutes later Alexander put down the telephone. "Stryker isn't on the Flagstaff field. And he hasn't yet been identified in their airspace."

"Ah. So his flight plan *was* a red herring."

"Unless he crashed between here and there," Alexander said hopefully.

Kennebeck grinned. "He didn't crash. But where the hell *did* he go?"

"Probably in the opposite direction," Alexander said. "Southern California."

"Ah. Los Angeles?"

"Or Santa Barbara. Burbank. Long Beach. Ontario. Orange County. There are a lot of airports within the range of that little Cessna."

They were both silent, thinking. Then Kennebeck said, "Reno. That's where they went. Reno."

"You were so sure they didn't know a thing about the Sierra labs," Alexander said. "Have you changed your mind?"

"No. I still think you could have avoided issuing all those termination orders. Look, they can't be going up to the mountains, because they don't know where the laboratories are. They don't know anything more about Project Pandora than what they picked up from that list of questions they took off Vince Immelman."

"Then why Reno?"

Pacing, Kennebeck said, "Now that we've tried to kill them, they *know* the story of the Sierra accident was entirely contrived. They figure there's something wrong with the little boy's body, something odd that we can't afford to let them see. So now they're *twice* as anxious to see it. They'd exhume it illegally if they could, but they can't get near the cemetery with us watching it. And Stryker knows for sure that we've got it staked out. So if they can't open the grave and see for themselves what we've done to Danny Evans, what are they going to do instead? They're going to do the next best thing—talk to the person who was supposedly the last one to see the boy's corpse before it was sealed in the coffin. They're going to ask him to describe the condition of the boy in minute detail."

"Richard Pannafin is the coroner in Reno. He issued the death certificate," Alexander said.

"No. They won't go to Pannafin. They'll figure he's involved in the cover-up."

"Which he is. Reluctantly."

"So they'll go to see the mortician who supposedly prepared the boy's body for burial."

"Bellicosti."

"Was that his name?"

"Luciano Bellicosti," Alexander said. "But if that's where they went, then they're not just hiding out, licking their wounds. Good God, they've actually gone on the offensive!"

"That's Stryker's military-intelligence training taking hold," Kennebeck said. "That's what I've been trying to tell you. He's not going to be an easy target. He could destroy the Network, given half a chance. And the woman's evidently not one to hide or run away from a problem either. We have to go after these two with more care than usual. What about this Bellicosti? Will he keep his mouth shut?"

"I don't know," Alexander said uneasily. "We have a pretty good hold on him. He's an Italian immigrant. He lived here for eight or nine years before he decided to apply for citizenship. He hadn't gotten his papers yet when we found ourselves needing a cooperative mortician. We put a freeze on his application with the Bureau of Immigration, and we threatened to have him deported if he didn't do what we wanted. He didn't like it. But citizenship was a big enough carrot to keep him motivated. However . . . I don't think we'd better rely on that carrot any longer."

"This is a hell of an important matter," Kennebeck said. "And it sounds to me as if Bellicosti knows too much about it."

"Terminate the bastard," Alexander said.

"Eventually, but not necessarily right now. If too many bodies pile up at once, we'll be drawing attention to—"

"Take no chances," Alexander insisted. "We'll terminate him. And the coroner too, I think. Scrub away the whole trail." He reached for the phone.

"Surely you don't want to take such drastic action until you're positive Stryker actually is headed for Reno. And you won't know for sure until he lands up there."

Alexander hesitated with his hand on the phone. "But if I wait, I'm just giving him a chance to keep one step ahead." Worried, he continued to hesitate, anxiously chewing his lip.

"There's a way to find out if it's really Reno he's headed

for. When he gets there, he'll need a car. Maybe he's already arranged for one to be waiting."

Alexander nodded. "We can call the rental agencies at the Reno airport."

"No need to call. The hacker geeks in computer operations can probably access all the rental agencies' data files long distance."

Alexander picked up the phone and gave the order.

Fifteen minutes later computer operations called back with its report. Elliot Stryker had a rental car reserved for late-night pickup at the Reno airport. He was scheduled to take possession of it shortly before midnight.

"That's a bit sloppy of him," Kennebeck said, "considering how clever he's been so far."

"He figures we're focusing on Arizona, not Reno."

"It's still sloppy," Kennebeck said, disappointed. "He should have built a double blind to protect himself."

"So it's like I said." Alexander's crooked smile appeared. "He *isn't* as sharp as he used to be."

"Let's not start crowing too soon," Kennebeck said. "We haven't caught him yet."

"We will," Alexander said, his composure restored. "Our people in Reno will have to move fast, but they'll manage. I don't think it's a good idea to hit Stryker and the woman in a public place like an airport."

What an uncharacteristic display of reserve, Kennebeck thought sourly.

"I don't even think we should put a tail on them as soon as they get there," Alexander said. "Stryker will be expecting a tail. Maybe he'll elude it, and then he'll be spooked."

"Get to the rental car before he does. Slap a transponder

on it. Then you can follow him without being seen, at your leisure."

"We'll try it," Alexander said. "We've got less than an hour, so there might not be time. But even if we don't get a beeper on the damn car, we're okay. We know where they're going. We'll just eliminate Bellicosti and set up a trap at the funeral home."

He snatched up the telephone and dialed the Network office in Reno.

I N RENO, WHICH BILLED ITSELF AS "THE BIGGEST Little City in the World," the temperature hovered at twenty-one degrees above zero as midnight approached. Above the lights that cast a frosty glow on the airport parking lot, the heavily shrouded sky was moonless, starless, perfectly black. Snow flurries were dancing on a changeable wind.

Elliot was glad they had bought a couple of heavy coats before leaving Las Vegas. He wished they'd thought of gloves; his hands were freezing.

He threw their single suitcase into the trunk of the rented Chevrolet. In the cold air, white clouds of exhaust vapor swirled around his legs.

He slammed the trunk lid and surveyed the snow-dusted cars in the parking lot. He couldn't see anyone in any of them. He had no feeling of being watched.

When they had landed, they'd been alert for unusual activity on the runway and in the private-craft docking yard—suspicious vehicles, an unusual number of ground crewmen—but they had seen nothing out of the ordinary.

Then as he had signed for the rental car and picked up the keys from the night clerk, he had kept one hand in a pocket of his coat, gripping the handgun he'd taken off Vince in Las Vegas—but there was no trouble.

Perhaps the phony flight plan had thrown the hounds off the trail. Now he went to the driver's door and climbed into the Chevy, where Tina was fiddling with the heater.

"My blood's turning to ice," she said.

Elliot held his hand to the vent. "We're getting some warm air already."

From his coat, he withdrew the pistol and put it on the seat between him and Christina, the muzzle pointed toward the dashboard.

"You really think we should confront Bellicosti at this hour?" she asked.

"Sure. It's not very late."

In an airport-terminal telephone directory, Tina had found the address of the Luciano Bellicosti Funeral Home. The night clerk at the rental agency, from whom they had signed out the car, had known exactly where Bellicosti's place was, and he had marked the shortest route on the free city map provided with the Chevy.

Elliot flicked on the overhead light and studied the map, then handed it to Tina. "I think I can find it without any trouble. But if I get lost, you'll be the navigator."

"Aye, aye, Captain."

He snapped off the overhead light and reached for the gearshift.

With a distant *click*, the light that he had just turned off now turned itself on.

He looked at Tina, and she met his eyes.

He clicked off the light again.

Immediately it switched on.

"Here we go," Tina said.

The radio came on. The digital station indicator began to sweep across the frequencies. Split-second blasts of music, commercials, and disc jockeys' voices blared senselessly out of the speakers.

"It's Danny," Tina said.

The windshield wipers started thumping back and forth at top speed, adding their metronomical beat to the chaos inside the Chevy.

The headlights flashed on and off so rapidly that they created a stroboscopic effect, repeatedly "freezing" the falling snow, so that it appeared as if the white flakes were descending to the ground in short, jerky steps.

The air inside the car was bitterly cold and growing colder by the second.

Elliot put his right hand against the dashboard vent. Heat was pushing out of it, but the air temperature continued to plunge.

The glove compartment popped open.

The ashtray slid out of its niche.

Tina laughed, clearly delighted.

The sound of her laughter startled Elliot, but then he had to admit to himself that he did not feel menaced by the work of this poltergeist. In fact, just the opposite was true. He sensed that he was witnessing a joyous display, a warm greeting, the excited welcome of a child-ghost. He was overwhelmed by the astonishing notion that he could actually feel goodwill in the air, a tangible radiation of love and affection. A not unpleasant shiver raced up his spine. Apparently, this was the same astonishing awareness of being buffeted by waves of love that had caused Tina's laughter.

She said, "We're coming, Danny. Hear me if you can, baby. We're coming to get you. We're coming."

The radio switched off, and so did the overhead light.

The windshield wipers stopped thumping.

The headlights blinked off and stayed off.

Stillness.

Silence.

Scattered flakes of snow collided softly with the windshield.

In the car, the air grew warm again.

Elliot said, "Why does it get cold every time he uses his . . . psychic abilities?"

"Who knows? Maybe he's able to move objects by harnessing the heat energy in the air, changing it somehow. Or maybe it's something else altogether. We'll probably never know. He might not understand it himself. Anyway, that isn't important. What's important is that my Danny is *alive*. There's no doubt about that. Not now. Not anymore. And I gather from your question, you've become a believer too."

"Yeah," Elliot said, still mildly amazed by his own change of heart and mind. "Yeah, I believe there's a chance you're right."

"I know I am."

"Something extraordinary happened to that expedition of scouts. And something downright uncanny has happened to your son."

"But at least he's not dead," Tina said.

Elliot saw tears of happiness shining in her eyes.

"Hey," he said worriedly, "better keep a tight rein on your

hopes. Okay? We've got a long, long way to go. We don't even know where Danny is or what shape he's in. We've got a gauntlet to run before we can find him and bring him back. We might both be killed before we even get close to him."

He drove away from the airport. As far as he could tell, no one followed them.

S**UFFERING** ONE OF HIS OCCASIONAL BOUTS OF claustrophobia, Dr. Carlton Dombey felt as though he had been swallowed alive and was trapped now in the devil's gut.

Deep inside the secret Sierra complex, three stories below ground level, this room measured forty feet by twenty. The low ceiling was covered with a spongy, pebbly, yellowish soundproofing, which gave the chamber a peculiar organic quality. Fluorescent tubes shed cold light over banks of computers and over worktables laden with journals, charts, file folders, scientific instruments, and two coffee mugs.

In the middle of the west wall—one of the two shorter walls—opposite the entrance to the room, was a six-foot-long, three-foot-high window that provided a view of another space, which was only half as large as this outer chamber. The window was constructed like a sandwich: Two one-inch-thick panes of shatterproof glass surrounded an inch-wide space filled with an inert gas. Two panes of ironlike glass. Stainless-steel frame. Four airtight rubber seals—one around the both faces of each pane. This viewport was designed to withstand everything from a gunshot to an earthquake; it was virtually inviolable.

Because it was important for the men who worked in the large room to have an unobstructed view of the smaller inner chamber at all times, four angled ceiling vents in both rooms bathed the glass in a continuous flow of warm, dry air to prevent condensation and clouding. Currently the system wasn't working, for three-quarters of the window was filmed with frost.

Dr. Carlton Dombey, a curly-haired man with a bushy mustache, stood at the window, blotting his damp hands on his medical whites and peering anxiously through one of the few frost-free patches of glass. Although he was struggling to cast off the seizure of claustrophobia that had gripped him, was trying to pretend that the organic-looking ceiling wasn't pressing low over his head and that only open sky hung above him instead of thousands of tons of concrete and steel rock, his own panic attack concerned him less than what was happening beyond the viewport.

Dr. Aaron Zachariah, younger than Dombey, clean-shaven, with straight brown hair, leaned over one of the computers, reading the data that flowed across the screen. "The temperature's dropped thirty-five degrees in there during the past minute and a half," Zachariah said worriedly. "That can't be good for the boy."

"Every time it's happened, it's never seemed to bother him," Dombey said.

"I know, but—"

"Check out his vital signs."

Zachariah moved to another bank of computer screens,

where Danny Evans's heartbeat, blood pressure, body temperature, and brainwave activity were constantly displayed. "Heartbeat's normal, maybe even slightly slower than before. Blood pressure's all right. Body temp unchanged. But there's something unusual about the EEG reading."

"As there always is during these cold snaps," Dombey said. "Odd brainwave activity. But no other indication he's in any discomfort."

"If it stays cold in there for long, we'll have to suit up, go in, and move him to another chamber," Zachariah said.

"There isn't one available," Dombey said. "All the others are full of test animals in the middle of one experiment or another."

"Then we'll have to move the animals. The kid's a lot more important than they are. There's more data to be gotten from him."

He's more important because he's a human being, not because he's a source of data, Dombey thought angrily, but he didn't voice the thought because it would have identified him as a dissident and as a potential security risk.

Instead, Dombey said, "We won't have to move him. The cold spell won't last." He squinted into the smaller room, where the boy lay motionless on a hospital bed, under a white sheet and yellow blanket, trailing monitor wires. Dombey's concern for the kid was greater than his fear of being trapped underground and buried alive, and finally his attack of claustrophobia diminished. "At least it's never lasted long. The temperature drops abruptly, stays down for two or three minutes, never longer than five, and then it rises to normal again."

"What the devil is wrong with the engineers? Why can't they correct the problem?"

Dombey said, "They insist the system checks out perfectly."

"Bullshit."

"There's no malfunction. So they say."

"Like hell there isn't!" Zachariah turned away from the video displays, went to the window, and found his own spot of clear glass. "When this started a month ago, it wasn't that bad. A few degrees of change. Once a night. Never during the day. Never enough of a variation to threaten the boy's health. But the last few days it's gotten completely out of hand. Again and again, we're getting these thirty- and forty-degree plunges in the air temperature in there. No malfunction, my ass!"

"I hear they're bringing in the original design team," Dombey said. "Those guys'll spot the problem in a minute."

"Bozos," Zachariah said.

"Anyway, I don't see what you're so riled up about. We're supposed to be testing the boy to destruction, aren't we? Then why fret about his health?"

"Surely you can't mean that," Zachariah said. "When he finally dies, we'll want to know for sure it was the injections that killed him. If he's subjected to many more of these sudden temperature fluctuations, we'll never be certain they didn't contribute to his death. It won't be clean research."

A thin, humorless laugh escaped Carlton Dombey, and he looked away from the window. Risky as it might be to express doubt to any colleague on the project, Dombey could not control himself: "Clean? This whole thing was never clean. It was a dirty piece of business right from the start."

Zachariah faced him. "You know I'm not talking about the morality of it."

"But I am."

"I'm talking about clinical standards."

"I really don't think I want to hear your opinions on either subject," Dombey said. "I've got a splitting headache."

"I'm just trying to be conscientious," Zachariah said, almost pouting. "You can't blame me because the work is dirty. I don't have much to say about research policy around here."

"You don't have *anything* to say about it," Dombey told him bluntly. "And neither do I. We're low men on the totem pole. That's why we're stuck with night-shift, baby-sitting duty like this."

"Even if I were in charge of making policy," Zachariah said, "I'd take the same course Dr. Tamaguchi has. Hell, he *had* to pursue this research. He didn't have any choice but to commit the installation to it once we found out the damn Chinese were deeply into it. And the Russians giving them a hand to earn some foreign currency. Our new friends the Russians. What a joke. Welcome to the new Cold War. It's China's nasty little project, remember. All we're doing is just playing catch-up. If you have to blame someone because you're feeling guilty about what we're doing here, then blame the Chinese, not me."

"I know. I know," Dombey said wearily, pushing one hand through his bush of curly hair. Zachariah would report their conversation in detail, and Dombey needed to assume a more balanced position for the record. "They scare me sure enough. If there's any government on earth capable of using a weapon like this, it's them—or the North Koreans or the Iraqis. Never a shortage of lunatic regimes. We don't have any choice but to maintain a strong defense. I really believe that. But sometimes . . . I wonder. While we're working so hard to keep ahead of our enemies, aren't we perhaps becoming more like them? Aren't we becoming a totalitarian state, the very thing we say we despise?"

"Maybe."

"Maybe," Dombey said, though he was sure of it.

"What choice do I have?"

"None, I guess."

"Look," Zachariah said.

"What?"

"The window's clearing up. It must be getting warm in there already."

The two scientists turned to the glass again and peered into the isolation chamber.

The emaciated boy stirred. He turned his head toward them and stared at them through the railed sides of the hospital bed in which he lay.

Zachariah said, "Those damn eyes."

"Penetrating, aren't they?"

"The way he stares . . . he gives me the creeps sometimes. There's something haunting about his eyes."

"You're just feeling guilty," Dombey said.

"No. It's more than that. His eyes are strange. They aren't the same as they were when he first came in here a year ago."

"There's pain in them now," Dombey said sadly. "A lot of pain and loneliness."

"More than that," Zachariah said. "There's something in those eyes . . . something there isn't any word for."

Zachariah walked away from the window. He went back to the computers, with which he felt comfortable and safe.

FRIDAY,

JANUARY 2

27

FOR THE MOST PART, RENO'S STREETS WERE CLEAN and dry in spite of a recent snowfall, though occasional patches of black ice waited for the unwary motorist. Elliot Stryker drove cautiously and kept his eyes on the road.

"We should almost be there," Tina said.

They traveled an additional quarter of a mile before Luciano Bellicosti's home and place of business came into sight on the left, beyond a black-bordered sign that grandiosely stated the nature of the service that he provided: FUNERAL DIRECTOR AND GRIEF COUNSELOR. It was an immense, pseudo-Colonial house, perched prominently on top of a hill, on a three- or four-acre property, and conveniently next door to a large, nondenominational cemetery. The long driveway curved up and to the right, like a width of black funeral bunting draped across the rising, snow-shrouded lawn. Stone posts and softly glowing electric lamps marked the way to the front door, and warm light radiated from several first-floor windows.

Elliot almost turned in at the entrance, but at the last moment he decided to drive by the place.

"Hey," Tina said, "that was it."

"I know."

"Why didn't you stop?"

"Storming right up to the front door, demanding answers from Bellicosti—that would be emotionally satisfying, brave, bold—and stupid."

"They can't be waiting for us, can they? They don't know we're in Reno."

"Never underestimate your enemy. They underestimated me and you, which is why we've gotten this far. We're not going to make the same mistake they did and wind up back in their hands."

Beyond the cemetery, he turned left, into a residential street. He parked at the curb, switched off the headlights, and cut the engine.

"What now?" she asked.

"I'm going to walk back to the funeral home. I'll go through the cemetery, circle around, and approach the place from the rear."

"*We* will approach it from the rear," she said.

"No."

"Yes."

"You'll wait here," he insisted.

"No way."

Pale light from a street lamp pierced the windshield, revealing a hard-edged determination in her face, steely resolution in her blue eyes.

Although he realized that he was going to lose the argument, Elliot said, "Be reasonable. If there's any trouble, you might get in the way of it."

"Now really, Elliot, talk sense. Am I the kind of woman who gets in the way?"

"There's eight or ten inches of snow on the ground. You aren't wearing boots."

"Neither are you."

"If they've anticipated us, set a trap at the funeral home—"

"Then you might need my help," she said. "And if they haven't set a trap, I've got to be there when you question Bellicosti."

"Tina, we're just wasting time sitting here—"

"Wasting time. Exactly. I'm glad you see it my way." She opened her door and climbed out of the car.

He knew then, beyond any shadow of a doubt, that he loved her.

Stuffing the silencer-equipped pistol into one of his deep coat pockets, he got out of the Chevy. He didn't lock the doors, because it was possible that he and Tina would need to get into the car in a hurry when they returned.

In the graveyard, the snow came up to the middle of Elliot's calves. It soaked his trousers, caked in his socks, and melted into his shoes.

Tina, wearing rubber-soled sneakers with canvas tops, was surely as miserable as he was. But she kept pace with him, and she didn't complain.

The raw, damp wind was stronger now than it had been a short while ago, when they'd landed at the airport. It swept through the graveyard, fluting between the headstones and the larger monuments, whispering a promise of more snow, much more than the meager flurries it now carried.

A low stone wall and a line of house-high spruce separated the cemetery from Luciano Bellicosti's property. Elliot and Tina climbed over the wall and stood in the tree shadows, studying the rear approach to the funeral home.

Tina didn't have to be told to remain silent. She waited beside him, arms folded, hands tucked into her armpits for warmth.

Elliot was worried about her, afraid for her, but at the same time he was glad to have her company.

The rear of Bellicosti's house was almost a hundred yards away. Even in the dim light, Elliot could see the fringe of icicles hanging from the roof of the long back porch. A few evergreen shrubs were clustered near the house, but none was of sufficient size to conceal a man. The rear windows were blank, black; a sentry might be standing behind any of them, invisible in the darkness.

Elliot strained his eyes, trying to catch a glimpse of movement beyond the rectangles of glass, but he saw nothing suspicious.

There wasn't much of a chance that a trap had been set for them so soon. And if assassins *were* waiting here, they would expect their prey to approach the funeral home boldly, confidently. Consequently, their attention would be focused largely on the front of the house.

In any case, he couldn't stand here all night brooding about it.

He stepped from beneath the sheltering branches of the trees. Tina moved with him.

The bitter wind was a lash. It skimmed crystals of snow off the ground and spun the stinging cold flecks at their reddened faces.

Elliot felt naked as they crossed the luminescent snow field. He wished that they weren't wearing such dark clothes. If anyone *did* glance out a back window, he would spot the two of them instantly.

The crunching and squeaking of the snow under their feet

seemed horrendously loud to him, though they actually were making little noise. He was just jumpy.

They reached the funeral home without incident.

For a few seconds they paused, touching each other briefly, gathering their courage.

Elliot took the pistol out of his coat jacket and held it in his right hand. With his left hand, he fumbled for the two safety catches, released them. His fingers were stiff from the cold. He wondered if he'd be able to handle the weapon properly if the need arose.

They slipped around the corner of the building and moved stealthily toward the front.

At the first window with light behind it, Elliot stopped. He motioned for Tina to stay behind him, close to the house. Cautiously he leaned forward and peeked through a narrow gap in a partly closed venetian blind. He nearly cried out in shock and alarm at what he saw inside.

A dead man. Naked. Sitting in a bathtub full of bloody water, staring at something fearsome beyond the veil between this world and the next. One arm trailed out of the tub; and on the floor, as if it had dropped out of his fingers, was a razor blade.

Elliot stared into the flat dead gaze of the pasty-faced corpse, and he knew that he was looking at Luciano Bellicosti. He also knew that the funeral director had not killed himself. The poor man's blue-lipped mouth hung in a permanent gape, as if he were trying to deny all of the accusations of suicide that were to come.

Elliot wanted to take Tina by the arm and hustle her back to the car. But she sensed that he'd seen something important, and she wouldn't go easily until she knew what it was. She pushed in front of him. He kept one hand on her back as she leaned toward the window, and he felt her go rigid when she glimpsed the dead man. When she turned to Elliot again, she was clearly ready to get the hell out of there, without questions, without argument, without the slightest delay.

They had taken only two steps from the window when Elliot saw the snow move no more than twenty feet from them. It wasn't the gauzy, insubstantial stirring of wind-blown flakes, but an unnatural and purposeful rising of an entire mound of white. Instinctively he whipped the pistol in front of him and squeezed off four rounds. The silencer was so effective that the shots could not be heard above the brittle, papery rustle of the wind.

Crouching low, trying to make as small a target of himself as possible, Elliot ran to where he had seen the snow move. He found a man dressed in a white, insulated ski suit. The stranger had been lying in the snow, watching them, waiting; now he had a wet hole in his chest. And a chunk of his throat was gone. Even in the dim, illusory light from the surrounding snow, Elliot could see that the sentry's eyes were fixed in the same unseeing gaze that Bellicosti was even now directing at the bathroom window.

At least one killer would be in the house with Bellicosti's corpse. Probably more than one.

At least one man had been waiting out here in the snow.

How many others?

Where?

Elliot scanned the night, his heart clutching up. He expected to see the entire white-shrouded lawn begin to move and rise in the forms of ten, fifteen, twenty other assassins.

But all was still.

He was briefly immobilized, dazed by his own ability to strike so fast and so violently. A warm, animal satisfaction rose in him, which was not an entirely welcome feeling, for he liked to think of himself as a civilized man. At the same time, he was hit by a wave of revulsion. His throat tightened, and a sour taste suddenly overwhelmed him. He turned his back on the man whom he had killed.

Tina was a pale apparition in the snow. "They know we're in Reno," she whispered. "They even knew we were coming here."

"But they expected us through the front door." He took her by the arm. "Let's get out of here."

They hurriedly retraced their path, moving away from the funeral home. With every step he took, Elliot expected to hear a shot fired, a cry of alarm, and the sounds of men in pursuit of quarry.

He helped Tina over the cemetery wall, and then, clambering after her, he was sure that someone grabbed his coat from behind. He gasped, jerked loose. When he was across the wall, he looked back, but he couldn't see anyone.

Evidently the people in the funeral home were not aware that their man outside had been eliminated. They were still waiting patiently for their prey to walk into the trap.

Elliot and Tina rushed between the tombstones, kicking up clouds of snow. Twin plumes of crystallized breath trailed behind them, like ghosts.

When they were nearly halfway across the graveyard, when Elliot was positive they weren't being pursued, he stopped, leaned against a tall monument, and tried not to take such huge, deep gulps of the painfully cold air. An image of his victim's torn throat exploded in his memory, and a shock wave of nausea overwhelmed him.

Tina put a hand on his shoulder. "Are you all right?"

"I killed him."

"If you hadn't, he would have killed us."

"I know. Just the same . . . it makes me sick."

"I would have thought . . . when you were in the army . . ."

"Yeah," he said softly. "Yeah, I've killed before. But like you said, that was in the army. This wasn't the same. That was soldiering. This was murder." He shook his head to clear it. "I'll be okay." He tucked the pistol into his coat pocket again. "It was just the shock."

They embraced, and then she said, "If they knew we were flying to Reno, why didn't they follow us from the airport? Then they would have known we weren't going to walk in the front door of Bellicosti's place."

"Maybe they figured I'd spot a tail and be spooked by it. And I guess they were so sure of where we were headed, they didn't think it was necessary to keep a close watch on us. They figured there wasn't anywhere else we *could* go but Bellicosti's funeral home."

"Let's get back to the car. I'm freezing."

"Me too. And we better get out of the neighborhood before they find that guy in the snow."

They followed their own footprints out of the cemetery, to the quiet residential street where the rented Chevrolet was parked in the wan light of the street lamp.

As Elliot was opening the driver's door, he saw movement out of the corner of his eye, and he looked up, already sure of what he would see. A white Ford sedan had just turned the corner, moving slowly. It drifted to the curb and braked abruptly. Two doors opened, and a pair of tall, darkly dressed men climbed out.

Elliot recognized them for what they were. He got into the Chevy, slammed the door, and jammed the key into the ignition.

"We *have* been followed," Tina said.

"Yeah." He switched on the engine and threw the car in gear. "A transponder. They must have just now homed in on it."

He didn't hear a shot, but a bullet shattered the rear side window behind his head and slammed into the back of the front seat, spraying gummy bits of safety glass through the car.

"Head down!" Elliot shouted.

He glanced back.

The two men were approaching at a run, slipping on the snow-spotted pavement.

Elliot stamped on the accelerator. Tires squealing, he pulled the Chevy away from the curb, into the street.

Two slugs ricocheted off the body of the car, each trailing away with a brief, high-pitched whine.

Elliot hunched low over the wheel, expecting a bullet through the rear window. At the corner, he ignored the stop sign and swung the car hard to the left, only tapping the brakes once, severely testing the Chevy's suspension.

Tina raised her head, glanced at the empty street behind them, then looked at Elliot. "Transponder. What's that? You mean we're bugged? Then we'll have to abandon the car, won't we?"

"Not until we've gotten rid of those clowns on our tail," he said. "If we abandon the car with them so close, they'll run us down fast. We can't get away on foot."

"Then what?"

They arrived at another intersection, and he whipped the

car to the right. "After I turn the next corner, I'll stop and get out. You be ready to slide over and take the wheel."

"Where are you going?"

"I'll fade back into the shrubbery and wait for them to come around the corner after us. You drive on down the street, but not too fast. Give them a chance to see you when they turn into the street. They'll be looking at you, and they won't see me."

"We shouldn't split up."

"It's the only way."

"But what if they get you?"

"They won't."

"I'd be alone then."

"They won't get me. But you have to move fast. If we stop for more than a couple of seconds, it'll show up on their receiver, and they might get suspicious."

He swung right at the intersection and stopped in the middle of the new street.

"Elliot, don't—"

"No choice." He flung open the door and scrambled out of the car. "Hurry, Tina!"

He slammed the car door and ran to a row of evergreen shrubs that bordered the front lawn of a low, brick, ranch-style house. Crouching beside one of those bushes, huddling in the shadows just beyond the circle of frosty light from a nearby street lamp, he pulled the pistol out of his coat pocket while Tina drove away.

As the sound of the Chevy faded, he could discern the roar of another vehicle, approaching fast. A few seconds later the white sedan raced into the intersection.

Elliot stood, extending the pistol in both hands, and snapped off three quick rounds. The first two clanged through sheet metal, but the third punctured the right front tire.

The Ford had rounded the corner too fast. Jolted by the blowout, the car careened out of control. It spun across the street, jumped the curb, crashed through a hedge, destroyed a plaster birdbath, and came to rest in the middle of a snow-blanketed lawn.

Elliot ran toward the Chevy, which Tina had brought to a stop a hundred yards away. It seemed more like a hundred miles. His pounding footsteps were as thunderous as drumbeats in the quiet night air. At last he reached the car. She had the door open. He leaped in and pulled the door shut. "Go, go!"

She tramped the accelerator into the floorboards, and the car responded with a shudder, then a surge of power.

When they had gone two blocks, he said, "Turn right at the next corner." After two more turns and another three blocks, he said, "Pull it to the curb. I want to find the bug they planted on us."

"But they can't follow us now," she said.

"They've still got a receiver. They can watch our progress on that, even if they can't get their hands on us till another chase car catches up. I don't even want them to know what direction we went."

She stopped the car, and he got out. He felt along the inner faces of the fenders, around the tire wells, where a transponder could have been stuck in place quickly and easily. Nothing. The front bumper was clean too. Finally he located the electronics package: The size of a pack of cigarettes, it was fixed magnetically to the underside of the rear bumper. He wrenched it loose, stomped it repeatedly underfoot, and pitched it away.

In the car again, with the doors locked and the engine running and the heater operating full-blast, they sat in stunned silence, basking in the warm air, but shivering nonetheless.

Eventually Tina said, "My God, they move fast!"

"We're still one step ahead of them," Elliot said shakily.

"Half a step."

"That's probably more like it," he admitted.

"Bellicosti was supposed to give us the information we need to interest a topnotch reporter in the case."

"Not now."

"So how do we get that information?"

"Somehow," he said vaguely.

"How do we build our case?"

"We'll think of something."

"Who do we turn to next?"

"It isn't hopeless, Tina."

"I didn't say it was. But where do we go from here?"

"We can't work it out tonight," he said wearily. "Not in our condition. We're both wiped out, operating on sheer desperation. That's dangerous. The best decision we can make is to make no decisions at all. We've got to hole up and get some rest. In the morning we'll have clearer heads, and the answers will all seem obvious."

"You think you can actually sleep?"

"Hell, yes. It's been a hard day's night."

"Where will we be safe?"

"We'll try the purloined letter trick," Elliot said. "Instead of sneaking around to some out-of-the-way motel, we'll march right into one of the best hotels in town."

"Harrah's?"

"Exactly. They won't expect us to be that bold. They'll be searching for us everywhere else."

"It's risky."

"Can you think of anything better?"

"No."

"*Everything* is risky."

"All right. Let's do it."

She drove into the heart of town. They abandoned the Chevrolet in a public parking lot, four blocks from Harrah's.

"I wish we didn't have to give up the car," Tina said as he took their only suitcase out of the trunk.

"They'll be looking for it."

They walked to Harrah's Hotel along windy, neon-splashed streets. Even at 1:45 in the morning, as they passed the entrances to casinos, loud music and laughter and the ringing of slot machines gushed forth, not a merry sound at that hour, a regurgitant noise.

Although Reno didn't jump all night with quite the same energy as Las Vegas, and although many tourists had gone to bed, the casino at Harrah's was still relatively busy. A young sailor apparently had a run going at one of the craps tables, and a crowd of excited gamblers urged him to roll an eight and make his point.

On this holiday weekend the hotel was officially booked to capacity; however, Elliot knew accommodations were always available. At the request of its casino manager, every hotel held a handful of rooms off the market, just in case a few regular customers—high rollers, of course—showed up by surprise, with no advance notice, but with fat bankrolls and no place to stay. In addition, some reservations were canceled at the last minute, and there were always a few no-shows. A neatly folded pair of twenty-dollar bills, placed without ostentation into the hand of a front-desk clerk, was almost certain to result in the timely discovery of a forgotten vacancy.

When Elliot was informed that a room was available, after all, for two nights, he signed the registration card as "Hank Thomas," a slight twist on the name of one of his favorite movie stars; he entered a phony Seattle address too. The clerk requested ID or a major credit card, and Elliot told a sad story of being victimized by a pickpocket at the airport. Unable to prove his identity, he was required to pay for both nights in advance, which he did, taking the money from a wad of cash he'd stuck in his pocket rather than from the wallet that supposedly had been stolen.

He and Tina were given a spacious, pleasantly decorated room on the ninth floor.

After the bellman left, Elliot engaged the deadbolt, hooked the security chain in place, and firmly wedged the heavy straight-backed desk chair under the knob.

"It's like a prison," Tina said.

"Except we're locked in, and the killers are running around loose on the outside."

A short time later, in bed, they held each other close, but neither of them had sex in mind. They wanted nothing more than to touch and to be touched, to confirm for each other that they were still alive, to feel safe and protected and cherished. Theirs was an animal need for affection and companionship, a reaction to the death and destruction that had filled the day. After encountering so many people with so little respect for human life, they needed to convince themselves that they really were more than dust in the wind.

After a few minutes he said, "You were right."

"About what?"

"About what you said last night, in Vegas."

"Refresh my memory."

"You said I was enjoying the chase."

"A part of you . . . deep down inside. Yes, I think that's truc."

"I know it is," he said. "I can see it now. I didn't want to believe it at first."

"Why not? I didn't mean it negatively."

"I know you didn't. It's just that for more than fifteen years, I've led a very ordinary life, a workaday life. I was convinced I no longer needed or wanted the kind of thrills that I thrived on when I was younger."

"I don't think you *do* need or want them," Tina said. "But now that you're in real danger again for the first time in years, a part of you is responding to the challenge. Like an old athlete back on the playing field after a long absence, testing his reflexes, taking pride in the fact that his old skills are still there."

"It's more than that," Elliot said. "I think . . . deep down, I got a sick sort of thrill when I killed that man."

"Don't be so hard on yourself."

"I'm not. In fact, maybe the thrill wasn't so deep down. Maybe it was really pretty near the surface."

"You should be glad you killed that bastard," she said softly, squeezing his hand.

"Should I?"

"Listen, if I could get my hands on the people who're trying to keep us from finding Danny, I wouldn't have any compunctions about killing them. None at all. I might even take a certain pleasure in it. I'm a mother lion, and they've stolen by cub. Maybe killing them is the most natural, admirable thing I could do."

"So there's a bit of the beast in all of us. Is that it?"

"It's not just me that has a savage trapped inside."

"But does that make it any more acceptable?"

"What's to accept?" she asked. "It's the way God made us. It's the way we were meant to be, so who's to say it isn't right?"

"Maybe."

"If a man kills only for the pleasure of it, or if he kills only for an ideal like some of these crackpot revolutionaries you read about, *that's* savagery . . . or madness. What you've done is altogether different. Self-preservation is one of the most powerful drives God gave us. We're built to survive, even if we have to kill someone in order to do it."

They were silent for a while. Then he said, "Thank you."

"I didn't do anything."

"You listened."

28

KURT HENSEN, GEORGE ALEXANDER'S RIGHT-hand man, dozed through the rough flight from Las Vegas to Reno. They were in a ten-passenger jet that belonged to the Network, and the aircraft took a battering from the high-altitude winds that blew across its assigned flight corridor. Hensen, a powerfully built man with white-blond hair and cat-yellow eyes, was afraid of flying. He could only manage to get on a plane after he had medicated himself. As usual he nodded off minutes after the aircraft lifted from the runway.

George Alexander was the only other passenger. He considered the requisitioning of this executive jet to be one of his most important accomplishments in the three years that he had been chief of the Nevada bureau of the Network. Although he spent more than half his time working in his Las Vegas office, he often had reason to fly to far points at the spur of the moment: Reno, Elko, even out of the state to Texas, California, Arizona, New Mexico, Utah. During the first year, he'd taken commercial flights or rented the services of a trustworthy private pilot who could fly the conventional twin-engine craft that Alexander's predecessor had managed to pry out of the Network's budget. But it had seemed absurd and shortsighted of the director to force a man of Alexander's position to travel by such relatively primitive means. His time was enormously valuable to the country; his work was sensitive and often required urgent decisions based upon first-hand examination of information to be found only in distant places. After long and arduous lobbying of the director, Alexander had at last been awarded this small jet; and immediately he put two full-time pilots, ex-military men, on the payroll of the Nevada bureau.

Sometimes the Network pinched pennies to its disadvantage. And George Lincoln Stanhope Alexander, who was an heir to both the fortune of the Pennsylvania Alexanders and to the enormous wealth of the Delaware Stanhopes, had absolutely no patience with people who were penurious.

It was true that every dollar had to count, for every dollar of the Network's budget was difficult to come by. Because its existence must be kept secret, the organization was funded out of misdirected appropriations meant for other government agencies. Three billion dollars, the largest single part of the Network's yearly budget, came from the Department of Health and Welfare. The Network had a deep-cover agent named Jacklin in the highest policy-making ranks of the Health bureaucracy. It was Jacklin's job to conceive new welfare programs, convince the Secretary of Health and Welfare that those programs were needed, sell them to the Congress, and then establish convincing bureaucratic shells to conceal the fact that the programs were utterly phony; and as federal funds flowed to these false-front operations, the money was diverted to the Network. Chipping three billion out of Health was the least risky of the Network's funding operations, for Health was so gigantic that it never missed such a petty sum. The Department of Defense, which was less flush than Health and Welfare these days, was nevertheless also guilty of waste, and it was good for at least another billion a year. Lesser amounts, ranging from only one hundred million to as much as half a billion, were secretly extracted from the Department of Energy, the Department of Education, and other government bodies on an annual basis.

The Network was financed with some difficulty, to be sure, but it was undeniably well funded. An executive jet for the chief of the vital Nevada bureau was not an extravagance, and Alexander believed his improved performance over the past year had convinced the old man in Washington that this was money well spent.

Alexander was proud of the importance of his position. But he was also frustrated because so few people were *aware* of his great importance.

At times he envied his father and his uncles. Most of them had served their country openly, in a supremely visible fashion, where everyone could see and admire their selfless public-spiritedness. Secretary of Defense, Secretary of State, the Ambassador to France . . . in positions of that nature, a man was appreciated and respected.

George, on the other hand, hadn't filled a post of genuine stature and authority until six years ago, when he was thirty-six. During his twenties and early thirties, he had labored at a variety of lesser jobs for the government. These diplomatic and intelligence-gathering assignments were never an insult to his family name, but they were always minor postings to embassies in smaller countries like

Iceland and Ecuador and Tonga, nothing for which *The New York Times* would deign to acknowledge his existence.

Then, six years ago, the Network had been formed, and the President had given George the task of developing a reliable South American bureau of the new intelligence agency. That had been exciting, challenging, important work. George had been directly responsible for the expenditure of tens of millions of dollars and, eventually, for the control of hundreds of agents in a dozen countries. After three years the President had declared himself delighted with the accomplishments in South America, and he had asked George to take charge of one of the Network's domestic bureaus—Nevada—which had been terribly mismanaged. This slot was one of the half-dozen most powerful in the Network's executive hierarchy. George was encouraged by the President to believe that eventually he would be promoted to the bureau chief of the entire western half of the country—and then all the way to the top, if only he could get the floundering western division functioning as smoothly as the South American and Nevada offices. In time he would take the director's chair in Washington and would bear full responsibility for all domestic and foreign intelligence operations. With that title he would be one of the most powerful men in the United States, more of a force to be reckoned with than any mere Secretary of State or Secretary of Defense could hope to be.

But he couldn't tell anyone about his achievements. He could never hope to receive the public acclaim and honor that had been heaped upon other men in his family. The Network was clandestine and must remain clandestine if it was to have any value. At least half of the people who worked for it did not even realize it existed; some thought they were employed by the FBI; others were sure they worked for the CIA; and still others believed that they were in the hire of various branches of the Treasury Department, including the Secret Service. None of those people could compromise the Network. Only bureau chiefs, their immediate staffs, station chiefs in major cities, and senior field officers who had proved themselves and their loyalty—only those people knew the true nature of their employers and their work. The moment that the news media became aware of the Network's existence, all was lost.

As he sat in the dimly lighted cabin of the fan-jet and watched the clouds racing below, Alexander wondered what his father and his uncles would say if they knew that his service to his country had often required him to issue kill orders. More shocking still to the sensibilities of patrician Easterners like them: on three occasions, in South America, Alexander had been in a position where it had been necessary for him to pull the assassin's trigger himself. He had enjoyed those murders so immensely, had been so profoundly thrilled by them, that he had, by choice, performed the executioner's role on half a dozen other assignments. What would the elder Alexanders, the famous statesmen, think if they knew he'd soiled his hands with blood? As for the fact that it was sometimes his job to order other men to kill, he supposed his family would understand. The Alexanders were all idealists when they were discussing the way things ought to be, but they were also hardheaded pragmatists when dealing with the way things actually were. They knew that the worlds of domestic military security and international espionage were not children's playgrounds. George liked to believe that they might even find it in their hearts to forgive him for having pulled the trigger himself.

After all, he had never killed an ordinary citizen or a person of real worth. His targets had always been spies, traitors; more than a few of them had been cold-blooded killers themselves. Scum. He had only killed scum. It wasn't a pretty job, but it also wasn't without a measure of real dignity and heroism. At least that was the way George saw it; he thought of himself as heroic. Yes, he was sure that his father and uncles would give him their blessings—if only he were permitted to tell them.

The jet hit an especially bad patch of turbulence. It yawed, bounced, shuddered.

Kurt Hensen snorted in his sleep but didn't wake.

When the plane settled down once more, Alexander looked out the window at the milky-white, moonlit, feminine roundness of the clouds below, and he thought of the Evans woman. She was quite lovely. Her file folder was on the seat beside him. He picked it up, opened it, and stared at her photograph. Quite lovely indeed. He decided he would kill her himself when the time came, and that thought gave him an instant erection.

He enjoyed killing. He didn't try to pretend otherwise with himself, no matter what face he had to present to the world. All of his life, for reasons he had never been able to fully ascertain, he had been fascinated by death, intrigued by the form and nature and possibilities of it, enthralled by the study and theory of its meaning. He considered himself a messenger of death, a divinely appointed headsman. Murder was, in many ways, more thrilling to him than sex. His taste for violence would not have been tolerated for long in the old FBI—perhaps not even in the new, thoroughly

politicized FBI—or in many other congressionally monitored police agencies. But in this unknown organization, in
this secret and incomparably cozy place, he thrived.

He closed his eyes and thought about Christina Evans.

29

In Tina's dream, Danny was at the far end of a long tunnel. He was in chains, sitting in the center of a small, well-lighted cavern, but the passageway that led to him was shadowy and reeked of danger. Danny called to her again and again, begging her to save him before the roof of his underground prison caved in and buried him alive. She started down the tunnel toward him, determined to get him out of there—and something reached for her from a narrow cleft in the wall. She was peripherally aware of a soft, firelike glow from beyond the cleft, and of a mysterious figure silhouetted against that reddish backdrop. She turned, and she was looking into the grinning face of Death, as if he were peering out at her from the bowels of Hell. The crimson eyes. The shriveled flesh. The lacework of maggots on his cheek. She cried out, but then she saw that Death could not quite reach her. The hole in the wall was not wide enough for him to step through, into her passageway; he could only thrust one arm at her, and his long, bony fingers were an inch or two short of her. Danny began calling again, and she continued down the dusky tunnel toward him. A dozen times she passed chinks in the wall, and Death glared out at her from every one of those apertures, screamed and cursed and raged at her, but none of the holes was large enough to allow him through. She reached Danny, and when she touched him, the chains fell magically away from his arms and legs. She said, "I was scared." And Danny said, "I made the holes in the walls smaller. I made sure he couldn't reach you, couldn't hurt you."

At eight-thirty Friday morning Tina came awake, smiling and excited. She shook Elliot until she woke him.

Blinking sleepily, he sat up. "What's wrong?"

"Danny just sent me another dream."

Taking in her broad smile, he said, "Obviously, it wasn't the nightmare."

"Not at all. Danny wants us to come to him. He wants us just to walk into the place where they're keeping him and take him out."

"We'd be killed before we could reach him. We can't just charge in like the cavalry. We've got to use the media and the courts to free him."

"I don't think so."

"The two of us can't fight the entire organization that's behind Kennebeck plus the staff of some secret military research center."

"Danny's going to make it safe for us," she said confidently. "He's going to use this power of his to help us get in there."

"That isn't possible."

"You said you believed."

"I do," Elliot said, yawning and stretching elaborately. "I do believe. But . . . how can he help us? How can he guarantee our safety?"

"I don't know. But that's what he was telling me in the dream. I'm sure of it."

She recounted the dream in detail, and Elliot admitted that her interpretation wasn't strained.

"But even if Danny could somehow get us in," he said, "we don't know where they're keeping him. This secret installation could be anywhere. And maybe it doesn't even exist. And if it does exist, they might not be holding him there anyway."

"It exists, and that's where he is," she said, trying to sound more certain than she actually was.

She was within reach of Danny. She felt almost as if she had him in her arms again, and she didn't want anyone to tell her that he might be a hair's breadth beyond her grasp.

"Okay," Elliot said, wiping at the corners of his sleep-matted eyes. "Let's say this secret installation exists. That doesn't help us a whole hell of a lot. It could be anywhere in those mountains."

"No," she said. "It has to be within a few miles of where Jaborski intended to go with the scouts."

"Okay. That's probably true. But that covers a hell of a lot of rugged terrain. We couldn't begin to conduct a thorough search of it."

Tina's confidence couldn't be shaken. "Danny will pinpoint it for us."

"Danny's going to tell us where he is?"

"He's going to try, I think. I sensed that in the dream."

"How's he going to do it?"

"I don't know. But I have this feeling that if we just find some way . . . some means of focusing his energy, channeling it . . ."

"Such as?"

She stared at the tangled bedclothes as if she were searching for inspiration in the creases of the linens. Her expression would have been appropriate to the face of a gypsy fortune-teller peering with a clairvoyant frown at tea leaves.

"Maps!" she said suddenly.

"What?"

"Don't they publish terrain maps of the wilderness areas? Backpackers and other nature lovers would need them. Not minutely detailed things. Basically maps that show the lay of the land—hills, valleys, the courses of rivers and streams, footpaths, abandoned logging trails, that sort of thing. I'm sure Jaborski had maps. I *know* he did. I saw them at the parent-son scout meeting when he explained why the trip would be perfectly safe."

"I suppose any sporting-goods store in Reno ought to have maps of at least the nearest parts of the Sierras."

"Maybe if we can get a map and spread it out . . . well, maybe Danny will find a way to show us exactly where he is."

"How?"

"I'm not sure yet." She threw back the covers and got out of bed. "Let's get the maps first. We'll worry about the rest of it later. Come on. Let's get showered and dressed. The stores will be open in an hour or so."

•   •   •

Because of the foul-up at the Bellicosti place, George Alexander didn't get to bed until five-thirty Friday morning. Still furious with his subordinates for letting Stryker and the woman escape again, he had difficulty getting to sleep. He finally nodded off around 7:00 A.M.

At ten o'clock he was awakened by the telephone. The

director was calling from Washington. They used an electronic scrambling device, so they could speak candidly, and the old man was furious and characteristically blunt.

As Alexander endured the director's accusations and demands, he realized that his own future with the Network was at stake. If he failed to stop Stryker and the Evans woman, his dream of assuming the director's chair in a few years would never become a reality.

After the old man hung up, Alexander called his own office, in no mood to be told that Elliot Stryker and Christina Evans were still at large. But that was exactly what he heard. He ordered men pulled off other jobs and assigned to the manhunt.

"I want them found before another day passes," Alexander said. "That bastard's killed one of us now. He can't get away with that. I want him eliminated. And the bitch with him. Both of them. Dead."

T WO SPORTING-GOODS STORES AND TWO GUN shops were within easy walking distance of the hotel. The first sporting-goods dealer did not carry the maps, and although the second usually had them, it was currently sold out. Elliot and Tina found what they needed in one of the gun shops: a set of twelve wilderness maps of the Sierras, designed with backpackers and hunters in mind. The set came in a leatherette-covered case and sold for a hundred dollars.

Back in the hotel room, they opened one of the maps on the bed, and Elliot said, "Now what?"

For a moment Tina considered the problem. Then she went to the desk, opened the center drawer, and withdrew a folder of hotel stationery. In the folder was a cheap plastic ballpoint pen with the hotel name on it. With the pen, she returned to the bed and sat beside the open map.

She said, "People who believe in the occult have a thing they call 'automatic writing.' Ever hear of it?"

"Sure. Spirit writing. A ghost supposedly guides your

hand to deliver a message from beyond. Always sounded like the worst sort of bunkum to me."

"Well, bunkum or not, I'm going to try something like that. Except, I don't need a ghost to guide my hand. I'm hoping Danny can do it."

"Don't you have to be in a trance, like a medium at a seance?"

"I'm just going to completely relax, make myself open and receptive. I'll hold the pen against the map, and maybe Danny can draw the route for us."

Elliot pulled a chair beside the bed and sat. "I don't believe for a minute it's going to work. Totally nuts. But I'll be as quiet as a mouse and give it a chance."

Tina stared at the map and tried to think of nothing but the appealing greens, blues, yellows, and pinks that the cartographers had used to indicate various types of terrain. She allowed her eyes to swim out of focus.

A minute passed.

Two minutes. Three.

She tried closing her eyes.

Another minute. Two.

Nothing.

She turned the map over and tried the other side of it.

Still nothing.

"Give me another map," she said.

Elliot withdrew another one from the leatherette case and handed it to her. He refolded the first map as she unfolded the second.

Half an hour and five maps later, Tina's hand suddenly skipped across the paper as if someone had bumped her arm.

She felt a peculiar pulling sensation that seemed to come from *within* her hand, and she stiffened in surprise.

Instantly the invasive power retreated from her.

"What was that?" Elliot asked.

"Danny. He tried."

"You're sure?"

"Positive. But he startled me, and I guess even the little bit of resistance I offered was enough to push him away. At least we know this is the right map. Let me try again."

She put the pen at the edge of the map once more, and she let her eyes drift out of focus.

The air temperature plummeted.

She tried not to think about the chill. She tried to banish *all* thoughts.

Her right hand, in which she held the pen, grew rapidly colder than any other part of her. She felt the unpleasant, inner pulling again. Her fingers ached with the cold. Abruptly her hand swung across the map, then back, then described a series of circles; the pen made meaningless scrawls on the paper. After half a minute, she felt the power leave her hand again.

"No good," she said.

The map flew into the air, as if someone had tossed it in anger or frustration.

Elliot got out of his chair and reached for the map—but it spun into the air again. It flapped noisily to the other end of the room and then back again, finally falling like a dead bird onto the floor at Elliot's feet.

"Jesus," he said softly. "The next time I read a story in the newspaper about some guy who says he was picked up in a flying saucer and taken on a tour of the universe, I won't be so quick to laugh. If I see many more inanimate objects dancing around, I'm going to start believing in *everything*, no matter how freaky."

Tina got up from the bed, massaging her cold right hand. "I guess I'm offering too much resistance. But it feels so weird when he takes control . . . I can't help stiffening a little. I guess you were right about needing to be in a trance."

"I'm afraid I can't help you with that. I'm a good cook, but I'm not a hypnotist."

She blinked. "Hypnosis! Of course! That'll probably do the trick."

"Maybe it will. But where do you expect to find a hypnotist? The last time I looked, they weren't setting up shops on street corners."

"Billy Sandstone," she said.

"Who?"

"He's a hypnotist. He lives right here in Reno. He has a stage act. It's a brilliant act. I wanted to use him in *Magyck!,* but he was tied up in an exclusive contract with a chain of Reno-Tahoe hotels. If you can get hold of Billy, he can hypnotize me. Then maybe I'll be relaxed enough to make this automatic writing work."

"Do you know his phone number?"

"No. And it's probably not listed. But I do know his agent's number. I can get through to him that way."

She hurried to the telephone.

31

BILLY SANDSTONE WAS IN HIS LATE THIRTIES, AS small and lean as a jockey, and his watchword seemed to be "neatness." His shoes shone like black mirrors. The creases in his slacks were as sharp as blades, and his blue sport shirt was starched, crisp. His hair was razor-cut, and he groomed his mustache so meticulously that it almost appeared to have been painted on his upper lip.

Billy's dining room was neat too. The table, the chairs, the credenza, and the hutch all glowed warmly because of the prodigious amount of furniture polish that had been buffed into the wood with even more vigor than he had employed when shining his dazzling shoes. Fresh roses were arranged in a cut-crystal vase in the center of the table, and clean lines of light gleamed in the exquisite glass. The draperies hung in perfectly measured folds. An entire battalion of nitpickers and fussbudgets would be hard-pressed to find a speck of dust in this room.

Elliot and Tina spread the map on the table and sat down across from each other.

Billy said, "Automatic writing is bunk, Christina. You must know that."

"I do, Billy. I know that."

"Well, then—"

"But I want you to hypnotize me anyway."

"You're a levelheaded person, Tina," Billy said. "This really doesn't seem like you."

"I know," she said.

"If you'd just tell me *why*. If you'd tell me what this is all about, maybe I could help you better."

"Billy," she said, "if I tried to explain, we would be here all afternoon."

"Longer," Elliot said.

"And we don't have much time," Tina said. "A lot's at stake here, Billy. More than you can imagine."

They hadn't told him anything about Danny. Sandstone didn't have the faintest idea why they were in Reno or what they were seeking in the mountains.

Elliot said, "I'm sure this seems ridiculous, Billy. You're probably wondering if I'm some sort of lunatic. You're wondering if maybe I've messed with Tina's mind."

"Which definitely isn't the case," Tina said.

"Right," Elliot said. "Her mind was messed up before I ever met her."

The joke seemed to relax Sandstone, as Elliot had hoped it would. Lunatics and just plain irrational people didn't intentionally try to amuse.

Elliot said, "I assure you, Billy, we haven't lost our marbles. And this *is* a matter of life and death."

"It really is," Tina said.

"Okay," Billy said. "You don't have time to tell me about

it now. I'll accept that. But will you tell me one day when you aren't in such a damn rush?"

"Absolutely," Tina said. "I'll tell you everything. Just please, please, put me in a trance."

"All right," Billy Sandstone said.

He was wearing a gold signet ring. He turned it around, so the face of it was on the wrong side—the palm side—of his finger. He held his hand in front of Tina's eyes.

"Keep your eyes on the ring and listen only to my voice."

"Wait a second," she said.

She pulled the cap off the red felt-tip pen that Elliot had purchased at the hotel newsstand just before they'd caught a taxi to Sandstone's house. Elliot had suggested a change in the color of ink, so they would be able to tell the difference between the meaningless scribbles that were already on the map and any new marks that might be made.

Putting the point of the pen to the paper, Tina said, "Okay, Billy. Do your stuff."

Elliot was not sure when Tina slipped under the hypnotist's spell, and he had no idea how this smooth mesmerism was accomplished. All Sandstone did was move one hand slowly back and forth in front of Tina's face, simultaneously speaking to her in a quiet, rhythmic voice, frequently using her name.

Elliot almost fell into a trance himself. He blinked his eyes and tuned out Sandstone's melodious voice when he realized that he was succumbing to it.

Tina stared vacantly into space.

The hypnotist lowered his hand and turned his ring around as it belonged. "You're in a deep sleep, Tina."

"Yes."

"Your eyes are open, but you are in a deep, deep sleep."

"Yes."

"You will stay in that deep sleep until I tell you to wake up. Do you understand?"

"Yes."

"You will remain relaxed and receptive."

"Yes."

"Nothing will startle you."

"No."

"You aren't really involved in this. You're just the method of transmission—like a telephone."

"Telephone," she said thickly.

"You will remain totally passive until you feel the urge to use the pen in your hand."

"All right."

"When you feel the urge to use the pen, you will not resist it. You will flow with it. Understood?"

"Yes."

"You will not be bothered by anything Elliot and I say to each other. You will respond to me only when I speak directly to you. Understood?"

"Yes."

"Now . . . open yourself to whoever wants to speak through you."

They waited.

A minute passed, then another.

Billy Sandstone watched Tina intently for a while, but at last he shifted impatiently in his chair. He looked at Elliot and said, "I don't think this spirit writing stuff is—"

The map rustled, drawing their attention. The corners curled and uncurled, curled and uncurled, again and again, like the pulse of a living thing.

The air was colder.

The map stopped curling. The rustling ceased.

Tina lowered her gaze from the empty air to the map, and her hand began to move. It didn't swoop and dart uncontrollably this time; it crept carefully, hesitantly across the paper, leaving a thin red line of ink like a thread of blood.

Sandstone was rubbing his hands up and down his arms to ward off the steadily deepening chill that had gripped the room. Frowning, glancing up at the heating vents, he started to get out of his chair.

Elliot said, "Don't bother checking the air-conditioning. It isn't on. And the heat hasn't failed either."

"What?"

"The cold comes from the . . . spirit," Elliot said, deciding to stick with the occult terminology, not wanting to get bogged down in the real story about Danny.

"Spirit?"

"Yes."

"Whose spirit?"

"Could be anyone's."

"Are you serious?"

"Pretty much."

Sandstone stared at him as if to say, *You're nuts, but are you dangerous?*

Elliot pointed to the map. "See?"

As Tina's hand moved slowly over the paper, the corners of the map began to curl and uncurl again.

"How is she doing that?" Sandstone asked.

"She isn't."

"The ghost, I suppose."

"That's right."

An expression of pain settled over Billy's face, as if he were suffering genuine physical discomfort because of Elliot's belief in ghosts. Apparently Billy liked his view of the world to be as neat and uncluttered as everything else about him; if he started believing in ghosts, he'd have to reconsider his opinions about a lot of other things too, and then life would become intolerably messy.

Elliot sympathized with the hypnotist. Right now he longed for the rigidly structured routine of the law office, the neatly ordered paragraphs of legal casebooks, and the timeless rules of the courtroom.

Tina let the pen drop from her fingers. She lifted her gaze from the map. Her eyes remained unfocused.

"Are you finished?" Billy asked her.

"Yes."

"Are you sure?"

"Yes."

With a few simple sentences and a sharp clap of his hands, the hypnotist brought her out of the trance.

She blinked in confusion, then glanced down at the route that she had marked on the map. She smiled at Elliot. "It worked. By God, it worked!"

"Apparently it did."

She pointed to the terminus of the red line. "That's where he is, Elliot. That's where they're keeping him."

"It's not going to be easy getting into country like that," Elliot said.

"We can do it. We'll need good, insulated outdoor clothes. Boots. Snowshoes in case we have to walk very far in open country. Do you know how to use snowshoes? It can't be that hard."

"Hold on," Elliot said. "I'm still not convinced your dream meant what you think it did. Based on what you said happened in it, I don't see how you reach the conclusion that Danny's going to help us get into the installation. We might get to this place and find we can't slip around its defenses."

Billy Sandstone looked from Tina to Elliot, baffled. "Danny? Your Danny, Tina? But isn't he—"

Tina said, "Elliot, it wasn't only what happened in the dream that led me to this conclusion. What I *felt* in it was far more important. I can't explain that part of it. The only way you could understand is if you had the dream yourself. I'm *sure* he was telling me that he could help us get to him."

Elliot turned the map to be able to study it more closely.

From the head of the table, Billy said, "But isn't Danny—"

Tina said, "Elliot, listen, I told you he would show us where he's being kept, and he drew that route for us. So far I'm batting a thousand. I also feel he's going to help us get into the place, and I don't see any reason why I should strike out on that one."

"It's just . . . we'd be walking into their arms," Elliot said.

"Whose arms?" Billy Sandstone asked.

Tina said, "Elliot, what happens if we stay here, hiding out until we can think of an alternative? How much time do we have? Not much. They're going to find us sooner or later, and when they get their hands on us, they'll kill us."

"Kill?" Billy Sandstone asked. "There's a word I don't like. It's right up there on the bad-word list beside *broccoli*."

"We've gotten this far because we've kept moving and we've been aggressive," Tina said. "If we change our approach, if we suddenly get too cautious, that'll be our downfall, not our salvation."

"You two sound like you're in a war," Billy Sandstone said uneasily.

"You're probably right," Elliot told Tina. "One thing I learned in the military was you have to stop and regroup your forces once in a while, but if you stop too long, the tide will turn and wash right over you."

"Should I maybe go listen to the news?" Billy Sandstone asked. "*Is* there a war on? Have we invaded France?"

To Tina, Elliot said, "What else will we need besides thermal clothing, boots, and snowshoes?"

"A Jeep," she said.

"That's a tall order."

"What about a tank?" Billy Sandstone asked. "Going to war, you might prefer a tank."

Tina said, "Don't be silly, Billy. A Jeep is all we need."

"Just trying to be helpful, love. And thanks for remembering I exist."

"A Jeep or an Explorer—anything with four-wheel drive," Tina told Elliot. "We don't want to walk farther than necessary. We don't want to walk at all if we can help it. There must be some sort of road into the place, even if it's well concealed. If we're lucky, we'll have Danny when we come out, and he probably won't be in any condition to trek through the Sierras in the dead of winter."

"I have an Explorer," Billy said.

"I guess I could have some money transferred from my Vegas bank," Elliot said. "But what if they're watching my accounts down there? That would lead them to us fast. And since the banks are closed for the holiday, we couldn't do anything until next week. They might find us by then."

"What about your American Express card?" she asked.

"You mean, *charge* a Jeep?"

"There's no limit on the card, is there?"

"No. But—"

"I read a newspaper story once about a guy who bought a Rolls-Royce with his card. You can do that sort of thing as long as they know for sure you're capable of paying the entire bill when it comes due a month later."

"It sounds crazy," Elliot said. "But I guess we can try."

"I have an Explorer," Billy Sandstone said.

"Let's get the address of the local dealership," Tina said. "We'll see if they'll accept the card."

"I have an Explorer!" Billy said.

They turned to him, startled.

"I take my act to Lake Tahoe a few weeks every winter," Billy said. "You know what it's like down there this time of year. Snow up to your ass. I hate flying the Tahoe-Reno shuttle. The plane's so damn small. And you know what a ticky-tacky airport they have at Tahoe. So I usually just drive down the day before I open. An Explorer's the only thing I'd want to take through the mountains on a bad day."

"Are you going to Tahoe soon?" Tina asked.

"No. I don't open until the end of the month."

"Will you be needing the Explorer in the next couple of days?" Elliot asked.

"No."

"Can we borrow it?"

"Well . . . I guess so."

Tina leaned across the corner of the table, grabbed Billy's head in her hands, pulled his face to hers, and kissed him. "You're a lifesaver, Billy. And I mean that literally."

"I'm a small circlet of hard candy?"

"Maybe things are breaking right for us," Elliot said. "Maybe we'll get Danny out of there after all."

"We will," Tina said. "I know it."

The roses in the crystal vase twirled around like a group of spinning, redheaded ballerinas.

Startled, Billy Sandstone jumped up, knocking over his chair.

The drapes drew open, slid shut, drew open, slid shut, even though no one was near the draw cords.

The chandelier began to swing in a lazy circle, and the dangling crystals cast prismatic patterns of light on the walls.

Billy stared, open-mouthed.

Elliot knew how disoriented Billy was feeling, and he felt sorry for the man.

After half a minute all of the unnatural movement stopped, and the room rapidly grew warm again.

"How did you *do* that?" Billy demanded.

"We didn't," Tina said.

"Not a ghost," Billy said adamantly.

"Not a ghost either," Elliot said.

Billy said, "You can borrow the Explorer. But first you've got to tell me what in hell's going on. I don't care how much of a hurry you're in. You can at least tell me a little of it. Otherwise, I'm going to shrivel up and die of curiosity."

Tina consulted Elliot. "Well?"

Elliot said, "Billy, you might be better off not knowing."

"Impossible."

"We're up against some damn dangerous people. If they thought you knew about them—"

"Look," Billy said, "I'm not just a hypnotist. I'm something of a magician. That's really what I most wanted to be, but I didn't really have the skill for it. So I worked up this act built around hypnotism. But magic—that's my one great love. I just have to know how you did that trick with the drapes, the roses. And the corners of the map! I just *have* to know."

Earlier this morning it had occurred to Elliot that he and Tina were the only people who knew that the official story of the Sierras accident was a lie. If they were killed, the truth would die with them, and the cover-up would continue. Considering the high price that they had paid for the pathetically insufficient information they had obtained, he couldn't tolerate the prospect of all their pain and fear and anxiety having been for naught.

Elliot said, "Billy, do you have a tape recorder?"

"Sure. It's nothing fancy. It's a little one I carry with me. I do some comedy lines in the act, and I use the recorder to develop new material, correct problems with my timing."

"It doesn't have to be fancy," Elliot said. "Just so it works. We'll give you a condensed version of the story behind all of this, and we'll record it as we go. Then I'll mail the tape to one of my law partners." He shrugged. "Not much insurance, but better than nothing."

"I'll get the recorder," Billy said, hurrying out of the dining room.

Tina folded the map.

"It's nice to see you smiling again," Elliot said.

"I must be crazy," she said. "We still have dangerous work ahead of us. We're still up against this bunch of cutthroats. We don't know what we'll walk into in those mountains. So why do I feel terrific all of a sudden?"

"You feel good," Elliot said, "because we're not running

anymore. We're going on the offensive. And foolhardy as that might be, it does a lot for a person's self-respect."

"Can a couple of people like us really have a chance of winning when we're up against something as big as the government itself?"

"Well," Elliot said, "I happen to believe that individuals are more apt to act responsibly and morally than institutions ever do, which at least puts us on the side of justice. And I also believe individuals are always smarter and better adapted to survival, at least in the long run, than any institution. Let's just hope my philosophy doesn't turn out to be half-baked."

•   •   •

At one-thirty Kurt Hensen came into George Alexander's office in downtown Reno. "They found the car that Stryker rented. It's in a public lot about three blocks from here."

"Used recently?" Alexander asked.

"No. The engine's cold. There's thick frost on the windows. It's been parked there overnight."

"He's not stupid," Alexander said. "He's probably abandoned the damn thing."

"You want to put a watch on it anyway?"

"Better do that," Alexander said. "Sooner or later they'll make a mistake. Coming back to the car might be it. I don't think so. But it might."

Hensen left the room.

Alexander took a Valium out of a tin that he carried in his jacket pocket, and he washed it down with a swallow of hot coffee, which he poured from the silver pot on his desk. This was his second pill since he'd gotten out of bed just three and a half hours ago, but he still felt edgy.

Stryker and the woman were proving to be worthy opponents.

Alexander never liked to have worthy opponents. He preferred them to be soft and easy.

Where were they?

32

THE DECIDUOUS TREES, STRIPPED OF EVERY LEAF, appeared to be charred, as if this particular winter had been more severe than others and as cataclysmic as a fire. The evergreens—pine, spruce, fir, tamarack—were flocked with snow. A brisk wind spilled over the jagged horizon under a low and menacing sky, snapping ice-hard flurries of snow against the windshield of the Explorer.

Tina was in awe of—and disquieted by—the stately forest that crowded them as they drove north on the narrowing county road. Even if she had not known that these deep woodlands harbored secrets about Danny and the deaths of the other scouts, she would have found them mysterious and unnervingly primeval.

She and Elliot had turned off Interstate 80 a quarter of an hour ago, following the route Danny had marked, circling the edge of the wilderness. On paper they were still moving along the border of the map, with a large expanse of blues and greens on their left. Shortly they would turn off the two-lane blacktop onto another road, which the map specified as "unpaved, nondirt," whatever that was.

After leaving Billy Sandstone's house in his Explorer, Tina and Elliot had not returned to the hotel. They shared a premonition that someone decidedly unfriendly was waiting in their room.

First they had visited a sporting-goods store, purchasing two Gore-Tex/Thermolite stormsuits, boots, snowshoes, compact tins of backpacker's rations, cans of Sterno, and other survival gear. If the rescue attempt went smoothly, as Tina's dream seemed to predict, they wouldn't have any need for much of what they bought. But if the Explorer broke down in the mountains, or if another hitch developed, they wanted to be prepared for the unexpected.

Elliot also bought a hundred rounds of hollow-point ammunition for the pistol. This wasn't insurance against the unforeseen; this was simply prudent planning for the trouble they could foresee all too well.

From the sporting-goods store they had driven out of town, west toward the mountains. At a roadside restaurant, they changed clothes in the rest rooms. His insulated suit was green with white stripes; hers was white with green and black stripes. They looked like a couple of skiers on their way to the slopes.

Entering the formidable mountains, they had become aware of how soon darkness would settle over the sheltered valleys and ravines, and they had discussed the wisdom of proceeding. Perhaps they would have been smarter to turn around, go back to Reno, find another hotel room, and get a fresh start in the morning. But neither wanted to delay. Perhaps the lateness of the hour and the fading light would work against them, but approaching in the night might actually be to their advantage. The thing was—they had momentum. They both felt as if they were on a good roll, and they didn't want to tempt fate by postponing their journey.

Now they were on a narrow county road, moving steadily higher as the valley sloped toward its northern end. Plows had kept the blacktop clean, except for scattered patches of hard-packed snow that filled the potholes, and snow was piled five or six feet high on both sides.

"Soon now," Tina said, glancing at the map that was open on her knees.

"Lonely part of the world, isn't it?"

"You get the feeling that civilization could be destroyed while you're out here, and you'd never be aware of it."

They hadn't seen a house or other structure for two miles. They hadn't passed another car in three miles.

Twilight descended into the winter forest, and Elliot switched on the headlights.

Ahead, on the left, a break appeared in the bank of snow that had been heaped up by the plows. When the Explorer reached this gap, Elliot swung into the turnoff and stopped. A narrow and forbidding track led into the woods, recently plowed but still treacherous. It was little more than one lane wide, and the trees formed a tunnel around it, so that after fifty or sixty feet, it disappeared into premature night. It was unpaved, but a solid bed had been built over the years by the generous and repeated application of oil and gravel.

"According to the map, we're looking for an 'unpaved, nondirt' road," Tina told him.

"I guess this is it."

"Some sort of logging trail?"

"Looks more like the road they always take in those old movies when they're on their way to Dracula's castle."

"Thanks," she said.

"Sorry."

"And it doesn't help that you're right. It *does* look like the road to Dracula's castle."

They drove onto the track, under the roof of heavy evergreen boughs, into the heart of the forest.

I N THE RECTANGULAR ROOM, THREE STORIES UNDER-
ground, computers hummed and murmured.

Dr. Carlton Dombey, who had come on duty twenty
minutes ago, sat at one of the tables against the north wall.
He was studying a set of electroencephalograms and digi-
tally enhanced sonograms and X rays.

After a while he said, "Did you see the pictures they took
of the kid's brain this morning?"

Dr. Aaron Zachariah turned from the bank of video
displays. "I didn't know there were any."

"Yeah. A whole new series."

"Anything interesting?"

"Yes," Dombey said. "The spot that showed up on the
boy's parietal lobe about six weeks ago."

"What about it?"

"Darker, larger."

"Then it's definitely a malignant tumor?"

"That still isn't clear."

"Benign?"

"Can't say for sure either way. The spot doesn't have all the spectrographic characteristics of a tumor."

"Could it be scar tissue?"

"Not exactly that."

"Blood clot?"

"Definitely not."

"Have we learned anything useful?"

"Maybe," Dombey said. "I'm not sure if it's useful or not." He frowned. "It's sure strange, though."

"Don't keep me in suspense," Zachariah said, moving over to the table to examine the tests.

Dombey said, "According to the computer-assigned analysis, the growth is consistent with the nature of normal brain tissue."

Zachariah stared at him. "Come again?"

"It could be a new lump of brain tissue," Dombey told him.

"But that doesn't make sense."

"I know."

"The brain doesn't all of a sudden start growing new little nodes that nobody's ever seen before."

"I know."

"Someone better run a maintenance scan on the computer. It has to be screwed up."

"They did that this afternoon," Dombey said, tapping a pile of printouts that lay on the table. "Everything's supposed to be functioning perfectly."

"Just like the heating system in that isolation chamber is functioning properly," Zachariah said.

Still poring through the test results, stroking his mustache with one hand, Dombey said, "Listen to this . . . the growth rate of the parietal spot is directly proportional to the number of injections the boy's been given. It appeared after his first series of shots six weeks ago. The more frequently the kid is reinfected, the faster the parietal spot grows."

"Then it must be a tumor," Zachariah said.

"Probably. They're going to do an exploratory in the morning."

"Surgery?"

"Yeah. Get a tissue sample for a biopsy."

Zachariah glanced toward the observation window of the isolation chamber. "Damn, there it goes again!"

Dombey saw that the glass was beginning to cloud again. Zachariah hurried to the window.

Dombey stared thoughtfully at the spreading frost. He said, "You know something? That problem with the window . . . if I'm not mistaken, it started at the same time the parietal spot first showed up on the X rays."

Zachariah turned to him. "So?"

"Doesn't that strike you as coincidental?"

"That's exactly how it strikes me. Coincidence. I fail to see any association."

"Well . . . could the parietal spot have a direct connection with the frost somehow?"

"What—you think the boy might be responsible for the changes in air temperature?"

"Could he?"

"How?"

"I don't know."

"Well, you're the one who raised the question."

"I don't know," Dombey said again.

"It doesn't make any sense," Zachariah said. "No sense at all. If you keep coming up with weird suggestions like that, I'll have to run a maintenance check on *you*, Carl."

34

THE OIL-AND-GRAVEL TRAIL LED DEEP INTO THE forest. It was remarkably free of ruts and chuckholes for most of its length, although the Explorer scraped bottom a few times when the track took sudden, sharp dips.

The trees hung low, lower, lower still, until, at last, the ice-crusted evergreen boughs frequently scraped across the roof of the Explorer with a sound like fingernails being drawn down a blackboard.

They passed a few signs that told them the lane they were using was kept open for the exclusive benefit of federal and state wildlife officers and researchers. Only authorized vehicles were permitted, the signs warned.

"Could this secret installation be disguised as a wildlife research center?" Elliot wondered.

"No," she said. "According to the map, that's nine miles into the forest on this track. Danny's instructions are to take a turn north, off this lane, after about five miles."

"We've gone almost five miles since we left the county road," Elliot said.

Branches scraped across the roof, and powdery snow cascaded over the windshield, onto the hood.

As the windshield wipers cast the snow aside, Tina leaned forward, squinting along the headlight beams. "Hold it! I think this is what we're looking for."

He was driving at only ten miles an hour, but she gave him so little warning that he passed the turnoff. He stopped, put the Explorer in reverse, and backed up twenty feet, until the headlights were shining on the trail that she had spotted.

"It hasn't been plowed," he said.

"But look at all the tire marks."

"A lot of traffic's been through here recently."

"This is it," Tina said confidently. "This is where Danny wants us to go."

"It's a damned good thing we have four-wheel drive."

He steered off the plowed lane, onto the snowy trail. The Explorer, equipped with heavy chains on its big winter-tread tires, bit into the snow and chewed its way forward without hesitation.

The new track ran a hundred yards before rising and turning sharply to the right, around the blunt face of a ridge. When they came out of this curve, the trees fell back from the verge, and open sky lay above for the first time since they had departed the county blacktop.

Twilight was gone; night was in command.

Snow began to fall more heavily—yet ahead of them, not a single flake lay in their way. Bizarrely, the unplowed trail had led them to a paved road; steam rose from it, and sections of the pavement were even dry.

"Heat coils embedded in the surface," Elliot said.

"Here in the middle of nowhere."

Stopping the Explorer, he picked up the pistol from the

seat between them, and he flicked off both safeties. He had loaded the depleted magazine earlier; now he jacked a bullet into the chamber. When he put the gun on the seat again, it was ready to be used.

"We can still turn back," Tina said.

"Is that what you want to do?"

"No."

"Neither do I."

A hundred and fifty yards farther, they reached another sharp turn. The road descended into a gully, swung hard to the left this time, and then headed up again.

Twenty yards beyond the bend, the way was barred by a steel gate. On each side of the gate, a nine-foot-high fence, angled outward at the top and strung with wickedly sharp coils of razor wire, stretched out of sight into the forest. The top of the gate was also wrapped with razor wire.

A large sign stood to the right of the roadway, supported on two redwood posts:

PRIVATE PROPERTY
ADMISSION BY KEY CARD ONLY
TRESPASSERS WILL BE PROSECUTED

"They make it sound like someone's hunting lodge," Tina said.

"Intentionally, I'm sure. Now what? You don't happen to have a key card, do you?"

"Danny will help," she said. "That's what the dream was all about."

"How long do we wait here?"

"Not long," she said as the gate swung inward.

"I'll be damned."

The heated road stretched out of sight in the darkness.

"We're coming, Danny," Tina said quietly.

"What if someone else opened the gate?" Elliot asked. "What if Danny didn't have anything to do with it? They might just be letting us in so they can trap us inside."

"It was Danny."

"You're so sure."

"Yes."

He sighed and drove through the gate, which swung shut behind the Explorer.

The road began to climb in earnest, hugging the slopes. It was overhung by huge rock formations and by wind-sculpted cowls of snow. The single lane widened to two lanes in places and switchbacked up the ridges, through more densely packed strands of larger trees. The Explorer labored ever higher into the mountains.

The second gate was one and a half miles past the first, on a short length of straightaway, just over the brow of a hill. It was not merely a gate, but a checkpoint. A guard shack stood to the right of the road, from which the gate was controlled.

Elliot picked up the gun as he brought the Explorer to a full stop at the barrier.

They were no more than six or eight feet from the lighted shack, close enough to see the guard's face as he scowled at them through the large window.

"He's trying to figure out who the devil we are," Elliot said. "He's never seen us or the Explorer, and this isn't the sort of place where there's a lot of new or unexpected traffic."

Inside the hut, the guard plucked a telephone handset from the wall.

"Damn!" Elliot said. "I'll have to go for him."

As Elliot started to open his door, Tina saw something that made her grab his arm. "Wait! The phone doesn't work."

The guard slammed the receiver down. He got to his feet, took a coat from the back of his chair, slipped into it, zippered up, and came out of the shack. He was carrying a submachine gun.

From elsewhere in the night, Danny opened the gate.

The guard stopped halfway to the Explorer and turned toward the gate when he saw it moving, unable to believe his eyes.

Elliot rammed his foot down hard on the accelerator, and the Explorer shot forward.

The guard swung the submachine gun into firing position as they swept past him.

Tina raised her hands in an involuntary and totally useless attempt to ward off the bullets.

But there were no bullets.

No torn metal. No shattered glass. No blood or pain.

They didn't even hear gunfire.

The Explorer roared across the straightaway and careened up the slope beyond, through the tendrils of steam that rose from the black pavement.

Still no gunfire.

As they swung into another curve, Elliot wrestled with the wheel, and Tina was acutely aware that a great dark void lay beyond the shoulder of the road. Elliot held the vehicle on the pavement as they rounded the bend, and then they were out of the guard's line of fire. For two hundred yards ahead, until the road curved once more, nothing threatening was in sight.

The Explorer dropped back to a safer speed.

Elliot said, "Did Danny do all of that?"

"He must have."

"He jinxed the guard's phone, opened the gate, and jammed the submachine gun. What *is* this kid of yours?"

As they ascended into the night, snow began to fall hard and fast in sheets of fine, dry flakes.

After a minute of thought Tina said, "I don't know. I don't know what he is anymore. I don't know what's happened to him, and I don't understand what he's become."

This was an unsettling thought. She began to wonder exactly what sort of little boy they were going to find at the top of the mountain.

35

WITH GLOSSY PHOTOGRAPHS OF CHRISTINA
Evans and Elliot Stryker, George Alexander's men circu-
lated through the hotels in downtown Reno, talking with
desk clerks, bellmen, and other employees. At four-thirty
they obtained a strong, positive identification from a maid at
Harrah's.

In room 918 the Network operatives discovered a cheap
suitcase, dirty clothes, toothbrushes, various toiletry items—
and eleven maps in a leatherette case, which Elliot and Tina,
in their haste and weariness, evidently had overlooked.

Alexander was informed of the discovery at 5:05. By 5:40
everything that Stryker and the woman had left in the hotel
room was brought to Alexander's office.

When he discovered the nature of the maps, when he
realized that one of them was missing, and when he
discovered that the missing map was the one Stryker would
need in order to find the Project Pandora labs, Alexander
felt his face flush with anger and chagrin. "The *nerve!*"

Kurt Hensen was standing in front of Alexander's desk,

picking through the junk that had been brought over from the hotel. "What's wrong?"

"They've gone into the mountains. They're going to try to get into the laboratory," Alexander said. "Someone, some damn turncoat on Project Pandora, must have revealed enough about its location for them to find it with just a little help. They went out and bought *maps*, for God's sake!"

Alexander was enraged by the cool methodicalness that the purchase of the maps seemed to represent. Who were these two people? Why weren't they hiding in a dark corner somewhere? Why weren't they scared witless? Christina Evans was only an ordinary woman. An ex-showgirl! Alexander refused to believe that a showgirl could be of more than average intelligence. And although Stryker had done some heavy military service, that had been ages ago. Where were they getting their strength, their nerve, their endurance? It seemed as if they must have some advantage of which Alexander was not aware. That had to be it. They had to have some advantage he didn't know about. What could it be? What was their edge?

Hensen picked up one of the maps and turned it over in his hands. "I don't see any reason to get too worked up about it. Even if they locate the main gate, they can't get any farther than that. There are thousands of acres behind the fence, and the lab is right smack in the middle. They can't get close to it, let alone inside."

Alexander suddenly realized what their edge was, what kept them going, and he sat up straight in his chair. "They can get inside easily enough if they have a friend in there."

"What?"

"That's it!" Alexander got to his feet. "Not only did someone on Project Pandora tell this Evans woman about her son. That same traitorous bastard is also up there in the labs right this minute, ready to open the gates and doors to them. Some bastard stabbed us in the back. He's going to help the bitch get her son out of there!"

Alexander dialed the number of the military security office at the Sierra lab. It neither rang nor returned a busy signal; the line hissed emptily. He hung up and tried again, with the same result.

He quickly dialed the lab director's office. Dr. Tamaguchi. No ringing. No busy signal. Just the same, unsettling hiss.

"Something's happened up there," Alexander said as he slammed the handset into the cradle. "The phones are out."

"Supposed to be a new storm moving in," Hensen said. "It's probably already snowing in the mountains. Maybe the lines—"

"Use your head, Kurt. Their lines are underground. And they have a cellular backup. No storm can knock out all communications. Get hold of Jack Morgan and tell him to get the chopper ready. We'll meet him at the airport as soon as we can get there."

"He'll need half an hour anyway," Hensen said.

"Not a minute more than that."

"He might not want to go. The weather's bad up there."

"I don't care if it's hailing iron basketballs," Alexander said. "We're going up there in the chopper. There isn't time to drive, no time at all. I'm sure of that. Something's gone wrong. Something's happening at the labs right now."

Hensen frowned. "But trying to take the chopper in there at night . . . in the middle of the storm . . ."

"Morgan's the best."

"It won't be easy."

"If Morgan wants to take it easy," Alexander said, "then he should be flying one of the aerial rides at Disneyland."

"But it seems suicidal—"

"And if *you* want it easy," Alexander said, "you shouldn't have come to work for me. This isn't the Ladies' Aid Society, Kurt."

Hensen's face colored. "I'll call Morgan," he said.

"Yes. You do that."

36

WINDSHIELD WIPERS BEATING AWAY THE SNOW, chain-wrapped tires clanking on the heated roadbed, the Explorer crested a final hill. They came over the rise onto a plateau, an enormous shelf carved in the side of the mountain.

Elliot pumped the brakes, brought the vehicle to a full stop, and unhappily surveyed the territory ahead.

The plateau was basically the work of nature, but man's hand was in evidence. This broad shelf in the mountainside couldn't have been as large or as regularly shaped in its natural state as it was now: three hundred yards wide, two hundred yards deep, almost a perfect rectangle. The ground had been rolled as flat as an airfield and then paved. Not a single tree or any other sizable object remained, nothing behind which a man could hide. Tall lampposts were arrayed across this featureless plain, casting dim, reddish light that was severely directed downward to attract as little attention as possible from aircraft that strayed out of the usual flight patterns and from anyone backpacking else-where in these remote mountains. Yet the weak illumination that the lamps provided was apparently sufficient for the security cameras to obtain clear images of the entire plateau, because cameras were attached to every lamppost, and not an inch of the area escaped their unblinking attention.

"The security people must be watching us on video monitors right now," Elliot said glumly.

"Unless Danny screwed up their cameras," Tina said. "And if he can jam a submachine gun, why couldn't he interfere with a closed-circuit television transmission?"

"You're probably right."

Two hundred yards away, at the far side of the concrete field, stood a one-story windowless building, approximately a hundred feet long, with a steeply pitched slate roof.

"That must be where they're holding him," Elliot said.

"I expected an enormous structure, a gigantic complex."

"It most likely *is* enormous. You're seeing just the front wall. The place is built into the next step of the mountain. God knows how far they cut back into the rock. And it probably goes down several stories too."

"All the way to Hell."

"Could be."

He took his foot off the brake and drove forward, through sheeting snow stained red by the strange light.

Jeeps, Land Rovers, and other four-wheel drive vehicles— eight in all—were lined up in front of the low building, side-by-side in the falling snow.

"Doesn't look like there's a lot of people inside," Tina said. "I thought there'd be a large staff."

"Oh, there is. I'm sure you're right about that too," Elliot said. "The government wouldn't go to all the trouble of hiding this joint out here just to house a handful of researchers or whatever. Most of them probably live in the installation for weeks or months at a time. They wouldn't want a lot of daily traffic coming in and out of here on a forest road that's supposed to be used only by state wildlife officers. That would draw too much attention. Maybe a few of the top people come and go regularly by helicopter. But if this is a military operation, then most of the staff is probably assigned here under the same conditions submariners have to live with. They're allowed to go into Reno for shore leave between cruises, but for long stretches of time, they're confined to this 'ship.' "

He parked beside a Jeep, switched off the headlights, and cut the engine.

The plateau was ethereally silent.

No one yet had come out of the building to challenge them, which most likely meant that Danny had jinxed the video security system.

The fact that they had gotten this far unhurt didn't make Elliot feel any better about what lay ahead of them. How long could Danny continue to pave the way? The boy appeared to have some incredible powers, but he wasn't God. Sooner or later he'd overlook something. He'd make a mistake. Just one mistake. And they would be dead.

"Well," Tina said, unsuccessfully trying to conceal her own anxiety, "we didn't need the snowshoes after all."

"But we might find a use for that coil of rope," Elliot said. He twisted around, leaned over the back of the seat, and quickly fetched the rope from the pile of outdoor gear in the cargo hold. "We're sure to encounter at least a couple of security men, no matter how clever Danny is. We have to be ready to kill them or put them out of action some other way."

"If we have a choice," Tina said, "I'd rather use rope than bullets."

"My sentiments exactly." He picked up the pistol. "Let's see if we can get inside."

They stepped out of the Explorer.

The wind was an animal presence, growling softly. It had teeth, and it nipped their exposed faces. On its breath were sprays of snow like icy spittle.

The only feature in the hundred-foot-long, one-story, windowless concrete facade was a wide steel door. The imposing door offered neither a keyhole nor a keypad. There was no slot in which to put a lock-deactivating ID card. Apparently the door could be opened only from within, after those seeking entrance had been scrutinized by the camera that hung over the portal.

As Elliot and Tina gazed up into the camera lens, the heavy steel barrier rolled aside.

Was it Danny who opened it? Elliot wondered. Or a grinning guard waiting to make an easy arrest?

A steel-walled chamber lay beyond the door. It was the size of a large elevator cab, brightly lighted and uninhabited.

Tina and Elliot crossed the threshold. The outer door slid shut behind them—*whoosh*—making an airtight seal.

A camera and two-way video communications monitor were mounted in the left-hand wall of the vestibule. The screen was filled with crazily wiggling lines, as if it was out of order.

Beside the monitor was a lighted glass plate against which the visitor was supposed to place his right hand, palm-down, within the existing outline of a hand. Evidently the installation's computer scanned the prints of visitors to verify their right to enter.

Elliot and Tina did not put their hands on the plate, but the inner door of the vestibule opened with another puff of compressed air. They went into the next room.

Two uniformed men were anxiously fiddling with the control consoles beneath a series of twenty wall-mounted video displays. All of the screens were filled with wiggling lines.

The youngest of the guards heard the door opening, and he turned, shocked.

Elliot pointed the gun at him. "Don't move."

But the young guard was the heroic type. He was wearing a sidearm—a monstrous revolver—and he was fast with it. He drew, aimed from the hip, and squeezed the trigger.

Fortunately Danny came through like a prince. The revolver refused to fire.

Elliot didn't want to shoot anyone. "Your guns are useless," he said. He was sweating in his Gore-Tex suit, praying that Danny wouldn't let him down. "Let's make this as easy as we can."

When the young guard discovered that his revolver wouldn't work, he threw it.

Elliot ducked, but not fast enough. The gun struck him alongside the head, and he stumbled backward against the steel door.

Tina cried out.

Through sudden tears of pain, Elliot saw the young guard rushing him, and he squeezed off one whisper-quiet shot.

The bullet tore through the guy's left shoulder and spun him around. He crashed into a desk, sending a pile of white and pink papers onto the floor, and then he fell on top of the mess that he had made.

Blinking away tears, Elliot pointed the pistol at the older guard, who had drawn his revolver by now and had found that it didn't work either. "Put the gun aside, sit down, and don't make any trouble."

"How'd you get in here?" the older guard asked, dropping his weapon as he'd been ordered. "Who are you?"

"Never mind," Elliot said. "Just sit down."

But the guard was insistent. "Who *are* you people?"

"Justice," Tina said.

•   •   •

Five minutes west of Reno, the chopper encountered snow. The flakes were hard, dry, and granular; they hissed like driven sand across the Perspex windscreen.

Jack Morgan, the pilot, glanced at George Alexander and said, "This will be hairy." He was wearing night-vision goggles, and his eyes were invisible.

"Just a little snow," Alexander said.

"A storm," Morgan corrected.

"You've flown in storms before."

"In these mountains the downdrafts and crosscurrents are going to be murderous."

"We'll make it," Alexander said grimly.

"Maybe, maybe not," Morgan said. He grinned. "But we're sure going to have fun trying!"

"You're crazy," Hensen said from his seat behind the pilot.

"When we were running operations against the drug lords down in Colombia," Morgan said, "they called me 'Bats,' meaning I had bats in the belfry." He laughed.

Hensen was holding a submachine gun across his lap. He

moved his hands over it slowly, as if he were caressing a woman. He closed his eyes, and in his mind he disassembled and then reassembled the weapon. He had a queasy stomach. He was trying hard not to think about the chopper, the bad weather, and the likelihood that they would take a long, swift, hard fall into a remote mountain ravine.

37

THE YOUNG GUARD WHEEZED IN PAIN, BUT AS FAR
as Tina could see, he was not mortally wounded. The bullet
had partially cauterized the wound as it passed through. The
hole in the guy's shoulder was reassuringly clean, and it
wasn't bleeding much.

"You'll live," Elliot said.

"I'm dying. Jesus!"

"No. It hurts like hell, but it isn't serious. The bullet
didn't sever any major blood vessels."

"How the hell would you know?" the wounded man
asked, straining his words through clenched teeth.

"If you lie still, you'll be all right. But if you agitate the
wound, you might tear a bruised vessel, and then you'll
bleed to death."

"Shit," the guard said shakily.

"Understand?" Elliot asked.

The man nodded. His face was pale, and he was sweating.

Elliot tied the older guard securely to a chair. He didn't
want to tie the wounded man's hands, so they carefully
moved him to a supply closet and locked him in there.

"How's your head?" Tina asked Elliot, gently touching the ugly knot that had raised on his temple, where the guard's gun had struck him.

Elliot winced. "Stings."

"It's going to bruise."

"I'll be all right," he said.

"Dizzy?"

"No."

"Seeing double?"

"No," he said. "I'm fine. I wasn't hit that hard. There's no concussion. Just a headache. Come on. Let's find Danny and get him out of this place."

They crossed the room, passing the guard who was bound and gagged in his chair. Tina carried the remaining rope, and Elliot kept the gun.

Opposite the sliding door through which she and Elliot had entered the security room was another door of more ordinary dimensions and construction. It opened onto a junction of two hallways, which Tina had discovered a few minutes ago, just after Elliot had shot the guard, when she had peeked through the door to see if reinforcements were on the way.

The corridors had been deserted then. They were deserted now too. Silent. White tile floors. White walls. Harsh fluorescent lighting.

One passageway extended fifty feet to the left of the door and fifty feet to the right; on both sides were more doors, all shut, plus a bank of four elevators on the right. The intersecting hall began directly in front of them, across from the guardroom, and bored at least four hundred feet into the mountain; a long row of doors waited on each side of it, and other corridors opened off it as well.

They whispered:

"You think Danny is on this floor?"

"I don't know."

"Where do we start?"

"We can't just go around jerking open doors."

"People are going to be behind some of them."

"And the fewer people we encounter—"

"—the better chance we have of getting out alive."

They stood, indecisive, looking left, then right, and then straight ahead.

Ten feet away, a set of elevator doors opened.

Tina cringed back against the corridor wall.

Elliot pointed the pistol at the lift.

No one got out.

The cab was at such an angle from them that they couldn't see who was in it.

The doors closed.

Tina had the sickening feeling that someone had been about to step out, had sensed their presence, and had gone away to get help.

Even before Elliot had lowered the pistol, the same set of elevator doors slid open again. Then slid shut. Open. Shut. Open. Shut. Open.

The air grew cold.

With a sigh of relief, Tina said, "It's Danny. He's showing us the way."

Nevertheless, they crept cautiously to the elevator and peered inside apprehensively. The cab was empty, and they boarded it, and the doors glided together.

According to the indicator board above the doors, they were on the fourth of four levels. The first floor was at the bottom of the structure, the deepest underground.

The cab controls would not operate unless one first inserted an acceptable ID card into a slot above them. But Tina and Elliot didn't need the computer's authorization to use the elevator; not with Danny on their side. The light on the indicator board changed from four to three to two, and the air inside the lift became so frigid that Tina's breath hung in clouds before her. The doors slid open three floors below the surface, on the next to the last level.

They stepped into a hallway exactly like the one they had left upstairs.

The elevator doors closed behind them, and around them the air grew warmer again.

Five feet away, a door stood ajar, and animated conversation drifted out of the room beyond. Men's and women's voices. Half a dozen or more, judging by the sound of them. Indistinct words. Laughter.

Tina knew that she and Elliot were finished if someone came out of that room and saw them. Danny seemed able to work miracles with inanimate objects, but he could not control people, like the guard upstairs, whom Elliot had been forced to shoot. If they were discovered and confronted by a squad of angry security men, Elliot's one pistol might not be enough to discourage an assault. Then, even with Danny jamming the enemy's weapons, she and Elliot would be able to escape only if they slaughtered their way out, and she knew that neither of them had the stomach for that much murder, perhaps not even in self-defense.

Laughter pealed from the nearby room again, and Elliot said softly, "Where now?"

"I don't know."

This level was the same size as the one on which they entered the complex: more than four hundred feet on one

side, and more than one hundred feet on the other. Forty
thousand or fifty thousand square feet to search. How many
rooms? Forty? Fifty? Sixty? A hundred, counting closets?

Just as she was beginning to despair, the air began to turn
cold again. She looked around, waiting for some sign from
her child, and she and Elliot twitched in surprise when the
overhead fluorescent tube winked off, then came on again.
The tube to the left of the first one also flickered. Then a
third tube sputtered, still farther to the left.

They followed the blinking lights to the end of the short
wing in which the elevators were situated. The corridor
terminated in an airtight steel door similar to those found on
submarines; the burnished metal glowed softly, and light
gleamed off the big round-headed rivets.

As Tina and Elliot reached that barrier, the wheel-like
handle in the center spun around. The door cycled open.
Because he had the pistol, Elliot went through first, but Tina
was close behind him.

They were in a rectangular room approximately forty feet
by twenty. At the far end a window filled the center of the
other short wall and apparently offered a view of a cold-
storage vault; it was white with frost. To the right of the
window was another airtight door like the one through
which they'd just entered. On the left, computers and other
equipment extended the length of the chamber. There were
more video displays than Tina could count at a glance; most
were switched on, and data flowed in the form of graphs,
charts, and numbers. Tables were arranged along the fourth
wall, covered with books, file folders, and numerous instruments that Tina could not identify.

A curly-haired man with a bushy mustache sat at one of
the tables. He was tall, broad-shouldered, in his fifties, and

he was wearing medical whites. He was paging through a book when they burst in. Another man, younger than the first, clean-shaven, also dressed in white, was sitting at a computer, reading the information that flashed onto the display screen. Both men looked up, speechless with amazement.

Covering the strangers with the menacing, silencer-equipped pistol, Elliot said, "Tina, close the door behind us. Lock it if you can. If security discovers we're here, at least they won't be able to get their hands on us for a while."

She swung the steel door shut. In spite of its tremendous weight, it moved more smoothly and easily than an average door in an average house. She spun the wheel and located a pin that, when pushed, prevented anyone from turning the handle back to the unlocked position.

"Done," she said.

The man at the computer suddenly turned to the keyboard and started typing.

"Stop that," Elliot advised.

But the guy wasn't going to stop until he had instructed the computer to trigger the alarms.

Maybe Danny could prevent the alarms from sounding, and maybe he could not, so Elliot fired once, and the display screen dissolved into thousands of splinters of glass.

The man cried out, pushed his wheeled chair away from the keyboard, and thrust to his feet. "Who the hell are you?"

"I'm the one who has the gun," Elliot said sharply. "If that's not good enough for you, I can shut you down the same way I did that damn machine. Now park your ass in that chair before I blow your fuckin' head off."

Tina had never heard Elliot speak in this tone of voice,

and his furious expression was sufficient to chill even her. He seemed to be utterly vicious and capable of anything.

The young man in white was impressed too. He sat down, pale.

"All right," Elliot said, addressing the two men. "If you cooperate, you won't get hurt." He waved the barrel of the gun at the older man. "What's your name?"

"Carl Dombey."

"What're you doing here?"

"I work here," Dombey said, puzzled by the question.

"I mean, what's your job?"

"I'm a research scientist."

"What science?"

"My degrees are in biology and biochemistry."

Elliot pointed at the younger man. "What about you?"

"What about me?" the younger one said sullenly.

Elliot extended his arm, lining up the muzzle of the pistol with the bridge of the guy's nose.

"I'm Dr. Zachariah," the younger man said.

"Biology?"

"Yes. Specializing in bacteriology and virology."

Elliot lowered the gun but still kept it pointed in their general direction. "We have some questions, and you two better have the answers."

Dombey, who clearly did not share his associate's compulsion to play hero, remained docile in his chair. "Questions about what?"

Tina moved to Elliot's side. To Dombey, she said, "We want to know what you've done to him, where he is."

"Who?"

"My boy. Danny Evans."

She could not have said anything else that would have

had a fraction as much impact on them as the words she'd spoken. Dombey's eyes bulged. Zachariah regarded her as he might have done if she had been dead on the floor and then miraculously risen.

"My God," Dombey said.

"How can you be here?" Zachariah asked. "You can't. You can't possibly be here."

"It seems possible to me," Dombey said. "In fact, all of a sudden, it seems inevitable. I knew this whole business was too dirty to end any way but disaster." He sighed, as if a great weight had been lifted from him. "I'll answer all of your questions, Mrs. Evans."

Zachariah swung toward him. "You can't do that!"

"Oh, no?" Dombey said. "Well, if you don't think I can, just sit back and listen. You're in for a surprise."

"You took a loyalty oath," Zachariah said. "A secrecy oath. If you tell them anything about this . . . the scandal . . . the public outrage . . . the release of military secrets . . ." He was sputtering. "You'll be a traitor to your country."

"No," Dombey said. "I'll be a traitor to this installation. I'll be a traitor to my colleagues, maybe. But not to my country. My country's far from perfect, but what's been done to Danny Evans isn't something that *my* country would approve of. The whole Danny Evans project is the work of a few megalomaniacs."

"Dr. Tamaguchi isn't a megalomaniac," Dr. Zachariah said, as if genuinely offended.

"Of course he is," Dombey said. "He thinks he's a great man of science, destined for immortality, a man of great works. And a lot of people around him, a lot of people protecting him, people in research and people in charge of project security—they're also megalomaniacs. The things done to Danny Evans don't constitute 'great work.' They won't earn anyone immortality. It's sick, and I'm washing my hands of it." He looked at Tina again. "Ask your questions."

"No," Zachariah said. "You damn fool."

Elliot took the remaining rope from Tina, and he gave her the pistol. "I'll have to tie and gag Dr. Zachariah, so we can listen to Dr. Dombey's story in peace. If either one of them makes a wrong move, blow him away."

"Don't worry," she said. "I won't hesitate."

"You're not going to tie me," Zachariah said.

Smiling, Elliot advanced on him with the rope.

• • •

A wall of frigid air fell on the chopper and drove it down. Jack Morgan fought the wind, stabilized the aircraft, and pulled it up only a few feet short of the treetops.

"Whoooooooeeeee!" the pilot said. "It's like breaking in a wild horse."

In the chopper's brilliant floodlights, there was little to see but driving snow. Morgan had removed his night-vision goggles.

"This is crazy," Hensen said. "We're not flying into an ordinary storm. It's a blizzard."

Ignoring Hensen, Alexander said, "Morgan, goddamn you, I know you can do it."

"Maybe," Morgan said. "I wish I was as sure as you. But I think maybe I can. What I'm going to do is make an indirect approach to the plateau, moving with the wind instead of across it. I'm going to cut up this next valley and then swing back around toward the installation and try to avoid some of these crosscurrents. They're murder. It'll take us a little longer that way, but at least we'll have a fighting chance. If the rotors don't ice up and cut out."

A particularly fierce blast of wind drove snow into the windscreen with such force that, to Kurt Hensen, it sounded like shotgun pellets.

38

Zachariah was on the floor, bound and gagged, glaring up at them with hate and rage.

"You'll want to see your boy first," Dombey said. "Then I can tell you how he came to be here."

"Where is he?" Tina asked shakily.

"In the isolation chamber." Dombey indicated the window in the back wall of the room. "Come on." He went to the big pane of glass, where only a few small spots of frost remained.

For a moment Tina couldn't move, afraid to see what they had done to Danny. Fear spread tendrils through her and rooted her feet to the floor.

Elliot touched her shoulder. "Don't keep Danny waiting. He's been waiting a long time. He's been calling you for a long time."

She took a step, then another, and before she knew it, she was at the window, beside Dombey.

A standard hospital bed stood in the center of the isolation chamber. It was ringed by ordinary medical equipment as well as by several mysterious electronic monitors.

Danny was in the bed, on his back. Most of him was covered, but his head, raised on a pillow, was turned toward the window. He stared at her through the side rails of the bed.

"Danny," she said softly. She had the irrational fear that, if she said his name loudly, the spell would be broken and he would vanish forever.

His face was thin and sallow. He appeared to be older than twelve. Indeed, he looked like a little old man.

Dombey, sensing her shock, said, "He's emaciated. For the past six or seven weeks, he hasn't been able to keep anything but liquids on his stomach. And not a lot of those."

Danny's eyes were strange. Dark, as always. Big and round, as always. But they were sunken, ringed by unhealthy dark skin, which was *not* the way they had always been. She couldn't pinpoint what else about his eyes made him so different from any eyes she had ever seen, but as she met Danny's gaze, a shiver passed through her, and she felt a profound and terrible pity for him.

The boy blinked, and with what appeared to be great effort, at the cost of more than a little pain, he withdrew one arm from under the covers and reached out toward her. His arm was skin and bones, a pathetic stick. He thrust it between two of the side rails, and he opened his small weak hand beseechingly, reaching for love, trying desperately to touch her.

Her voice quivering, she said to Dombey, "I want to be with my boy. I want to hold him."

As the three of them moved to the airtight steel door that led into the room beyond the window, Elliot said, "Why is he in an isolation chamber? Is he ill?"

"Not now," Dombey said, stopping at the door, turning to

them, evidently disturbed by what he had to tell them. "Right now he's on the verge of starving to death because it's been so long since he's been able to keep any food on his stomach. But he's not infectious. He *has* been very infectious, off and on, but not at the moment. He's had a unique disease, a man-made disease created in the laboratory. He's the only person who's ever survived it. He has a natural antibody in his blood that helps him fight off this particular virus, even though it's an artificial bug. That's what fascinated Dr. Tamaguchi. He's the head of this installation. Dr. Tamaguchi drove us very hard until we isolated the antibody and figured out why it was so effective against the disease. Of course, when that was accomplished, Danny was of no more scientific value. To Tamaguchi, that meant he was of no value at all . . . except in the crudest way. Tamaguchi decided to test Danny to destruction. For almost two months they've been reinfecting his body over and over again, letting the virus wear him down, trying to discover how many times he can lick it before it finally licks him. You see, there's no permanent immunity to this disease. It's like strep throat or the common cold or like cancer, because you can get it again and again . . . if you're lucky enough to beat it the first time. Today, Danny just beat it for the fourteenth time."

Tina gasped in horror.

Dombey said, "Although he gets weaker every day, for some reason he wins out over the virus faster each time. But each victory drains him. The disease *is* killing him, even if indirectly. It's killing him by sapping his strength. Right now he's clean and uninfected. Tomorrow they intend to stick another dirty needle in him."

"My God," Elliot said softly. "My God."

Gripped by rage and revulsion, Tina started at Dombey. "I can't believe what I just heard."

"Brace yourself," Dombey said grimly. "You haven't heard half of it yet."

He turned away from them, spun the wheel on the steel door, and swung that barrier inward.

Minutes ago, when Tina had first peered through the observation window, when she had seen the frighteningly thin child, she had told herself that she would not cry. Danny didn't need to see her cry. He needed love and attention and protection. Her tears might upset him. And judging from his appearance, she was concerned that any serious emotional disturbance would literally destroy him.

Now, as she approached his bed, she bit her lower lip so hard that she tasted blood. She struggled to contain her tears, but she needed all her willpower to keep her eyes dry.

Danny became excited when he saw her drawing near, and in spite of his terrible condition, he shakily thrust himself into a sitting position, clutching at the bed rails with one frail, trembling hand, eagerly extending his other hand toward her.

She took the last few steps haltingly, her heart pounding, her throat constricted. She was overwhelmed with the joy of seeing him again but also with fear when she realized how hideously wasted he was.

When their hands touched, his small fingers curled tightly around hers. He held on with a fierce, desperate strength.

"Danny," she said wonderingly. "Danny, Danny."

From somewhere deep inside of him, from far down beneath all the pain and fear and anguish, Danny found a smile for her. It wasn't much of a smile; it quivered on his lips as if sustaining it required more energy than lifting a hundred-pound weight. It was such a tentative smile, such a vague ghost of all the broad warm smiles she remembered, that it broke her heart.

"Mom."

Tina could hardly recognize his weary, cracking voice.

"Mom."

"It's all right," she said.

He shuddered.

"It's all over, Danny. It's all right now."

"Mom . . . Mom . . ." His face spasmed, and his brave smile dissolved, and an agonized groan escaped him. "Ooooohhhhh, *Mommy* . . ."

Tina pushed down the railing and sat on the edge of the bed and carefully pulled Danny into her arms. He was a rag doll with only meager scraps of stuffing, a fragile and timorous creature, nothing whatsoever like the happy, vibrant, active boy that he had once been. At first she was afraid to hug him, for fear he would shatter in her embrace. But he hugged her very hard, and again she was surprised by how much strength he could still summon from his devastated body. Shaking violently, snuffling, he put his face against her neck, and she felt his scalding tears on her skin. She couldn't control herself any longer, so she allowed her own tears to come, rivers of tears, a flood. Putting one hand on the boy's back to press him against her, she discovered how shockingly spindly he was: each rib and vertebra so prominent that she seemed to be holding a skeleton. When she pulled him into her lap, he trailed wires that led from electrodes on his skin to the monitoring machines around the bed, like an abandoned marionette. As his legs came out from under the covers, the hospital gown slipped off them, and Tina saw that his poor limbs were too bony and fleshless to safely support him. Weeping, she cradled him, rocked him, crooned to him, and told him that she loved him.

Danny was alive.

39

JACK MORGAN'S STRATEGY OF FLYING WITH THE land instead of over it was a smashing success. Alexander was increasingly confident that they would reach the installation unscathed, and he was aware that even Kurt Hensen, who hated flying with Morgan, was calmer now than he had been ten minutes ago.

The chopper hugged the valley floor, streaking northward, ten feet above an ice-blocked river, still forced to make its way through a snowfall that nearly blinded them, but sheltered from the worst of the storm's turbulence by the walls of mammoth evergreens that flanked the river. Silvery, almost luminous, the frozen river was an easy trail to follow. Occasionally wind found the aircraft and pummeled it, but the chopper bobbed and weaved like a good boxer, and it no longer seemed in danger of being dealt a knockout punch.

"How long?" Alexander asked.

"Ten minutes. Maybe fifteen," Morgan said. "Unless."

"Unless what?"

"Unless the blades cake up with ice. Unless the drive shaft and the rotor joints freeze."

"Is that likely?" Alexander asked.

"It's certainly something to think about," Morgan said. "And there's always the possibility I'll misjudge the terrain in the dark and ram us right into the side of a hill."

"You won't," Alexander said. "You're too good."

"Well," Morgan said, "there's always the chance I'll screw up. That's what keeps it from getting boring."

* * *

Tina prepared Danny for the journey out of his prison. One by one, she removed the eighteen electrodes that were fixed to his head and body. When she gingerly pulled off the adhesive tape, he whimpered, and she winced when she saw the rawness of his skin under the bandage. No effort had been made to keep him from chafing.

While Tina worked on Danny, Elliot questioned Carl Dombey. "What goes on in this place? Military research?"

"Yes," Dombey said.

"Strictly biological weapons?"

"Biological and chemical. Recombinant DNA experiments. At any one time, we have thirty to forty projects underway."

"I thought the U.S. got out of the chemical and biological weapons race a long time ago."

"For the public record, we did," Dombey said. "It made the politicians look good. But in reality the work goes on. It has to. This is the only facility of its kind we have. The Chinese have three like it. The Russians . . . they're now supposed to be our new friends, but they keep developing bacteriological weapons, new and more virulent strains of viruses, because they're broke, and this is a lot cheaper than other weapons systems. Iraq has a big bio-chem warfare project, and Libya, and God knows who else. Lots of people out there in the rest of the world—they believe in chemical and biological warfare. They don't see anything immoral about it. If they felt they had some terrific new bug that we didn't know about, something against which we couldn't retaliate in kind, they'd use it on us."

Elliot said, "But if racing to keep up with the Chinese—or the Russians or the Iraqis—can create situations like the one we've got here, where an innocent child gets ground up in the machine, then aren't we just becoming monsters too? Aren't we letting our fears of the enemy turn *us* into *them*? And isn't that just another way of losing the war?"

Dombey nodded. As he spoke, he smoothed the spikes of his mustache. "That's the same question I've been wrestling with ever since Danny got caught in the gears. The problem is that some flaky people are attracted to this kind of work because of the secrecy and because you really do get a sense of power from designing weapons that can kill millions of people. So megalomaniacs like Tamaguchi get involved. Men like Aaron Zachariah here. They abuse their power, pervert their duties. There's no way to screen them out ahead of time. But if we closed up shop, if we stopped doing this sort of research just because we were afraid of men like Tamaguchi winding up in charge of it, we'd be conceding so much ground to our enemies that we wouldn't survive for long. I suppose we have to learn to live with the lesser of the evils."

Tina removed an electrode from Danny's neck, carefully peeling the tape off his skin.

The child still clung to her, but his deeply sunken eyes were riveted on Dombey.

"I'm not interested in the philosophy or morality of biological warfare," Tina said. "Right now I just want to know how the hell Danny wound up in this place."

"To understand that," Dombey said, "you have to go back twenty months. It was around then that a Chinese scientist named Li Chen defected to the United States, carrying a diskette record of China's most important and dangerous new biological weapon in a decade. They call the stuff 'Wuhan-400' because it was developed at their RDNA labs outside of the city of Wuhan, and it was the four-hundredth viable strain of man-made microorganisms created at that research center.

"Wuhan-400 is a perfect weapon. It afflicts only human beings. No other living creature can carry it. And like syphilis, Wuhan-400 can't survive outside a living human body for longer than a minute, which means it can't permanently contaminate objects or entire places the way anthrax and other virulent microorganisms can. And when the host expires, the Wuhan-400 within him perishes a short while later, as soon as the temperature of the corpse drops below eighty-six degrees Fahrenheit. Do you see the advantage of all this?"

Tina was too busy with Danny to think about what Carl Dombey had said, but Elliot knew what the scientist meant. "If I understand you, the Chinese could use Wuhan-400 to wipe out a city or a country, and then there wouldn't be any need for them to conduct a tricky and expensive decontamination before they moved in and took over the conquered territory."

"Exactly," Dombey said. "And Wuhan-400 has other, equally important advantages over most biological agents.

For one thing, you can become an infectious carrier only four hours after coming into contact with the virus. That's an incredibly short incubation period. Once infected, no one lives more than twenty-four hours. Most die in twelve. It's worse than the Ebola virus in Africa—infinitely worse. Wuhan-400's kill-rate is one hundred percent. No one is supposed to survive. The Chinese tested it on God knows how many political prisoners. They were never able to find an antibody or an antibiotic that was effective against it. The virus migrates to the brain stem, and there it begins secreting a toxin that liberally eats away brain tissue like battery acid dissolving cheesecloth. It destroys the part of the brain that controls all of the body's automatic functions. The victim simply ceases to have a pulse, functioning organs, or any urge to breathe."

"And that's the disease Danny survived," Elliot said.

"Yes," Dombey said. "As far as we know, he's the only one who ever has."

Tina had pulled the blanket off the bed and folded it in half, so she could wrap Danny in it for the trip out to the Explorer. Now she looked up from the task of bundling the child, and she said to Dombey, "But why was he infected in the first place?"

"It was an accident," Dombey said.

"I've heard that one before."

"This time it's true," Dombey said. "After Li Chen defected with all the data on Wuhan-400, he was brought here. We immediately began working with him, trying to engineer an exact duplicate of the virus. In relatively short order we accomplished that. Then we began to study the bug, searching for a handle on it that the Chinese had overlooked."

"And someone got careless," Elliot said.

"Worse," Dombey said. "Someone got careless and *stupid*. Almost thirteen months ago, when Danny and the other boys in his troop were on their winter survival outing, one of our scientists, a quirky son of a bitch named Larry Bollinger, accidentally contaminated himself while he was working alone one morning in this lab."

Danny's hand tightened on Christina's, and she stroked his head, soothing him. To Dombey, she said, "Surely you have safeguards, procedures to follow when and if—"

"Of course," Dombey said. "You're trained what to do from the day you start to work here. In the event of accidental contamination, you immediately set off an alarm. Immediately. Then you seal the room you're working in. If there's an adjoining isolation chamber, you're supposed to go into it and lock the door after yourself. A decontamination crew moves in swiftly to clean up whatever mess you've made in the lab. And if you've infected yourself with something curable, you'll be treated. If it's not curable . . . you'll be attended to in isolation until you die. That's one reason our pay scale is so high. Hazardous-duty pay. The risk is part of the job."

"Except this Larry Bollinger didn't see it that way," Tina said bitterly. She was having difficulty wrapping Danny securely in the blanket because he wouldn't let go of her. With smiles, murmured assurances, and kisses planted on his frail hands, she finally managed to persuade him to tuck both of his arms close to his body.

"Bollinger snapped. He just went right off the rails," Dombey said, obviously embarrassed that one of his colleagues would lose control of himself under those circumstances. Dombey began to pace as he talked. "Bollinger knew how fast Wuhan-400 claims its victims, and he just panicked. Flipped out. Apparently, he convinced himself he could run away from the infection. God knows, that's exactly what he tried to do. He didn't turn in an alarm. He walked out of the lab, went to his quarters, dressed in outdoor clothes, and left the complex. He wasn't scheduled for R and R, and on the spur of the moment he couldn't think of an excuse to sign out one of the Range Rovers, so he tried to escape on foot. He told the guards he was going snowshoeing for a couple of hours. That's something a lot of us do during the winter. It's good exercise, and it gets you out of this hole in the ground for a while. Anyway, Bollinger wasn't interested in exercise. He tucked the snowshoes under his arm and took off down the mountain road, the same one I presume you came in on. Before he got to the guard shack at the upper gate, he climbed onto the ridge above, used the snowshoes to circle the guard, returned to the road, and threw the snowshoes away. Security eventually found them. Bollinger was probably at the bottom gate two and a half hours after he walked out of the door here, three hours after he was infected. That was just about the time that another researcher walked into his lab, saw the cultures of Wuhan-400 broken open on the floor, and set off the alarm. Meanwhile, in spite of the razor wire, Bollinger climbed over the fence. Then he made his way to the road that serves the wildlife research center. He started out of the forest, toward the county lane, which is about five miles from the turnoff to the labs, and after only three miles—"

"He ran into Mr. Jaborski and the scouts," Elliot said.

"And by then he was able to pass the disease on to

them," Tina said as she finished bundling Danny into the blanket.

"Yeah," Dombey said. "He must have reached the scouts five or five and a half hours after he was infected. By then he was worn out. He'd used up most of his physical reserves getting out of the lab reservation, and he was also beginning to feel some of the early symptoms of Wuhan-400. Dizziness. Mild nausea. The scoutmaster had parked the expedition's minibus on a lay-by about a mile and a half into the woods, and he and his assistant and the kids had walked in another half-mile before they encountered Larry Bollinger. They were just about to move off the road, into the trees, so they would be away from any sign of civilization when they set up camp for their first night in the wilderness. When Bollinger discovered they had a vehicle, he tried to persuade them to drive him all the way into Reno. When they were reluctant, he made up a story about a friend being stranded in the mountains with a broken leg. Jaborski didn't believe Bollinger's story for a minute, but he finally offered to take him to the wildlife center where a rescue effort could be mounted. That wasn't good enough for Bollinger, and he got hysterical. Both Jaborski and the other scout leader decided they might have a dangerous character on their hands. That was when the security team arrived. Bollinger tried to run from them. Then he tried to tear open one of the security men's decontamination suits. They were forced to shoot him."

"The spacemen," Danny said.

Everyone stared at him.

He huddled in his yellow blanket on the bed, and the memory made him shiver. "The spacemen came and took us away."

"Yeah," Dombey said. "They probably did look a little bit like spacemen in their decontamination suits. They brought everyone here and put them in isolation. One day later all of them were dead . . . except Danny." Dombey sighed. "Well . . . you know most of the rest."

40

THE HELICOPTER CONTINUED TO FOLLOW THE FROzen river north, through the snow-swept valley.

The ghostly, slightly luminous winter landscape made George Alexander think of graveyards. He had an affinity for cemeteries. He liked to take long, leisurely walks among the tombstones. For as long as he could remember, he had been fascinated with death, with the mechanics and the meaning of it, and he had longed to know what it was like on the other side—without, of course, wishing to commit himself to a one-way journey there. He didn't want to die; he only wanted to *know*. Each time that he personally killed someone, he felt as if he were establishing another link to the world beyond this one; and he hoped, once he had made enough of those linkages, that he would be rewarded with a vision from the other side. One day maybe he would be standing in a graveyard, before the tombstone of one of his victims, and the person he had killed would reach out to him from beyond and let him see, in some vivid clairvoyant fashion, exactly what death was like. And then he would know.

"Not long now," Jack Morgan said.

Alexander peered anxiously through the sheeting snow into which the chopper moved like a blind man running full-steam into endless darkness. He touched the gun that he carried in a shoulder holster, and he thought of Christina Evans.

To Kurt Hensen, Alexander said, "Kill Stryker on sight. We don't need him for anything. But don't hurt the woman. I want to question her. She's going to tell me who the traitor is. She's going to tell me who helped her get into the labs even if I have to break her fingers one at a time to make her open up."

　　　•　　•　　•

In the isolation chamber, when Dombey finished speaking, Tina said, "Danny looks so awful. Even though he doesn't have the disease anymore, will he be all right?"

"I think so," Dombey said. "He just needs to be fattened up. He couldn't keep anything on his stomach because recently they've been reinfecting him, testing him to destruction, like I said. But once he's out of here, he should put weight on fast. There is one thing . . ."

Tina stiffened at the note of worry in Dombey's voice. "What? What one thing?"

"Since all these reinfections, he's developed a spot on the parietal lobe of the brain."

Tina felt ill. "No."

"But apparently it isn't life-threatening," Dombey said quickly. "As far as we can determine, it's not a tumor. Neither a malignant nor a benign tumor. At least it doesn't have any of the characteristics of a tumor. It isn't scar tissue either. And not a blood clot."

"Then what is it?" Elliot asked.

Dombey pushed one hand through his thick, curly hair. "The current analysis says the new growth is consistent with the structure of normal brain tissue. Which doesn't make sense. But we've checked our data a hundred times, and we can't find anything wrong with that diagnosis. Except it's impossible. What we're seeing on the X rays isn't within our experience. So when you get him out of here, take him to a brain specialist. Take him to a dozen specialists until someone can tell you what's wrong with him. There doesn't appear to be anything life-threatening about the parietal spot, but you sure should keep a watch on it."

Tina met Elliot's eyes, and she knew that the same thought was running through both their minds. Could this spot on Danny's brain have anything to do with the boy's psychic power? Were his latent psychic abilities brought to the surface as a direct result of the man-made virus with which he had been repeatedly infected? Crazy—but it didn't seem any more unlikely than that he had fallen victim to Project Pandora in the first place. And as far as Tina could see, it was the only thing that explained Danny's phenomenal new powers.

Apparently afraid that she would voice her thoughts and alert Dombey to the incredible truth of the situation, Elliot consulted his wristwatch and said, "We ought to get out of here."

"When you leave," Dombey said, "you should take some files on Danny's case. They're on the table closest to the outer door—that black box full of diskettes. They'll help support your story when you go to the press with it. And for God's sake, splash it all over the newspapers as fast as you can. As long as you're the only ones outside of here who know what happened, you're marked people."

"We're painfully aware of that," Elliot acknowledged.

Tina said, "Elliot, you'll have to carry Danny. He can't walk. He's not too heavy for me, worn down as he is, but he's still an awkward bundle."

Elliot gave her the pistol and started toward the bed.

"Could you do me a favor first?" Dombey asked.

"What's that?"

"Let's move Dr. Zachariah in here and take the gag out of his mouth. Then you tie me up and gag me, leave me in the outer room. I'm going to make them believe he was the one who cooperated with you. In fact, when you tell your story to the press, maybe you could slant it that way."

Tina shook her head, puzzled. "But after everything you said to Zachariah about this place being run by megalomaniacs, and after you've made it so clear you don't agree with everything that goes on here, why do you want to stay?"

"The hermit's life agrees with me, and the pay is good," Dombey said. "And if I don't stay here, if I walk away and get a job at a civilian research center, that'll be just one less rational voice in this place. There are a lot of people here who have some sense of social responsibility about this work. If they all left, they'd just be turning the place over to men like Tamaguchi and Zachariah, and there wouldn't be anyone around to balance things. What sort of research do you think they might do *then*?"

"But once our story breaks in the papers," Tina said, "they'll probably just shut this place down."

"No way," Dombey said. "Because the work has to be

done. The balance of power with totalitarian states like China has to be maintained. They might pretend to close us down, but they won't. Tamaguchi and some of his closest aides will be fired. There'll be a big shake-up, and that'll be good. If I can make them think that Zachariah was the one who spilled the secrets to you, if I can protect my position here, maybe I'll be promoted and have more influence." He smiled. "At the very least, I'll get more pay."

"All right," Elliot said. "We'll do what you want. But we've got to be fast about it."

They moved Zachariah into the isolation chamber and took the gag out of his mouth. He strained at his ropes and cursed Elliot. Then he cursed Tina and Danny and Dombey. When they took Danny out of the small room, they couldn't hear Zachariah's shouted invectives through the airtight steel door.

As Elliot used the last of the rope to tie Dombey, the scientist said, "Satisfy my curiosity."

"About what?"

"Who told you your son was here? Who let you into the labs?"

Tina blinked. She couldn't think what to say.

"Okay, okay," Dombey said. "You don't want to rat on whoever it was. But just tell me one thing. Was it one of the security people, or was it someone on the medical staff? I'd like to think it was a doctor, one of my own, who finally did the right thing."

Tina looked at Elliot.

Elliot shook his head: *no*.

She agreed that it might not be wise to let anyone know what powers Danny had acquired. The world would regard him as a freak, and everyone would want to gawk at him, put him on display. And for sure, if the people in this installation got the idea that Danny's newfound psychic abilities were a result of the parietal spot caused by his repeated exposure to Wuhan-400, they would want to test him, poke and probe at him. No, she wouldn't tell anyone what Danny could do. Not yet. Not until she and Elliot figured out what effect that revelation would have on the boy's life.

"It was someone on the medical staff," Elliot lied. "It was a doctor who let us in here."

"Good," Dombey said. "I'm glad to hear it. I wish I'd had enough guts to do it a long time ago."

Elliot worked a wadded handkerchief into Dombey's mouth.

Tina opened the outer airtight door.

Elliot picked up Danny. "You hardly weigh a thing, kid. We'll have to take you straight to McDonald's and pack you full of burgers and fries."

Danny smiled weakly at him.

Holding the pistol, Tina led the way into the hall. In the room near the elevators, people were still talking and laughing, but no one stepped into the corridor.

Danny opened the high-security elevator and made the cab rise once they were in it. His forehead was furrowed, as if he were concentrating, but that was the only indication that he had anything to do with the elevator's movement.

The hallways were deserted on the top floor.

In the guardroom, the older of the two security men was still bound and gagged in his chair. He watched them with anger and fear.

Tina, Elliot, and Danny went through the vestibule and stepped into the cold night. Snow lashed them.

Over the howling of the wind, another sound arose, and Tina needed a few seconds to identify it.

A helicopter.

She squinted up into the snow-shipped night and saw the chopper coming over the rise at the west end of the plateau. What madman would take a helicopter out in this weather?

"The Explorer!" Elliot shouted. "Hurry!"

They ran to the Explorer, where Tina took Danny out of Elliot's arms and slid him into the backseat. She got in after him.

Elliot climbed behind the wheel and fumbled with the keys. The engine wouldn't turn over immediately.

The chopper swooped toward them.

"Who's in the helicopter?" Danny asked, staring at it through the side window of the Explorer.

"I don't know," Tina said. "But they're not good people, baby. They're like the monster in the comic book. The one you sent me pictures of in my dream. They don't want us to get you out of this place."

Danny stared at the oncoming chopper, and lines appeared in his forehead again.

The Explorer's engine suddenly turned over.

"Thank God!" Elliot said.

But the lines didn't fade from Danny's forehead.

Tina realized what the boy was going to do, and she said, "Danny, wait!"

*   *   *

Leaning forward to view the Explorer through the bubble window of the chopper, George Alexander said, "Put us down right in front of them, Jack."

"Will do," Morgan said.

To Hensen, who had the submachine gun, Alexander said, "Like I told you, waste Stryker right away, but not the woman."

Abruptly the chopper soared. It had been only fifteen or twenty feet above the pavement, but it rapidly climbed forty, fifty, sixty feet.

Alexander said, "What's happening?"

"The stick," Morgan said. An edge of fear sharpened his voice, fear that hadn't been audible throughout the entire, nightmarish trip through the mountains. "Can't control the damn thing. It's frozen up."

Eighty, ninety, a hundred feet they soared, soared straight up into the night.

Then the engine cut out.

"What the hell?" Morgan said.

Hensen screamed.

Alexander watched death rushing up at him and knew his curiosity about the other side would shortly be satisfied.

•　•　•

As they drove off the plateau, around the burning wreckage of the helicopter, Danny said, "They were bad people. It's all right, Mom. They were real bad people."

To everything there is a season, Tina reminded herself. A time to kill and a time to heal.

She held Danny close, and she stared into his dark eyes, and she wasn't able to comfort herself with those words from the Bible. Danny's eyes held too much pain, too much knowledge. He was still her sweet boy—yet he was changed. She thought about the future. She wondered what lay ahead for them.

AFTERWORD

The Eyes of Darkness is one of five novels that I wrote under the pen name "Leigh Nichols," which I no longer use. Although it was the second of the five, it is the fifth and final in the series to be reissued in paperback under my real name. The previous four were *The Servants of Twilight, Shadowfires, The House of Thunder,* and *The Key to Midnight.* Demand from my readers made it possible for these books to be republished, and I'm grateful to all of you for your interest.

As you know if you have read the afterwords in *The Funhouse* and *The Key to Midnight,* I like to amuse myself by revealing the tragic deaths of the various pen names I used early in my career. Somewhat to my embarrassment, I must admit that I've not always been truthful with you in these matters. Previously, I told you that Leigh Nichols drank too much champagne one evening on a Caribbean cruise ship and was decapitated in a freak limbo accident. I was touched by your sympathy cards and accounts of the memorial services you held, but now that Berkley Books has brought you this fifth and final of the Nichols novels, I must confess that I was lying in order not to have to reveal Nichols's true—and more disturbing—fate. One bleak and wintry night Leigh Nichols was abducted by extraterrestrials, taken on a tour of our solar system, introduced to the alien Nest Queen, and forced to undergo a series of horrifying surgeries. Though eventually returned to Earth, the author was too traumatized to continue a career as a novelist—but finally built a new life as the current dictator of Iraq.

The Eyes of Darkness was one of my early attempts to write a cross-genre novel mixing action, suspense, romance, and a touch of the paranormal. While it doesn't have the intensity, depth of characterization, complexity of theme, or pace of later novels such as *Watchers* and *Mr. Murder*, and while it doesn't go for your throat as fearsomely as a book like *Intensity*, readers who have found it under the Nichols name in used-book stores have expressed favorable opinions of it. I suppose they like it because the device of the lost child—and the dedicated mother who will do anything to find out what has happened to her little boy—strikes a primal chord in all of us.

As I revised the book for this new edition, I resisted the urge to transform the story entirely into a novel of the type that I would write today. I updated cultural and political references, polished away a few of the more egregious stylistic inadequacies, and trimmed excess wordage here and there. I enjoyed revisiting *Eyes*, which remains a basically simple tale that relies largely on plot and on the strangeness of the premise to engage the reader. I hope you *were* engaged, and that you have enjoyed taking this five-book voyage through the career of Leigh Nichols. If you're ever in Iraq, the surgically altered author will probably be happy to sign copies of these books for you—or will denounce you as an infidel and have you thrown into a prison cell as vile as any sewer. Inquire at your own risk.